KU-268-388

THE HANGING TREE

Also by Paul Doherty

The Margaret Beaufort mysteries

DARK QUEEN RISING *
DARK QUEEN WAITING *
DARK QUEEN WATCHING *

The Brother Athelstan mysteries

THE NIGHTINGALE GALLERY
THE HOUSE OF THE RED SLAYER
MURDER MOST HOLY
THE ANGER OF GOD
BY MURDER'S BRIGHT LIGHT
THE HOUSE OF CROWS
THE ASSASSIN'S RIDDLE
THE DEVIL'S DOMAIN
THE FIELD OF BLOOD
THE HOUSE OF SHADOWS
BLOODSTONE *
THE STRAW MEN *
CANDLE FLAME *
THE BOOK OF FIRES *
THE HERALD OF HELL *
THE GREAT REVOLT *
A PILGRIMAGE TO MURDER *
THE MANSIONS OF MURDER *
THE GODLESS *
THE STONE OF DESTINY *

* *available from Severn House*

THE HANGING TREE

Paul Doherty

SEVERN
HOUSE

First world edition published in Great Britain and the USA in 2022
by Severn House, an imprint of Canongate Books Ltd,
14 High Street, Edinburgh EH1 1TE.

Trade paperback edition first published in Great Britain and the USA in 2022
by Severn House, an imprint of Canongate Books Ltd.

severnhouse.com

British Library Cataloguing-in-Publication Data
A CIP catalogue record for this title is available from the British Library.

ISBN-13: 978-1-78029-139-0 (cased)
ISBN-13: 978-1-4483-0895-8 (trade paper)
ISBN-13: 978-1-4483-0896-5 (e-book)

All Severn House titles are printed on acid-free paper.

Typeset by Palimpsest Book Production Ltd.,
Falkirk, Stirlingshire, Scotland.
Printed and bound in Great Britain by
TJ Books, Padstow, Cornwall.

To Rose Lavin, a woman who loves history, intrigue and
a good murder, this book is dedicated to you.
You are a wonderful Nan and I would like to thank you for all you do.
Love Thomas.

HISTORICAL NOTE

By the early winter of 1382, London and the surrounding shires had recovered from the chaos and turbulence caused by the Great Revolt the previous summer. Law and order had been reimposed and London, which had borne the brunt of the uprising, returned to its usual business of making money. England was a prosperous nation. The wars in France had ended and trade was flourishing.

England possessed a most treasured commodity, its beautiful wool, needed by the great textile industry of Europe and no more so than the wealthy cities of Northern Italy. English wool was most prized and Italian bankers flocked to London, creating their own quarter, as they did business with the English Crown. The Lombard bankers became an integral part of London society so that even streets and highways were named after them.

Of course where there's money, there's also murder. Greed and the desire to seize what was precious lay at the heart of city life and the business carried on there. Vast sums of money were to be had and everybody wanted a share, be they those dwelling in the underworld of Whitefriars or in the stately mansions along Cheapside. Fortunes were to be had, fortunes to be made, even though the consequences of failure could be too hideous even to contemplate . . .

(The quotations before each part or chapter are from Chaucer's *Canterbury Tales*: 'The Pardoner's Prologue').

THE PROLOGUES

'The Love of money is the root of all evil.'

Magister Henry Beaumont of Colchester, Custos or Keeper in the Exchequer of Coin, gazed around the small antechamber just within the doorway of the House or Mansion of the Exchequer. Beaumont needed no reminding, being a trained clerk for many years, that this was England's great treasury. The personal property of young King Richard II. Of course, that was the theory. For on that day, the feast of St Hilary, 13 January in the year of our Lord 1382, such treasure was also the property of the King's uncle, John of Gaunt, Duke of Lancaster and self-styled regent to the kingdom during 'the minority of his beloved nephew'. Gaunt, however, was like the other great lords. He never, in the words of St Paul, allowed his hands to be stained with 'filthy lucre'. Such matters were best left to the likes of Beaumont.

'Magister?'

Ralph Calpurne gently tapped the table as he peered through the gaps of the shuttered window.

'Magister,' he repeated. 'It will be Prime soon and then we begin to move the treasure.'

'We certainly do.' Beaumont stared around at his small company, the Clerks of the Light gathered about him. They were all waiting for the first sliver of dawn; this would be greeted by a peal of bells from Westminster Abbey nearby, summoning the Blackrobes, the Benedictine monks, to chant the lilting melodies of the Office of Prime.

'Oh yes an important day.' Beaumont scratched at his close-shorn head, his lean, sallow face with its sharp eyes and determined mouth and chin, all tense and anxious. Despite the troubles the day might bring, it was also his birthday. Beaumont steeled himself against what the future might hold. He was about to reach an important crossroads in his life.

'Magister, will the Tower archers be here soon?'

Beaumont smiled at Luke Whitby, the young clerk, fresh-faced though sharp as a razor.

'Of course, my friend. We are going to move tens of thousands of pounds sterling in gold and silver. It's to be carted to Queenshithe.'

'And then?' Philip Crossley, the oldest of the clerks, thin as a whippet with the face of a lean, hungry weasel asked. 'What then, Magister?'

'There's a great fighting cog, the *Ludovico*, brought in by the Frescobaldi.' Beaumont half smiled and wafted a hand to still the usual moans and complaints about the Frescobaldi. The Italian bankers were notorious for loaning the English Crown vast sums, then milking the profits accrued through high interest charges. 'Anyway,' Beaumont continued, 'the treasure will be taken to the *Ludovico*. It will be safe there; the cog's a veritable floating fortress.'

'So there will be a formidable escort?'

'Well of course.'

'Where's Adrian?' Whitby demanded. 'We'll have to move soon, so where is Adrian?'

'Master Adrian Bloxhall,' Beaumont replied caustically, 'is on a most vital errand.' He grinned as the three clerks stiffened. 'He's gone to the buttery. It's going to be a long, arduous day. I have asked Bloxhall to fetch us morning ales, fresh bread, rissoles and a pot of butter.' Beaumont spread his hands. 'We shall celebrate my birthday both at the beginning and at the end of our day.' Beaumont's declaration was greeted with murmurs of approval. Further discussion ended as the bells of Westminster boomed out the summons to Prime. All four clerks hurriedly rose to their feet, preparing themselves for the climb up to the treasury. They adjusted belts, fastened cloaks, making sure their boots were securely pulled on.

Beaumont approached the door and glanced through the eyelets. He then opened the door built into the wall of the antechamber and led his entourage into the stairwell of Flambard's Tower, an ancient edifice built with hard granite blocks. The walls of the tower were at least a yard thick and expertly built. Iron-hard cement had held the slabs fast ever since the time of Flambard, William the Conqueror's master mason, who had personally supervised the tower's construction. Flambard's skill was unique, so much so that legend had it that Flambard had been taught the masons' art by the demon lords of the air. The tower was at least three hundred years old, yet it showed no signs of wear. The stones, the cement, the wood, seemed as strong as when they were first laid. The tower certainly reflected its creator: dark, forbidding and foreboding. Cold, even on a hot summer's day. A gloomy, damp place. Cresset torches blazed against the murk, braziers glowed fiercely, yet to no avail. The chill from the stones hung like a veil enveloping the clerks, who shivered as Magister Beaumont produced his unique set of keys and approached the heavy, iron-barred, metal-studded door. Above this, carved into the stones, its letters picked out in scarlet, ran the verse 'And the Gates of Hell shall not prevail against thee'. The clerks privately prayed that this was so. Beaumont opened the top lock and, with another key, the bottom one. He swung open the heavy door and stepped into a stairwell about three yards across. To the left, built under the bulk of the twisting, narrow, spiral staircase, was a door leading to an ancient cellar or crypt. The door to this was firmly bolted.

Beaumont paused before walking towards the staircase. Above the first step hung a bell under its coping, fastened securely against the wall. Beaumont gave three vigorous tugs in honour of the Trinity, so the bell pealed noisily through the cavernous stairwell. Once the peals died away, Beaumont began his climb up the steep, sharp-edged steps. He moved cautiously. This was truly a treacherous stairway, deliberately so, a sure defence against any fleet-footed thief. Some safety was afforded by the stout, coarse guide rope fastened to the wall. Beaumont gripped this tightly and paused to glance over his shoulder at his three companions, following close behind.

'Never trust this place,' Beaumont rasped. 'And never forget the traps.' He climbed one more step, then glanced to his right at the small red cross painted on the wall just above the guide rope. Beaumont stretched out, moving his hand until he touched the trip cord still tautly fastened across the eighth step. A simple, but very clever device, to bring any unwary intruder crashing down. Beaumont moved his hand, following the cord to its end, looped through a small metal peg driven into the wall. Beaumont undid this then left the loosened cord for his comrades to see before moving on. He continued his climb patiently, now and again pausing to release further trip cords. The three clerks, trailing cautiously behind, quietly cursed Flambard and all his devilish machinations to protect this tower. Beaumont eventually reached the thirty-ninth step and loosened the last trip cord.

'Magister!'

Beaumont turned, wiping the sheen of sweat from his face. 'What is it, Whitby?'

'The bell! Magister, you sounded the bell but there's been no response! Our plainchant,' Whitby murmured, 'has been sorely disturbed.'

The others behind Whitby also expressed their surprise. Beaumont, quietly cursing, nodded in agreement.

'We take it for granted,' he murmured. 'But you are correct. Despencer should have pealed his bell in reply so, let us see. Let us see.'

He climbed onto the fortieth step, which led into a narrow stairwell dominated by a heavy, iron-barred door very similar to the one below. Once again Beaumont, using two separate keys, opened the top and bottom locks. He pushed at the door and it swung back to be caught by the thick, blood-red sheet of the finest Moroccan leather. The draught excluder, held down by small weights sewn into its hem, blocked his way.

'Strange,' Whitby murmured. 'The arras has not been pulled back. Surely Despencer knew we were on our way up?'

'I know, I know.' Beaumont turned and struggled with the heavy leather curtain. He glanced over his shoulder. The treasure chamber was shadow-filled. The torches and most of the candles had petered out. Beaumont, however, concentrated on pulling back the arras, dragging it free of the door. He now swung this open so the other clerks could join him. Once inside, however, all four clerks just stood staring around in amazement.

'Where are they?' Whitby gasped. 'In God's name.' Whitby pointed to the five window embrasures, each partially cordoned off by a sheet of Moroccan leather similar to the arras hanging before the door.

'Magister, what should we do?'

'I must lock us in,' Beaumont retorted. 'That's what the protocols stipulate.' Beaumont then shook his head. 'Oh, never mind the protocols, let's open these.'

The clerks hastened to obey, pulling back each curtain to exclamations of horror and surprise. The treasure chamber was a paved roundel. Facing the door were five window embrasures, small chambers in themselves, each with a chancery desk and leather-cushion-backed chair. Small coffers stood stacked either side of the chancery desks. The window in each embrasure was a long arrow-slit, filled with stiffened horn polished to a sheen. All the lancets were heavily barred both within and without. The little light they afforded was augmented by a huge lanternhorn hanging on a chain above each desk. This now shed a dancing glow over the horrors perpetrated in each chamber. Indeed, none of Beaumont's retinue could break free from the terrors which now assailed them. They'd pulled back the arras stretching across each enclave, as well as that over the middle embrasure; this enclave was much larger than the rest and sealed off by a heavy iron-barred gate, which stretched from floor to ceiling.

'Nothing,' Crossley exclaimed, 'nothing's out of place, except that.' He gestured towards the enclaves. In all of these, a Clerk of the Dark sat slumped in his chair.

'Even the Magister.' Whitby pointed to the central embrasure, where Despencer slouched in his treasury chair.

'I don't . . .' Calpurne's voice died away as the entrance bell below echoed noisily through the tower. Beaumont strode back to the door and tugged hard at the bell rope to send a peal of acknowledgement. A short while later, Adrian Bloxhall, face all sweaty, bustled through the door carrying a large food hamper.

'In heaven's name.' Bloxhall exclaimed. 'What . . .'

'Put the hamper down.' Beaumont became all assertive. 'Adrian, put the hamper down and come with me. The rest of you stand back.'

The other three clerks were only too pleased to remain stock still. This chamber, their daily workplace, now terrified them. The deathly silence and those five comrades, Clerks of the Dark, sitting so eerily at their desks, their very posture proclaiming something truly heinous had occurred here. The clerks watched as Magister Beaumont and his henchman Bloxhall moved from one embrasure to the next. On one occasion they had to pause when Beaumont put his face in his hands, as if to control his stomach. The inspection continued. Beaumont and Bloxhall eventually walked over to the great central pillar. The Magister leaned against this, staring down as he tried to control his breathing. Bloxhall hurried off to the jakes cupboard in a narrow enclave close to the door. After some noisy retching, he staggered back, wiping his mouth on the back of his hand.

'They're dead.' Beaumont lifted his head. 'They are all dead.'

'How?' Whitby gasped. 'In heaven's name, Magister, how?'

'And there's more.' He gasped. 'The treasury boxes have been emptied; the coins are gone. Nothing there but bags of spent charcoal.'

His companions could only gaze fearfully back.

'I will check again but undoubtedly,' Beaumont flailed a hand, 'all of our comrades have been murdered, garrotted, and the treasure plundered. We must leave this now and send for Master Thibault.'

Clement the Key-Master, once a leading figure in the Guild, a true craftsman, was, on that day, 13 January, the Year of Our Lord 1382, absorbed by depictions of the power of Hell. He stood hidden deep in the shadows to the right of the main door of St Erconwald's Church in Southwark. Clement had become totally distracted, fascinated by the freshly painted fresco which now covered that stretch of wall between the door and the shadow-filled north transept. Clement knew all about the parish of St Erconwald, as well as one of its leading parishioners, the Hangman of Rochester. This most notable of executioners had been held over the font and baptized Giles of Sempringham, his true name. Giles, however, had followed a tortuous path through life to become Southwark's leading hangman. An executioner who could despatch a felon in the twinkling of an eye, a sheer drop from the gallows' ladder so the condemned fellow's neck snapped as sharp as that of a chicken bound for the oven. The hangman was also a most gifted painter. What fascinated Clement on this particular occasion was the fresco entitled by a scroll spat out of a demon's mouth. It proclaimed one word, 'Murder!' The nightmare painting reflected Clement's own dark mood and deep anxieties. The fresco was a graphic, vivid depiction of a meeting between Lord Satan and Cain, Adam's son and the world's first murderer, who had slain his own brother Abel out of sheer jealousy. In the painting Satan was flanked by three henchmen, Murder, Lust and Greed. The person Satan wished to do business with was a handsome young man with golden hair, garbed in a silver-blue robe studded with diamonds. Cain, the master of murder, was also protected by evil spirits. The first was a ferocious cat-faced demon with a curled tail and clawed feet. The demon's monstrous head was turned slightly to glare out of the painting, so his globulous white eyes, with no pupils, seemed to be staring at Clement, as if wondering whether he should pounce and drag Clement's soul down to a hellish banquet where he could sit and sup with demons. Clement peered closer at a second evil spirit, a demon assassin with spiked hair and pointed ears, its black tongue thrust out through yellow, rotting teeth. The demon was garbed like a knight for combat, with a peaked helmet nestling in the crook of his arm. The demon wore a long daggered surcoat, gloriously festooned with skulls, whilst long-toed sollets sheathed the demon's claw-like feet. Behind this master of Hell, half concealed in the murk, stood more of the devil's squires: grotesque, horned, pot-bellied demons all armoured for war. Above this hellish host hovered Death, an evil-looking crone with a dire face and dreadful body. The crone, undoubtedly the Angel of Death, was sharp-kneed and sharp-elbowed, her skin roughly crinkled. The crone's shift was pulled back to reveal long, ghastly shanks. Now absorbed in this story from Hell, Clement wondered where the hangman had learnt his art. Did this fascination with the dead and the life beyond the veil have its roots in his work as a hangman? Clement closed his eyes and whispered a prayer. He must remember why he came here.

'Murder is . . .' he whispered to himself. 'Murder is and murder does. Did you . . .' He broke off as he heard a sound behind him. He tensed and caught his breath, only to relax as the parish cat, the great, one-eyed Bonaventure, emerged from the shadows of the transept, a wriggling mouse caught firmly in its jaw. Clement hurriedly opened the postern in the main door so the cat could slide, swift and silent as any assassin, into the dark. Clement closed the door and returned to study the painting. So absorbed in the artist's work, Clement was totally unaware that his own sudden, silent death was being plotted by the figure lurking deep in the shadows of the nave. Murder truly intended to make its presence felt, not just in paintings and frescos but in the very sinews of life.

Clement himself appreciated the dangers which sprang from

the secrets he was beginning to unravel. He repressed a sudden sharp shiver of fear. Clement turned and looked back down the long, empty, hollow-sounding nave, where only a few sconce torches and the fast-fading day provided slivers of light. Clement breathed out noisily. He'd discussed his jumbled thoughts with his good friend and distant kinsman Crispin the Carpenter, who had advised him to come here. Brother Athelstan, the Dominican parish priest of St Erconwald's, would celebrate his Mass and speak to those such as Clement, who needed words of advice. Clement had hurried to St Erconwald's, only to be informed by Benedicta the Beautiful that Brother Athelstan had been summoned by Sir John Cranston to meet him at Westminster. Dreadful murders had occurred there. Nevertheless, Benedicta had added, Brother Athelstan would surely return, so would Clement, whom she recognized, wish to stay in the church, bearing in mind the freezing weather outside? Clement had accepted the widow woman's kind offer, along with a jug of ale and a dish of scones from The Piebald tavern. Benedicta had brought the drink and food herself, as well as wafers from Merrylegs' pastry shop. Benedicta had encouraged her visitor to eat, drink, then relax. Clement certainly needed to do that, warming himself over one of the wheeled fire-baskets placed judiciously around the church. Clement had both eaten and drank then warmed himself, moving a brazier close to the wall painting he was scrutinizing.

Clement continued his reflection, totally unaware of murder, creeping like a spider towards him, slowly, measuredly, listening to the different sounds from the church and outside. Clement himself felt an awful chill of loneliness, as well as a premonition that all might not go well. Clement wondered what he should do but then closed his eyes as he clutched his stomach. It was time that he was gone. There was some malignancy in his belly; he was bleeding from inside and growing weaker by the day. Clement suspected that he was grievously ill and that was another reason for coming here today. He breathed in, clutching his cloak more closely and, at the same time, brushing the pommel of his dagger. Clement continued to ignore the pain in his belly, that sharp disturbance of his humours. He just wished he had come earlier to consult with the small, dark-faced, innocent-looking friar. Crispin the Carpenter had urged him to seek out Athelstan and so, eventually, he had.

Clement realized this was all so different from the glory days when he was a true craftsman, a high-ranking official of the guild, a time when architects from all over Europe consulted with him over this issue or that. Clement would tell Athelstan about his lovely wife Anna, now gone to God. How the old King and his warlike sons had patronized Clement and showered the Key-Master with favour, rewards and sweet inducements. The old King had chosen him to fashion special locks for the treasury at Westminster. Locks which would control two important doors. Each door would have two locks, one at the top and one at the bottom. The King wanted a work of craftsmanship, a subtle piece of workmanship so the locks were unique, as were the keys. Clement had risen to the challenge, creating four such locks. Plaudits and congratulations had rained down on him and his family . . . and then disaster! One morning, long before the city mist had dissipated and the bells tolled out, Master Thibault, Keeper of the King's Secrets, had unleashed his searchers. They had broken into both Clement's house and workshop, confiscating his coffers, caskets and, of course, the fruits of his own stupidity. He should not have kept those plans, charts and drawings, the pieces of wood and metal all connected with the creation of those special locks. In truth, he had meant well, but Clement had been caught with documents and artefacts which should have been destroyed.

Clement closed his eyes and leaned his hot forehead against the cold plaster. Death and Destruction, those infernal twins, had swept into his life, and the blight had spread like some baleful mist. Anna, his beloved wife, had died of a bloody flux, now very similar to the one which weakened him. Clement had been dismissed from both the Guild and the royal service, no fees, no wages, no pension, no house or home, and then Columba! Columba, his one and only beloved son, a master craftsman in the making. Columba had met and married Isabella Fleming, and then what? In truth, Columba had been sorely affected by his father's disgrace and matters slipped from bad to worse. Rumours even ran rife about Columba's marriage, then silence. Nothing! Columba had just disappeared. No trace or sign of him. Clement had grieved for his son every day over the last few years. He and Columba had lost something, and Clement just wished that he could rectify what was wrong. But Columba had vanished, as completely and as swiftly as dew on a bright summer's morning. Columba had apparently fled his narrow house in Crooked Lane near St Michaels, Dowgate. He had taken his clothes and all his valuables, except for one.

'He didn't take the Walsingham,' Clement whispered into the darkness. 'Columba would never have left the Walsingham. He took it with him everywhere. So why hadn't he on that last great venture?' Clement tightened his fist as a spasm of razor-sharp pain swept his stomach. Clement ignored this. There were more important matters. Over the last few days, so much had become manifest. Issues he had ignored now fell into place, both about Columba and other mysteries. So pressingly important, Clement had needed to have urgent word with Crispin the Carpenter, who had advised him to attend the dawn Mass here at St Erconwald. Brother Athelstan would be only too willing to hear his confession then shrive him. Moreover, Crispin had urged, once Clement had knelt at the mercy stool under the sign of the five-petalled rose, anything he said to the priest was locked and sealed under the sacrament. For a short while, Clement had objected, but Crispin, a shrewd man, had reassured Clement about their dark-faced Dominican friar. Crispin had explained how Athelstan had once been a soldier and campaigned with his brother in France. Athelstan might well be a man of God but he was also a man of the world. He had been through suffering. He knew how fraught families could become. After all, Athelstan's brother had been killed in France. Athelstan blamed himself and brought back his brother's corpse, but this proved futile; the tragic news had hastened the death of Athelstan's parents. The shock and consternation this caused compelled Athelstan to reflect on his life. In the end this former soldier, in reparation for his misdeeds, had renounced the world and entered the Dominican Order.

'For his sins,' Crispin laughingly added. 'Athelstan was appointed parish priest of St Erconwald's. Just as importantly, the friar had been appointed as secretarius, personal clerk to the almighty Sir John Cranston, Lord High Coroner of London, a man of sharp mind and keen wit.

'So you see,' Crispin had whispered to Clement, 'Athelstan is a man of the Holy Spirit. Speak to him, my friend. Inform him about all you have seen, heard and experienced. All those matters you cannot tell me. What you suspect, how you feel. Pour it out, as you would water from a jar. Seek comfort and absolution, Athelstan will certainly provide these.'

That was a matter of days ago. Yesterday Clement had plucked up courage. He had met Crispin at The Hanging Tree, where they had both feasted on fresh fish cooked in a sauce. Clement had insisted on meeting there. He did not wish to cross to Southwark and join Crispin in The Piebald, owned by that master of mischief, Joscelyn the one-armed former river pirate. In Crispin's view, The Piebald was too noisy, whilst its customers were highly inquisitive of any newcomer. No, The Hanging Tree, despite its macabre title and chilling sign, was the most comfortable place to meet. This morning he had risen early. He had met Crispin, once again listened to his advice, then hurried across to Southwark. Clement startled as he heard a sound and turned to stare down the hollow nave, surely a haunted place, with its occasional flaring torch licking the encroaching darkness. Was he alone? Clement wondered. Benedicta said the church would be securely locked behind her. Surely, no one else was here, whilst the only way out was through the postern in the main door, by which the great tomcat had just left. What was that cat's name, Clement wondered? Ah yes, Bonaventure!

Clement walked down the nave. Again, he heard a sound, a cough, low and gravelly. Clement stopped, grimaced, and gently banged the heel of his hand against his forehead. Of course, he had forgotten! Blodwyn the Blessed, the thief who, according to Benedicta, had fled into the parish a short while after Athelstan left. Blodwyn had apparently crept in, pleading for sanctuary, after Bladdersmiff the beadle had caught Blodwyn pilfering loaves and a few coins from a nearby common bakery. Benedicta had ushered the thief into the sanctuary and served him some morning ale, along with slices of the stolen bread Blodwyn had dropped just outside the church.

Clement walked up the nave, under the crudely carved rood screen and into the sanctuary. Blodwyn, clearly distinguished by his bright blond hair and tattered, blood-red jerkin, lay stretched out in the enclave of the apse behind the high altar. The sanctuary man was fast asleep, as snug as a pig in its sty. Beside him on the floor lay a small flattened wineskin, the obvious cause of Blodwyn's deep sleep.

Clement turned and walked back into the shadows. Perhaps it was time he left. He could always come back. Clement glimpsed another painting on one of the squat, drum-like pillars and moved across to peer more closely. He clutched his belly as a sharp spasm of pain seared his stomach. He just wished Athelstan would return.

'So much,' Clement whispered into the darkness, 'so much I have recently seen and reflected on. What went before was not the truth!' A further spasm of pain caught him. Clement's head went back and the assassin, now close behind him, looped the garrotte around Clement's scrawny neck. The Key-Master, shocked as any rabbit in a snare, could only gape and splutter, his flailing hand catching his dagger sheath. He drew the blade but it was futile. He was too weak. Clement fell slack and let himself sink into the roaring darkness.

'We have robbed the royal treasury.' The leader of the Carbonari, gathered on the wasteland close to Westminster, was almost beside himself with glee. 'We have robbed the royal treasury.' He repeated and, lifting his arms, he performed a Tuscan country dance which provoked laughter from his comrades. He stopped all breathless and, lifting his mask, wiped away the sweat. He shivered and quietly cursed the hideous English winter, which seemed to fasten tight on everything. The leader walked over to the huge wheelbarrow. He and others had used this to carry the great sack containing the freshly minted gold and silver coins plundered from the treasure chamber. The leader turned, sitting on the edge of the barrow as he watched more of his comrades lead across two powerful dray horses to hitch them to the high-sided cart.

'Isn't this dangerous?' One of them asked. 'Surely . . .'

'Nonsense,' the leader replied. He gestured across the mist-shrouded common land which stretched for miles to the north of the hallowed precincts of Westminster. 'Some of us will go back into the city,' he declared, 'to report our great news. A few of you will accompany me. Now!' He plucked at his own filthy jerkin. 'We have been chosen because we speak the tongue, so we will tramp from this place like surly mouthed peasants, carting sacks of miserable vegetables to this market or that. We shall always be on the move. We'll camp out in the cold and act the part. I mean, who would want to steal sacks of vegetables? Coarse plants plucked from their meagre soil.' He paused at the laughter. 'We shall go all shabby and shuffling as we trundle the trackways and coffin paths of this benighted place.'

'And where are we going?'

'Oh, my friend, that secret will remain so until our masters decide otherwise. Suffice to say we shall travel due east and eventually—'

'Our masters will join us?'

'Precisely, my friend, so,' the leader pushed himself off the barrow, 'let us load the treasure onto the cart, hide it well, keep our weapons concealed and so move on.'

'And the mistake? I heard you mention it in that brief conversation. A mistake was made during the robbery. Can it be rectified?'

'Yes yes, my friend. A mistake was certainly made and, perhaps, we will have to deal with that swiftly and ruthlessly.' The leader narrowed his eyes. 'We have been alerted about the mistake – a singularly stupid one, but our masters will take care of that one way or another.'

'And the fat coroner and his sharp-eyed friar? It's no great secret,' the man continued, 'that when the English Crown learns that its treasure has been stolen, Cranston and his familiar will be assigned to hunt us down.'

'And it's no great secret,' the leader replied, 'that our masters strived to have them removed peaceably from Westminster in a subtly clever way but,' he shrugged, 'that failed. However, rest assured, if the fat coroner and his little friar pry and prod, a more lasting solution might have to be found.'

'We would plot the assassination of Sir John Cranston, Lord High Coroner of London, and Brother Athelstan, priest of St Erconwald's? A dangerous move, surely? Both the coroner and the Dominican are highly regarded by my Lord of Gaunt, his Master of Secrets and, of course, the young King himself! That could have dire consequences.'

'Yet what choice do we have but to secure a treasure which is rightfully ours? Remember . . .' the leader held up a black mittened hand, 'we did not begin this dance, Master Thibault did. He nursed his own secret designs on the treasure and, for all I know, still does. However, although we have stolen the King of England's treasure, and this is the delightful contradiction, we have simply seized what is rightfully ours. So, my friend, the likes of Gaunt and Thibault can go hang, as they certainly might when the news of this robbery sweeps the city. But that is their concern. We have the treasure and we shall keep it . . .'

PART ONE

'If any soul in church this day, is guilty of an act so hideous.'

'So.' Brother Athelstan truly wished he was back in Southwark. Once again he was about to cross the murky meadows of murder to confront a monster, some malignancy lurking deep in the gloaming.

'So what, little monk?'

'Friar, Sir John.'

'My apologies.' Sir John Cranston, Lord High Coroner of London, certainly looked the part. Cranston's rubicund face beamed with good health, his snow-white moustache and beard expertly cut and crimped. He was dressed in a field-green gown over a cambric shirt and black leggings of the purest and thickest wool. The coroner turned to raise a well-booted foot onto a stool. Cranston's warbelt and earth-brown military cloak lay tossed over the table which separated him from his secretarius, clerk, confidant and close friend, Brother Athelstan. Cranston studied the little Dominican's freshly shaven, olive-skinned face, his night-black hair shorn on all three sides, although the tonsure on the crown was clearly marked.

'Not like so many priests . . .' Cranston spoke his thoughts loudly. He then coughed and plucked his miraculous wineskin from the chair beside him.

'You don't finish sentences, little friar, so don't give me that querying look.'

'In which case, Sir John, I am in very good company. Yes, my Lord Coroner?'

'To answer you bluntly, Athelstan. Many of your kind – priests, monks and friars sworn to chastity – allow their hair to grow and so hide their celibate status with the set purpose of having their wicked way with some hapless lady.'

'Sir John, the cowl doesn't make the monk or the tonsure a celibate.'

'I agree. So what, little friar, were you about to say?'

'Why are we here, sitting in a small antechamber in the House of the Exchequer at Westminster?'

'Patience, my little friar. Let us be prudent and wait.' Athelstan caught Cranston's glance, followed by the coroner raising a stubby finger to his lips. Athelstan breathed out noisily. Of course, they were at Westminster, the centre of John of Gaunt's web, the arena in which the powerful and the rich fought each other, be it in the council chamber or on the field of battle. A constant, never-ending struggle for power. In such a place, the walls had eyes as well as ears. A place where informants, spies and Judas men gathered, as Sir John tersely put it, like flies to a turd. Nevertheless, Athelstan was finding it hard to control his curiosity, and he wondered yet again why he and Sir John had been summoned here. The noble coroner had whispered about rumours of a most daring robbery and of clerks being found strangled in their chairs. How Flambard's Tower, that massive concentric, black-stoned donjon, enjoyed the most macabre reputation, so it was hardly surprising that some dreadful mishap had occurred in or around it. Athelstan, who had visited the tower some years previously, could only agree with such stories. Moreover Sir John, who was writing his great History of London, had discovered and collected all the legends and lore about Flambard's great keep, built like the massive peel towers to be found in Scotland and Ireland. Apparently, the donjon enjoyed a most sinister reputation.

Ah well, Athelstan reflected, all would be revealed soon enough. He closed his eyes and let his mind float like a cloud against the sky. Flambard's Tower made him think of his own recent building, a simple affair yet important in the life of a parish. Athelstan had ordered Matthew the Mason to construct a sturdy, red-bricked, black-tiled cottage on the site of the old death house in the middle of God's Acre, the sprawling cemetery adjoining St Erconwald's. In truth, the cemetery was a rambling stretch of common land, strewn with gorse, bramble, derelict flower beds, tortuous coffin paths and clumps of ancient trees: oak, sycamore and yew. It was also a lonely, haunted place, and St Erconwald's cemetery had become the favourite hunting ground for wizards, warlocks, a whole coven of midnight hags and demon worshippers. All kinds of sorcerers had flocked in, eager to plunder graves and so use human remains for their midnight masses. The newly built cottage was a defence against these. Once finished, Athelstan had consecrated the place and given it the title of 'The House of the Faithfully Departed'. More importantly, Athelstan had handed the property over to Thomas the Toad. Athelstan smiled to himself; ah yes, Thomas the Toad, to be distinguished from Thomas the Turd, one of Watkin the dung collector's henchmen. In fact . . .

Athelstan opened his eyes and shook Cranston's arm as he heard footsteps outside. The door opened and three men swept into the antechamber. Athelstan immediately recognized all three. Thibault was Gaunt's one and only loyal henchman, a Master of Secrets, a man with the angelic looks of a cherub, which masked a cunning second to none. This morning, however, Thibault could not repress the rage seething within him, or hide the hot marks of anger on his smooth, pale face. Thibault's bright blue eyes were cold and unblinking, hard as glass, the usual smiling mouth all pursed and prim. He clasped hands with both Cranston and Athelstan, then sat down at the head of the table as the coroner and friar greeted the other two arrivals. Henry Beaumont, Magister in the royal chancery, and Signor Giovanni Conteza, a leading light in the Lombard bank of the Bardi. Athelstan had met both men during the many times he had accompanied Sir John and the Lady Maud to Westminster or some other royal palace. They were hardly seated when Master Thibault, who didn't give a fig about the courtesies, rapped the table for their attention.

'Gentlemen,' he declared in his well-modulated voice. 'The candle burns, time passes, so take your seats.'

They did so. Athelstan caught Cranston's eye and winked, warning the coroner to stay prudent. Thibault was, despite his best efforts, truly suffused with rage; the Master of Secrets came swiftly to the point.

'All the treasure chests in the Exchequer of Coin, kept so safe in the great arca of Flambard's Tower, have been ransacked, plundered. Bags of spent charcoal left mockingly in return.' Thibault paused at Cranston's gasp of surprise.

'Everything?' the coroner asked.

'Everything. Listen now,' Thibault pressed on, 'tens of thousands of good pound sterling in the finest gold and silver have been stolen. Those,' he glanced spitefully at Beaumont, 'whose sacred task was to protect such a treasure hold, have been garrotted, strangled like chickens in their coop. This may . . .' Thibault was unable to continue. He paused to catch his breath, gesturing at Conteza to continue.

'Gentlemen,' the banker declared, his voice only betraying a slight accent, 'I am Giovanni Conteza. You know that, as you do that our bank, the Bardi, loaned the English Crown vast sums . . .'

Athelstan coughed to catch Cranston's attention. A warning not to comment. Cranston, like many leading Londoners, knew that the loans the Bardi had provided went straight into the Regent's purse. Conteza's stark declaration only emphasized a fact everyone knew but nobody dared mention.

'The English Crown,' the banker continued, 'agreed to repay their loans by Easter this year.' Conteza's long, narrow face puckered in concern as he combed his well-tended, night-black beard with his fingers.

'That,' he declared, 'is what was planned. Now, however, our gold, our silver, have been taken and, with all due respect to His Grace the King and his beloved uncle my Lord of Gaunt, we shall insist on repayment.' Conteza's words rang like a warning bell through the chamber.

'Master Thibault.' Beaumont lifted his head, positively squirming in his chair. 'Master Thibault,' he repeated, 'the corpses, the bodies of my colleagues are stiffening, beginning to bloat.' Thibault just glared at his clerk. He turned, lips twisted in a snarl, only to stop and catch his breath.

'I hear what you say, Magister, and my Lord Conteza must meet His Grace.' Thibault's voice faded. He blinked, lips moving soundlessly, then abruptly rose to his feet.

'My Lord Conteza,' he declared, 'come with me. Master Beaumont,' he gestured at Cranston and Athelstan, 'let them view what we have seen. Only God knows what my Lord of Gaunt will think.'

Master Thibault plucked Conteza by the sleeve and both men swept out of the chamber. Athelstan heard Thibault berating whoever was waiting in the stairwell. Beaumont, his face twisted in anger, retook his seat.

'We will be blamed for all of this,' he snarled. 'Master Thibault will—'

'Hush now,' Athelstan murmured. 'Let us proceed in peace and quiet.'

'Peace and quiet,' Beaumont snorted.

'Yes, peace and quiet,' Cranston rasped. 'The swiftest way to trap and unmask a felon. So let us begin.' Beaumont nodded, rubbed his face, forced a smile and stood up.

'I am sorry,' he declared. 'My humours are disturbed. It's best if I fetch my colleagues.'

Beaumont left and returned with four other clerks whom he introduced: Luke Whitby, Adrian Bloxhall, Philip Crossley and Ralph Calpurne.

'So Brother Athelstan,' Beaumont declared as the introductions were made, 'Sir John. Here we are, the Clerks of the Light.'

The friar swiftly scrutinized Beaumont's comrades. He recognized them for what they were. Royal clerks confident in themselves, garbed in sober but costly tunics, cloak and boots, around their waist a chancery belt with cups and sheaths for inkpots and quills. They were sharp-faced and hawk-eyed, restless, impatient to proceed, moving from foot to foot whilst the Magister finished the introductions. Once completed, Beaumont added that all the clerks who worked in the Exchequer of Coin, including Despencer, had served in the royal array, both in the kingdom and across the Narrow Seas.

'What is the matter?' Athelstan asked as Luke Whitby abruptly stepped forward.

'Sir John Cranston is well known.' Whitby bowed to the coroner. 'As is his secretarius, Brother Athelstan. I do not wish to be rude but, gentlemen, our comrades upstairs, their corpses will soon be . . .'

'Let us begin,' Athelstan declared. 'The day fades. Master Beaumont, I have been reflecting on the way here. Sir John has described Flambard's Tower as an arca, a treasure chest, securely locked. And yet robbers broke in to plunder, steal and murder. Somehow, these dire depredations must spring from some fault in how Flambard's Tower was secured. Consequently I want you to faithfully repeat exactly what happened this morning. Omit no detail. Try and ignore,' Athelstan smiled, 'if you can, myself and Sir John. We will just ask questions. So, as I said, let us begin.'

Beaumont led them to a door to the side of the antechamber.

Athelstan, standing on tiptoe, peered through the eyelet high in the door before following Sir John into a dusty, cobweb-filled stairwell. Once there he watched as Beaumont turned the two locks at top and bottom. The Magister swung the door open and they entered the tower stairwell. Beaumont then pulled three times at the bell rope hanging above the bottom step. The peals echoed through the cavernous tower.

'Wait.'

The stairwell was now so thronged that Athelstan asked the clerks to go back outside. Once they had, the friar scrupulously examined the heavy, fortified door with its strong hinges. The front of the door was strengthened with metal studs and bars. The two locks certainly seemed very intricate, the work of some city guildsman, a master locksmith. Athelstan summoned Beaumont back.

'And each of these locks has its own key?' he asked.

'Yes.'

'And these are held by?'

'Master Thibault. I collect them from him at the start of my horarium and return them immediately once I have finished, as did Despencer, Magister of the Clerks of the Dark.'

'Explain that to me.'

'There are two cohorts: the Clerks of the Light who work here from Prime to Vespers, and those of the dark who take over from Vespers to Prime.'

'You do alternate weeks?'

'Yes, of course.'

Athelstan stared around. The tower was a circular arca; its stone walls must be yards thick, its doors strongly fortified. The floor was of hard paving, stretching up to the bottom step of the staircase. Athelstan suspected this was a steep spiral built into the wall, another line of defence. Athelstan had seen the same before. Anyone using these steps either going up or down would have to be most careful and prudent.

'And so this morning?'

'As normal.'

'Which means?'

'My comrades and I came into the tower. We unlocked the door and I rang the bell.' He pointed to where it hung on the wall beneath its coping, the rope dangling down.

'And that was pealed?'

'Yes, three times in honour of the Trinity, the agreed sign that we had entered the tower. I locked the door behind me and waited for Despencer to reply with the three peals from the bell hanging in the treasure chamber.'

'And did he?'

'Of course not, my Lord Coroner, he was dead.'

Cranston turned swiftly and glared at the other clerks, whose sniggers abruptly died away.

'But at the time you did not know that?' Athelstan retorted. 'Anyway, let's continue. You came into the tower, the bell has been rung, you've opened the door and locked it behind you. Then what?'

'There are thirty-nine steps up,' Beaumont declared. 'Brother Athelstan, Sir John.' Beaumont brushed by them. 'It's best if I go first. There are narrow lancets high in the staircase wall. They afford some light but, in truth, despite the windows and the torches, the staircase is truly cloaked in perpetual night. And there's more . . .' Beaumont led them up the spiral staircase; the steps were steep and sharp. Beaumont abruptly paused, holding a hand up. 'As I said,' he remarked over his shoulder, 'there are thirty-nine steps. This spiral staircase was specially designed to make it very difficult for anyone to hasten up or down. Believe me, it is almost impossible to carry anything up or down, unless you do so very slowly and carefully. You need to clutch this guide cord fastened to the wall.' Beaumont patted the thick, coarse rope threaded through iron loops screwed into the stone. 'More importantly . . .' Beaumont walked up a few more steps and crouched down. He touched the red cross painted on the right-hand wall. 'This is a warning to myself and other exchequer clerks.'

Cranston whistled under his breath. 'A trip cord.'

'Correct, Sir John, known only to us. There is one across every eighth step. The small red cross painted on the wall indicates a trip cord is there. See?' Beaumont stretched into the dark on his right and removed the cord with a stout hook on the end. 'Nice and taut,' he declared. 'Enough to bring the unwary, or uninvited, crashing down, and so alert anyone in the treasure chamber.'

'And these trip cords,' Cranston demanded. 'What happened last night?'

'Well, once Master Despencer had begun to climb, he loosened these. On our descent I went last, replacing them.'

'And they were still there this morning when you arrived to begin your day?'

'Oh yes, nothing was disturbed . . .'

They continued their climb. Athelstan realized how steep and dangerous the staircase truly was. A redoubtable defence of the treasure chamber. He could hear Sir John and the others gasping for breath. They moved gingerly up. At last they reached the top. Beaumont took his ring of keys from a hook on his chancery belt.

'As I said,' he gasped, 'two locks, a separate key for each, no more, no less. Brother Athelstan, Sir John, prepare yourselves. You will find the chamber as we found it. Not one thing has been moved or altered.' He turned the bottom lock and pushed the door open, leading them inside, shoving back the heavy draught excluder so that the door swung free.

'And that was pulled across this morning?' Athelstan asked.

'Yes, yes it was.'

Athelstan blessed himself. He stood staring around, eager to catch the very essence of this place; and he sensed it. This was a murder room. A chamber of swift, savage slaughter. He bowed his head and recited a prayer to the Holy Spirit, to the Lord of Life, before walking forward. He then turned, gesturing Cranston closer, and pointed back at the clerks standing just within the doorway.

'Master Beaumont, I would appreciate it if you and your clerks would stay where you are.' Athelstan plucked Cranston's sleeve, leading the coroner to the great central pillar, a squat, barrel-shaped column of hard granite, its only decoration being acanthus leaves carved at both top and bottom. Athelstan leaned against this, staring across at the five embrasures. The thick sheaths of Moroccan leather, like that across the doorway, had been pulled back. Each embrasure or enclave was a chamber in itself, with a huge lantern-horn hanging on its chain above the chancery desk. More light was provided by the long lancet windows but, even from where he stood, Athelstan could see these were closely barred. The friar stared around, not yet daring to approach the embrasures where five royal clerks slumped in their chairs, their backs to him, heads down, as if they had all slipped into some eerie trance.

'Sleep is the brother of death, Sir John, and no more true than here.' Athelstan glanced to his right and glimpsed the palliasses, probably used by the Clerks of the Dark if they wished to snatch a little sleep. He beat his heel against the floor, which was covered with stout rope matting to lessen the chill of this grim chamber. A buttery table stood against the far wall to the right of Athelstan. He walked over. There was a platter of bread, cold meats, pots of butter, cheese, a jug of wine, a water butt, goblets, platters, and a small tun of Bordeaux fitted with a tap. He noticed how little of this repast had been consumed.

'Is this chamber used every day?' Athelstan walked back to Beaumont. 'Is such sustenance always given?' He gestured at the buttery table.

'No.' The Magister shook his head. 'Flambard's Tower is only used when gold and silver coin are to be counted, coffered and carried away. On this occasion, and it was almost complete, the Crown was preparing to repay its loan to the Bardi bankers. They have a great warship . . .'

'The *Ludovico*,' Cranston intervened. 'A majestic, well-armed battle cog.'

'And so,' Athelstan continued, 'the coins are brought here from the Tower Mint?'

'Under very close guard,' Cranston declared. 'Indeed, I have some responsibility for that. The journey is safe enough; it's only a short walk down to the quayside followed by a swift river passage to Westminster.'

'We took possession of the last of the bullion some days ago,' Beaumont declared. 'And we were meant to finish it today.'

'Finish what?'

'Scrutinizing the freshly minted coins, weighing them.' He pointed towards one of the embrasures. 'Counting carefully, making sure there were one hundred coins in each bag before they were placed in the coffers. Of course, we check each other's work. We also ensure no one takes any of the coins.'

'In other words, you search each other?'

'Yes, that's the last thing we do before we leave this chamber. Moreover, Master Thibault insists we leave all purses and satchels in our quarters.' Beaumont grinned and patted his stomach. 'Whilst any pockets in our jerkins and other items of clothing must all be sewn up.'

'Yes, yes,' Cranston declared wearily. 'Only Master Thibault would think of that.'

'And the food and drink?'

'Master Thibault supplies that, an entire tun of Bordeaux to keep us all happy, whilst a sealed butt of water and a hamper of dried food is available for us from the great buttery before we begin our watch.'

'And who carries that up?'

'Oh, one of us. This morning we came in here to discover the great robbery, Bloxhall joined us later. I'd sent him to the buttery to secure a hamper of food for the day. Any of my comrades can do that, provided the trip cords have been removed. Once that's done and the Clerks of the Dark have gone, we are sealed in until Vespers.'

'On the question of food, the provender on the buttery table is hardly touched. Which means,' Athelstan declared, 'these clerks were murdered early in their watch.'

'So it would seem.'

'And the hamper Bloxhall brought?'

'Oh, he took it back as soon as we left the chamber to summon Master Thibault.'

'And so.' Athelstan beckoned Sir John to follow him over to the central enclave. Athelstan coughed and gagged at the foul smell and gratefully accepted the small pomander, which Cranston always carried on him. Burying his mouth and nose into the sweet-smelling cloth, Athelstan crouched beside the corpse slouched in the chancery chair. Death. A sharp, cruel death had certainly disfigured Despencer's face. Popping eyes, ghastly looking skin, the lips around the half-opened mouth were swollen, as was the tongue, savagely bitten between clenched teeth. Athelstan took the pomander away and flinched at the fetid smell.

'Poor man,' Cranston whispered. 'Garrotted.' The coroner tilted back Despencer's head to reveal the savage deep cut across the throat.

'Garrotted,' Cranston repeated, 'his throat closed, neck twisted. The shock would loosen his belly and empty his bladder; the same will be true of the rest.' Cranston and Athelstan soon established that every one of the other clerks had been garrotted, with virtually no sign of disturbance or defence. It was as if all five clerks had offered their throats to the assassin, who had toppled them into the dark. Once they had scrutinized the corpses, both coroner and friar inspected each of the embrasures.

'No coins, nothing,' Athelstan explained. 'Nothing on the desks or the weighing scales or in any other sack, except for these.' Athelstan walked into the central embrasure, taking care not to brush the corpse. He leaned down, and drew from one of the chests next to Despencer's chancery table a small dirty sack, its neck twisted with a filthy piece of string. He took three similar sacks from other chests, and placed all four on the floor before opening them, using Cranston's dagger to slice the cord. Athelstan emptied the dirty, grey charcoal onto the floor. All the coins had been taken, but four sacks of this rubbish placed in one of the treasure chests. What was the significance of that? Athelstan wondered. A mark of contempt? Some form of message?

'Master Beaumont,' Athelstan called out. 'You and your comrades, come! What is all this?'

The clerks gathered round. Beaumont leaned down and plucked up a piece of spent charcoal.

'In heaven's name,' the clerk murmured, and glanced anxious-eyed at his companions, who just shook their heads.

'Brother Athelstan, Sir John.' Beaumont measured his words. 'We do not know what this means. A pile of spent charcoal means nothing to us. Why it was put in those sacks and placed in the treasure chests, well, it's like the rest of all this, a true mystery, nothing . . .' Beaumont fell silent as the bell below pealed out, followed by the murmur of voices and slow, heavy steps on the staircase outside.

'That, I promise you,' Cranston declared, taking a generous gulp from his miraculous wineskin,' must be my chief bailiff, Master Henry Flaxwith, and his beautiful boys.'

'Then let us wait,' Athelstan declared. He walked over to the jakes cupboard which stood just to the left of the door. Athelstan pulled back the leather curtain and opened the closet. The interior was clean. A bench with a turd hole in the middle and a small lavarium with a jug of water, a bowl and a napkin. A sack of plunging rods stood next to this. The whitewashed walls on either side of the jakes bench had candle niches, but the tapers looked as if they had burnt away some time ago. Athelstan closed the door as Flaxwith and his burly bailiffs strode into the chamber, gasping and breathless, moaning about the steep climb. This seemed to have had little effect on Samson, Flaxwith's mastiff, which – Athelstan secretly maintained – was the ugliest dog in the kingdom. Notwithstanding that, Samson openly adored Cranston. Immediately the dog leapt to greet his hero, only to be pulled back by a quietly cursing Flaxwith. Once order had been established, Cranston asked Flaxwith and his bailiffs to remove the five corpses from their chairs and lay them out on the floor. The bailiffs began their gruesome tasks, lifting the cadavers and placing them on the cork matting side by side. The movement of the corpses grew even more macabre: the bellies of the dead men had bloated slightly, and air trapped in their gut now broke out, one corpse even jerking as if desperate to revive. The bailiffs moved carefully. They brought out Despencer's corpse. Athelstan glimpsed the key ring attached to the man's chancery belt. He knelt, unhooked the ring, and studied the four keys. Each had its own unique set of teeth. He summoned Beaumont over.

'These are the keys to the four locks?'

'Yes.'

'And you hold a similar set?'

'Yes.'

'Then hand them to me, please,' Athelstan insisted. 'I need to bring this chamber firmly under my control.'

Beaumont reluctantly handed the keys over and went back to stand with his silent, pale-faced colleagues near the door. At last Flaxwith and his cohort had all five corpses, faces gruesomely disfigured by violent death, lying next to each other. Athelstan recited the '*De Profundis*' – 'Out of the depths do I cry to thee, oh Lord.' Cranston and the clerks joined in the sombre verses of the death song, the words ringing mournfully across the chamber. Athelstan finished with the 'Requiem'. He then blessed all five corpses and asked Flaxwith to search the dead men's clothing. Little was found, and Athelstan recalled how the clerks were forbidden purses and pockets. Once satisfied with the search, Athelstan, joined by Cranston, scrutinized as far as they could each corpse. They looked for anything which might explain the violent, silent murder of five mailed clerks, yet they could discover nothing. No trace of any binding, or ligature. No wound, no fresh bruises. Nothing but the bloody, deep brutal cut of the garrotte, which had choked off their life breath. Athelstan moved to kneel by one corpse after the other. He then rose, patted the keys in his pocket and called Beaumont over.

'When you left the Clerks of the Dark yesterday evening, all was well?'

'Of course.'

Again Athelstan patted the keys he had pocketed. 'And when you left, you kept these close by?'

'No.'

'*What?*'

'Brother Athelstan, Master Thibault is the most cunning of men.'

'I know that.'

'He insists that as soon as we lock the door into the steps, we leave Flambard's Tower and hand the keys directly over to him. All my comrades will bear witness to that. They will testify that I did the same last night. Indeed, we cannot leave for home until these keys are firmly in Master Thibault's hands.'

'And in the morning?'

'Oh yes, my clerks and I had to dance attendance on Master Thibault until he handed the keys back to us. My friends,' Beaumont turned to the other clerks, 'is that not true?'

A chorus of agreement answered his question. Athelstan scratched at his face. So many questions, so many problems. He realized that, for the moment, there was little point in further questioning. Athelstan clapped his hands to gain attention.

'Sir John, we should prepare to leave. Master Flaxwith, please take all five corpses to the common crypt, the great mortuary close by the convent of the Friars of the Sack. I want you to strip each cadaver, search the clothing, and look for anything suspicious, apart from the wounds caused by the garrotte.' He paused. 'The door will remain unlocked, though this chamber is now sealed against any trespassers. No one can come in here except myself, Sir John and you, Master Flaxwith, or someone carrying my personal writ. Understood? I repeat. Understood?' Athelstan demanded, gazing around. 'This chamber is now the court's property in every sense of the word, and that,' Athelstan pointed at the buttery table, 'includes the wine goblets, jug, and whatever food is left. So, Master Flaxwith, I want you to take everything that can be eaten or drunk, mix it in a bowl and have it served to the rats in the Guildhall cellars.'

'The four-legged ones,' Cranston intervened. 'Though I'd love to include some of the two-legged.'

'Sir John, I hear what you say, but the four-legged will suffice. I want the provender put in that cellar and its door firmly locked and sealed. Oh yes.' Athelstan pointed to the embrasure. 'Keep the small sacks of charcoal dust!' Athelstan went over to stand by the five corpses. 'Take these, as I have said, to the common crypt.' Athelstan broke off at the sound of footsteps hurrying up the staircase. Flaxwith went towards the door, Samson barking loudly enough to raise the dead. The chief bailiff paused to scold him as the royal courier pushed his breathless way into the chamber.

'Sir John, Brother Athelstan,' he gasped, wiping sweat-soaked hands on his gorgeous blue, gold and scarlet tabard. 'Sir John, Brother Athelstan.'

'You've already said that,' the coroner snapped. 'What is it?'

'Master Thibault and His Grace the Regent insist that they must meet you after the Angelus bell in the council chamber of the Secret Chancery.'

'Tell Master Thibault we'll be there. Now,' Cranston turned back to Athelstan, 'little friar, is there anything else? Flaxwith will ensure that the corpses are moved.'

Athelstan repeated his instructions on what was to be done. He then waited for the clerks to leave the chamber, escorted by the bailiffs. Cranston and Athelstan followed a short while later, making their way carefully down the steps. At the bottom, Athelstan tapped Flaxwith on the chest.

'No one, Master Henry,' he whispered hoarsely, 'and I mean *no one*, apart from myself, Sir John and you, or someone authorized by us, enters that chamber.' Flaxwith promised he would strictly observe that.

Cranston and Athelstan left. Once away from Flambard's Tower, Athelstan stopped and placed one hand on the coroner's arm.

'Little friar.'

'Sir John? Let us feed the inner man.'

Cranston clapped the friar on the shoulder. 'Wonderful words.' He breathed. 'Wonderful! The inner man certainly needs feeding.

We are too far from The Lamb of God, so it's God's speed to The Ink Pot and Pen, the best eating place in this benighted spot.'

Cranston and Athelstan left the royal precincts and entered the narrow streets of Westminster, a small city in itself, and an ancient one. The trackways, runnels and alleys were little more than coffin paths, which snaked past houses and tenements three storeys high. Once imposing mansions, these buildings were so decayed that they had lost all their struts, so the upper storeys on either side leaned drunkenly forward, as if to touch each other, blocking out both light and air. The streets certainly reeked of every stench. The sewers down the centre were crammed with the filth of both man and beast. Huge midden heaps awaited the dung collectors; in the meantime these had become a ghastly battleground. Large rats scurried and slithered, whilst feral cats and dogs hunted the vermin, oblivious to the ragged children playing about these mounds of mouldering mess. The narrow streets were also very busy, being thronged with shops and stalls. A noisy place: signs creaked; doors clattered in the harsh cold breeze; shutters were flung open so cess pots, stool jars and urine bottles could be emptied to loud raucous shouts. The stink forced Cranston and Athelstan to cover mouth and nose as they made their way, sharp-eyed for any filth in the street as well as any from on high.

Westminster, despite the early hour, was busy enough. Clerks hurried to their work in the great offices of state. Some of these thronged the pastry shops and alehouses, hungry, thirsty, eager to break their fast. A few clerks, still inebriated from the night before, indulged in macabre mischief. One cohort of these madcaps had bought a cage of mice into the streets and released them. This immediately attracted the horde of cats and dogs. In their terror, some of the mice fled to where they could, including up the skirts of women: the women screamed stridently whilst their menfolk drew dagger and cudgel to beat and wound the offending clerks. Bailiffs intervened.

Cranston, grabbing Athelstan by the elbow, pushed his way through the increasingly dangerous affray. They continued down the main runnel but had to halt again. A crowd had gathered to watch a housebreaker caught red-handed, being hanged immediately from a pole sign above an apothecary shop. City bailiffs, garbed in black and red, had forced the thief to stand on a stool, then fastened a noose tightly around his throat. Once ready, they'd kicked the stool away, leaving the captured thief to kick and dance to the cries and catcalls of the mob. A bailiff, loudly proclaiming the rights of Infangentheof, which allowed law officers to immediately execute those caught in the very act. A woman, probably related to the condemned man, was desperately trying to grab the felon's legs and pull him down so as to lessen his agony with a swift death. The hanged man twisted and turned on the rope, his face turning blue, his tongue, all swollen, desperately thrust out.

'Satan's tits,' Cranston murmured, 'it's Culpeper!' The coroner drew his sword, pushed his way through the throng and, with one slicing thrust, cut the rope. The felon crashed onto the shit-strewn cobbles. Cranston knelt beside him and cut the noose. The coroner then turned the man's head so Athelstan could recognize Culpeper, who only recently had helped both himself and Sir John to solve a mystery at The Piebald tavern. The bailiffs, at first uncertain about what to do, hung back, but then the leader of the comitatus crouched down and peered at Sir John, who was now helping Culpeper to recover.

'Heaven bless you,' the bailiff shouted. 'It's old Jack, Jack Cranston, the Lord High Coroner.'

'And you?'

'Glaves. We stood together with the Black Prince at Poitiers.'

Athelstan could feel the tension dissipate. Cranston got to his feet, dragging the hapless Culpeper to his. The coroner gave the felon a shake.

'How on God's earth were you caught so easily?'

'Made a mistake, Sir John,' Culpeper croaked, rubbing his scarred throat. 'Didn't expect so many bailiffs. In fact, I didn't expect any at all.'

'Your mistake,' Glaves retorted. 'Sir John, what should we do with him?' Cranston thrust Culpeper away for the bailiff to seize.

'Newgate for you, m'lad.' Cranston tapped Culpeper on the top of his head. 'Put him in a holding cell till I decide what to do with him. Believe it or not, Master Culpeper did good work for me and the Crown some weeks ago, and that may well save him from a hanging. But tell me,' the coroner continued, 'Culpeper's right, why so many of you?'

'Haven't you heard, Sir John? A great robbery at the Exchequer of Coin. A veritable treasure mysteriously stolen. Thousands of freshly minted gold and silver coin. Master Thibault has issued writs to market bailiffs and beadles, surveyors, watchmen, indeed any street official, be it shit collector or stone paver, to be alert over anyone trading in freshly minted coin. To do so is now considered High Treason. Not to report it is High Treason and to knowingly hold such coins . . .'

'Is High Treason.' Cranston finished the sentence. 'And of course, the heralds of the alleyway, the street-swallows and the squires of the sewer, have all been promised pardons and wealth for any information.'

'Precisely, Sir John. Now we must deal with our own little treasure here.'

Cranston agreed. The comitatus swept around him. Culpeper, firmly gripped by the hair, was hauled away, still shouting praises about 'the merciful Lord High Coroner'.

'Lucifer's bollocks!' Cranston breathed, staring around at the stalls and shops. 'I am truly surprised. Thibault is already on the hunt. He hopes that whoever robbed the Exchequer will try to pass the freshly minted coins as soon as possible.'

'Do you think that's true?'

'Do you?'

'No, my Lord Coroner,' Athelstan replied flatly. 'I think . . .' The friar broke off as a bellman, accompanied two horn heralds, came swaggering through the thong. They paused close to Cranston, the bellman ringing his bell. Once he'd finished, the horn heralds blew their small trumpets. The noise of the market swiftly abated. The bellman, in a hoarse proclamation, loudly declared how all good, honest and loyal subjects, on his or her allegiance to the Crown, were to report anyone trading in freshly minted coin of the realm. A similar scene awaited them outside The Inkpot and Pen. A tale-bearer walked on stilts, escorted by two attendants, who were grotesquely garbed like ferocious, cat-faced demons. This wandering minstrel had paused in his usual farrago of nonsense about the devil and a cohort of demons supping at a banquet along the Canterbury Road. Instead, he too was proclaiming, 'News, dire and dreadful, of a great robbery in the royal precincts at Westminster.'

'Master Thibault has been busy,' Cranston growled. 'But he will have to wait, my belly is empty.'

The coroner led Athelstan into the taproom and over to a window seat, a comfortable enclave with its cushions, bench and stools. Athelstan knew Cranston's choice was dictated by a love of dining in some well-kept garden. Cranston often talked about his stay in Italy, and the beautiful countryside outside Florence where, he claimed, he could eat and drink from dusk to dawn. The English climate however, on a sharp January morning, was another matter; the closest Cranston could get to his ideal was to stare through the window, counting how many shrubs and trees he could recognize. He did so now as Athelstan stared around. The taproom was a warm, welcoming place, with its long buttery table; its rafter baskets, full of cured meats, exuded a mouth-watering fragrance. The floor was scrubbed free of dirty rushes, whilst its whitewashed walls were brilliantly festooned with depictions of different quills, pens, inkpots, and other items of the chancery. Delicious smells drifted from the tall vertical hearth with its huge stone stew pot hanging just above the coals. A scullion informed them that a delicious soup was maturing slowly.

'But I will devour it quickly,' Cranston declared, and ordered two deep bowls, along with fresh bread, butter, a dish of stewed vegetables and two blackjacks of morning ale. Once served, Athelstan blessed the food and the two sat eating quietly, lost in their own thoughts. Cranston, his horned spoon constantly dipping into the soup, soon finished his bowl. Athelstan caught his eye, grinned and pushed his half-full bowl across the table.

'Really, little friar?'

'Really, my Lord Coroner.'

Cranston needed no second bidding but fair cleared the table. He then leaned back, cradling his blackjack, his rubicund face creased in pleasure.

'Oh Lord be thanked,' he murmured.

'Oh Lord help us, my Lord Coroner.'

'What do we have here?'

Athelstan picked up the napkin and dabbed his lips. 'We have, Sir John, a truly challenging mystery. Two locked, fortified doors, a spiral staircase made even more dangerous by trip cords. We have five fighting clerks. We have a treasure, bulky and heavy to carry, and yet the robber passes through those two doors like some disembodied spirit. They managed to float up those steps without tripping or alerting anyone. Sir John, they went up, then they came down. As for the clerks, they were fairly young men, skilled in arms, yet there is no sign of resistance. If someone attacked me, Sir John, you would come to my assistance. Nevertheless, there is not a shred of evidence to indicate any of those clerks defended either themselves or their comrades. All five appeared to have just sat there and almost welcomed a cruel death. One thing does bother me slightly.'

'What's that, little friar?'

'We know about the doors, the steps and the clerks, but was there any other guard? After all, Flambard's Tower stands in a lonely, desolate part of the royal precincts. If you leave the antechamber and turn left, there are the exchequer buildings; Flambard's Tower stands in its own ground to the right. And that overlooks what? Common land? Indeed, something like God's Acre at St Erconwald's. An untilled and unused stretch of countryside, where only gorse, bramble, briar and other weeds prosper, along with the occasional copse of ancient oak or sycamore.'

'I see what you mean, little friar, but what did you expect? A comitatus of men-at-arms camped out there? Mounted archers on constant patrol? But to what purpose? Anyone attacking the tower would soon alert the rest of the royal precincts, where you have soldiers enough. What's the use of bringing an army against such a tower? At the end of the day, you have to get through those two doors, plunder whatever's there and leave. No, no, placing some comitatus around Flambard would not make matters better, though I take your point, Athelstan. It wouldn't hurt for a mounted patrol or some other cohort to be present and vigilant during the night watches. Ah well, what's the use of speculating about that? The treasury was robbed and we are still faced with that question: what do we have here?'

PART TWO

'I labour to fetch them in and not to punish vice or sin.'

Master Thibault asked the same a few hours later when Cranston and Athelstan met him, Signor Conteza and, in Cranston's words, 'Lord God Almighty, John of Gaunt, self-styled Regent of the kingdom'. They gathered in the council chamber of the Secret Seal, deep in the chancery mansion at Westminster. A cold, stark room, its whitewashed walls bereft of any ornament except for bleak black crosses, nailed on the walls either end of the chamber. A retainer, garbed in black and gold, served small beakers of chilled white wine and slices of buttered bread. Athelstan used the occasion to study those sitting across the highly polished chancery table.

Lord Gaunt looked very angry, his usual smooth, fair skin suffused with red spots of fury. The Regent kept clawing at his hair, golden as ripe corn, his eerie light blue eyes flitting, full red lips moving soundlessly. Athelstan couldn't decide whether this Plantagenet Prince was praying or quietly cursing. Elegantly garbed in a gorgeous surcoat depicting the royal arms, his fingers and wrists festooned with jewelled rings and bracelets, Gaunt looked what he was: the master of the royal house which had just been plundered of its treasure. Thibault, garbed as usual in black from head to toe, looked his angelic self, his furious temper now carefully hidden, like the true Master of Secrets he proclaimed to be. Signor Conteza was swathed in a thick, heavy military cloak. From the moment they met, the banker constantly complained about the cold. He insisted that more braziers should be brought in, and extra logs thrown on the fire that was now raging in the black stone hearth. The Lombard's face was harsh, sour and unforgiving. Athelstan suspected the banker had a heart of stone and a will of iron. Oh, Conteza would be full of sympathy for the plight of those who borrowed from him and his associates. Nevertheless, Conteza and his pack of wolves would still insist on repayment of every penny of their loan, and this must be sooner rather than later.

Once the servants had left and a guard had been set up outside, Master Thibault, bowing towards Gaunt, posed the question that Athelstan had. 'What do we have here?'

A wall of silence greeted his question so he repeated it, pointing at Athelstan.

'My Lord,' the friar replied. 'We have just been admitted to the place of murder. What can we say?'

'Whatever you say is important. Therefore, whatever you have on your mind, say it. Yes, Sir John?'

'Some questions first.' The coroner leaned across the table. 'The Exchequer of Coin is not like any other office of state. It gathers only when bullion, royal treasure, is being moved, yes? Quite a long process, which begins with gold and silver being taken to the Tower Mints, and so the journey begins, yes?' Cranston simply pressed on, not waiting for an answer. 'The Mint does its work; the coins are weighed, counted, and poured into small treasury bags, which are fastened with twine at the neck and sealed with a wax signet.'

'That is correct,' Thibault murmured.

'Once ready, the money is taken and handed over to whoever it is intended for?'

'Of course,' Thibault snapped.

'And this present business?' Cranston demanded.

'Oh, it's been a few months in preparation,' Thibault replied.

'So,' Athelstan intervened, 'yesterday evening, the Clerks of the Dark arrived to take over from the Clerks of the Light. Magister Despencer received a set of four keys from you, Master Thibault?'

'Of course. They always do and, before you ask, Brother Athelstan, each key is as unique as the lock it turns. There are three such sets. One for me, the other two being used on a daily or nightly basis by either Magister Beaumont or Despencer. They collect the keys at Prime or Vespers from me alone, then return them immediately once their horarium is complete.'

'To you alone?'

'As I have said, Brother Athelstan, to me alone.'

'Nothing strange or out of the ordinary has occurred in or around the Exchequer of Coin?'

'Nothing, Brother Athelstan, I assure you of that.'

'So this morning Beaumont collected the keys from you? Oh, by the way . . .' Athelstan opened the chancery satchel he had placed on the table. 'I have Beaumont's keys, Master Thibault. I will need them, yes?' The master simply shrugged. 'And these are the keys taken from Despencer.' Athelstan plucked out a second set.

'Note the royal arms on the head of the key,' Gaunt rasped.

'I have, my Lord.'

'That means,' Gaunt beat his fist against the table, 'no copy can be made. Such an act would be treasonable.'

'Treason or not,' Athelstan retorted, 'could it be done?'

'No.' Cranston picked up the keys, pointing to the teeth. 'These are specially made by a skilled craftsman.'

'I must inform you,' Thibault said, 'that we had the keys fashioned by a leading member of the Guild. He was supposed to destroy all drawings and anything to do with the fashioning of the twelve keys – three sets of four. It took months to complete. Our intention was to create perfect replicas, so each of the three sets could open the four locks. Unfortunately, our Key-Master did not destroy everything associated with this enterprise.'

'And what happened?' Athelstan's curiosity was pricked. One of his parishioners, Crispin the Carpenter, had mentioned someone called Clement the Key-Master, surely? As a friend, kinsman or both? Was it this person?

'That was years ago,' Thibault continued. 'We raided the Key-Master's house and workshop.'

'How did you know?'

'Oh, some informant left a note with one of the guards of the Secret Chancery. A stark, simple message that the Key-Master was, perhaps, intending to make a fourth set, for he had certainly not destroyed everything.'

'Oh yes, I heard about this.' Cranston spoke up. 'Yet it came to nothing surely?'

'It came to nothing, my Lord Coroner.' Thibault half smiled. 'As I said, we ransacked Clement's house and workshop. We found items he should have destroyed but nothing more. Clement fell from grace. It's not really a matter for our present concern.' Thibault jabbed a finger at Athelstan. 'I tell you this, my good friar, keep safe the two sets of keys you have. One day,' he breathed out noisily, 'the treasure chamber will be used again. But not now.' Thibault shook his head. 'So, Brother Athelstan, tell us what you have learnt from our good clerks.'

'According to Beaumont, the Clerks of the Light opened the first door, pulled at the bell rope and began their climb. On their slow way up, Beaumont carefully removed the trip cords stretched across each step.'

'None of these had been cut or loosed?'

'Apparently not. Beaumont and his companions reached the door to the treasure chamber. No one greeted them. No bell had been pealed in response to theirs. He unlocked the door and entered the treasury.' Athelstan then emphasized his points on the fingers of his right hand. 'All five clerks sat garrotted, each in their enclave, their flesh cold with a faint odour of putrefaction.' Athelstan paused. 'I believe the murders took place shortly after Despencer and his clerks arrived in the treasure chamber: this would explain why the food had barely been touched whilst their corpses had started to stink.'

'And no other sign of violence?'

'Apparently none whatsoever.'

'No evidence of poison or some other noxious powder?'

'No sign, though I have ordered every scrap of food and drink to be taken to the Guildhall for the most thorough scrutiny.'

'Good, good,' Thibault murmured.

'And so?' Gaunt demanded.

'And so,' Athelstan retorted, 'we come to the heart of the mystery. The treasury chamber is formidably fortified, sealed by two heavy, reinforced doors, which can only be unlocked with special keys. No other obvious aperture exists. There are windows but these are heavily barred, sheeted with horn, and they manifest no sign of forced entry or violence. Then, of course, there's the latrine.' Athelstan waved a hand. 'A stool closet, a garderobe, it houses nothing more than a narrow stone chute. I scrutinized that but have yet to inspect where the chute actually ends.'

'In the cellar below,' Thibault replied. 'There's a cesspit, a shit barrel. This is periodically taken away and replaced with another, all scrubbed and drenched with pinewood juice.'

'Has it been replaced recently?'

'In Heaven's name,' Thibault shouted, 'I don't know when shit buckets are emptied, but I will investigate as you,' Thibault smirked, 'must examine what's there. Indeed, Sir John, Brother Athelstan, I thought you would have done that already.'

'We will. We will,' Athelstan replied softly, gently pressing a sandalled foot against the toe of Cranston's boot. A reminder to the coroner not to be provoked or riled by men Cranston secretly despised.'

'My Lord of Gaunt,' Athelstan continued, 'we plan to return to the treasury chamber, but in the meantime we must define the mystery confronting us. How did the assassin enter that chamber? Were doors deliberately left open? However, that would have been noticed, surely? One door perhaps, but two?' Athelstan pulled a face. 'How did the assassin climb those steps and not be tripped by the cords? If not going up, surely on his way down, carrying how many sacks?'

'At least forty,' Thibault wearily replied.

'Someone may have had new keys fashioned,' Gaunt murmured.

'Impossible, my Lord,' Thibault hurriedly whispered. 'How could they, they would need the locks.' Thibault rapped a fist against the tablecloth. 'Never mind the doors, or the trip cords; all those killed were young, able-bodied clerks who served in the royal array.'

'So they were soldiers, more than capable of defending themselves,' Athelstan declared. 'Yet there is nothing to demonstrate they offered the least resistance. How could it be done? So how could all five be killed so expertly without the others intervening?'

'Could they have been poisoned beforehand?'

'It's possible, my Lord Gaunt,' Cranston declared. 'But we detected no sign of poison. No symptoms on their face. What I saw of the food and drink, I would say it was untainted but, of course, we will have to wait to establish that.'

'And Beaumont and his comrades are trustworthy?' Athelstan demanded.

'Royal clerks,' Thibault replied. 'I trust them as much as I trust anyone. Indeed, once they had finished in the Exchequer of Coin, I was going to ask Beaumont and Despencer to investigate a string of murders committed across the city.' He shrugged. 'But that will have to wait. I shall come back to it.' He smiled thinly. 'We are going to need your help – Sir John, Brother Athelstan – to resolve this string of murders but, for the moment, let us concentrate on the present mayhem. Our treasure has been stolen,' he continued flatly. 'Sack after sack,' Thibault swallowed hard, 'of gold and silver coin. But how was it moved?'

'They could have dropped it down the chute in the garderobe,' Cranston offered.

'But the bags must have been bulky,' Athelstan retorted. 'It would be so easy for one to become stuck, caught fast further down the chute. Even human waste can block a latrine. How it was moved is a further mystery.'

'More importantly,' Gaunt drew himself up, 'we do not know who was responsible.'

'I do,' Conteza spat out.

'In a while, signor,' Thibault declared. 'Let my lord finish.'

'We do not know who or how,' Gaunt declared. 'A king's treasure was taken and five royal clerks slaughtered in one of this kingdom's most secure chambers, an arca in itself—'

'As for the who,' Conteza intervened, 'I understand that sacks of spent charcoal were left? Some sort of mocking farewell? This raises the possibility that the Carbonari were involved in the robbery. Indeed, even responsible for it.'

'What!' Cranston declared. 'Who in God's name are the Carbonari?'

'Charcoal burners,' Athelstan declared. 'That's what Carbonari means, isn't it, charcoal burners?'

'And more, Brother Athelstan. The Carbonari are a secret,' Conteza pulled a face, 'or perhaps not so secret, society.' Conteza shrugged. 'They are a close-knit federation of Italian families, be it in Florence or Naples. Unlike other secret societies, they are not against church or state, prince or prelate. They are just thieves, expert and skilled in all kinds of robbery, and they are very proud of what they do. They would regard the plundering of the royal treasury chamber at Westminster as a great achievement. Two years ago, they raided the treasure house of the Knights Hospitallers in Venice. A year later, they plundered the Duke of Milan's jewel house.'

'And the dusty charcoal?'

'Their insignia, their escutcheon. It symbolizes their so-called poverty, which compels them to steal from the rich.' Conteza wiped his lips on the back of his hand. 'They are no poorer than I am. They are certainly much richer this morning. The Carbonari have struck again, I am sure of it.'

'But they are far from Italy,' Athelstan protested. 'Are you saying the Carbonari would cross land and sea to rob this kingdom's secure treasury? To make such a journey is challenging enough. Moreover, as you have just pointed out, there are enough palaces in Italy to keep them plundering for many a day.'

'No, no.' Conteza plucked at a hair on his costly jerkin. 'I am a banker, Brother Athelstan, but I could also be a member of the Carbonari.' He shook his head and laughed. 'I am not, but remember how many of us Italians – what you call money men – live along your Lombard Street in this city. A great number of households; families, together with their servants and retainers, not to mention the crews of our ships, berthed along London's quayside. We Italians flow in and out of this kingdom. For God's sake, Brother Athelstan, we even have a street named after us, a part of the city retained for our banking activities. A good many of our merchant bankers are powerful lords. They have large retinues, many of them fighting men.'

'In other words, there are hundreds of possible suspects amongst the Lombard community here in London?'

'In truth yes, Brother Athelstan. Indeed, I do assure you, we will keep a sharp eye out and an open ear for any evidence which might suggest that the perpetrators of this murderous mystery are members of our community.'

'Master Thibault.' Cranston made to bring the wineskin from his cloak but thought again when Athelstan nudged him.

'Sir John?'

'All the details of the robbery are being voiced along the streets by tale-tellers, heralds of the alleyway, ballad-mongers and the rest. Meanwhile beadles and bailiffs are making careful search for anyone offering freshly minted silver or gold coin. Is it wise? I mean, such publicity?'

'News of the robbery is all over the city, Sir John. You know how these things play out – servitors, servants, retainers, guards.' Thibault pulled a face. 'They will get to know anyway. We have described what happened, be it the wealth taken or the sacks of charcoal left. Anyway,' Thibault drew a deep breath, 'what more is there to say? Sir John, we have to alert the city, the merchants of Cheapside and others. A great robbery has taken place, and I hope, I pray, that the perpetrators, or at least one of them, makes a mistake. Gold and silver coin carry their own message.' He smiled. 'Spend me!'

'There is little more we can say about the robbery,' Athelstan agreed. 'At this moment on God's good candle, we can do nothing but question and search. Which means we have to return to the treasury probably time and again.' Athelstan paused and stared up at the ceiling. He was tempted to ask about whether there had been other guards and, if there had been, why hadn't Thibault mentioned them? Athelstan decided to leave that for the moment, however, as other matters were more immediate.

'Brother Athelstan?'

'My Lords, I am sorry, I daydream. But you mention another problem. You talked of murders . . .?'

'Too true,' Thibault replied. We have in this city, as Sir John Cranston knows, a Guild of Hangmen. Most of these are old soldiers, who accompanied our chevauchées into France. The hangmen are servants of the Crown. To cut to the quick, at least six have been murdered over the last few months, their corpses tossed on dunghills around the city. They've been completely stripped of every scrap of clothing. Their death wound is always the same, a knife thrust through the heart. Pinned on each corpse is a scrawled note.' Thibault opened his belt wallet and slid a dirty piece of parchment across the table. Athelstan studied this and then passed it onto Cranston.

'Oh yes, as I said, I have heard about this,' Cranston murmured. 'I'd have thought the sheriffs would have caught the assassin and hanged him out of hand.'

'They certainly haven't,' Thibault retorted. 'I was about to issue a commission, set up an inquisition under my most trusted clerks, Beaumont and Despencer. Now, because of what has happened, I must turn to you, Sir John. You'll have to meet the Guild of Hangmen. They are housed at The Hanging Tree, a spacious, well-furnished hostelry on Bridge Street, close to the Thames.'

'Yes, yes I know it. We should go there. Yes, we should go

there,' Athelstan repeated, lost in his own reverie. He blinked and whispered a prayer, aware of the deepening silence. He did fleetingly wonder if all of this was a sham. Could Gaunt and Thibault be responsible for the robbery? An audacious attempt to line their own deep pockets. Is that why there was no mention made of other guards? Yet, on reflection, Flambard's Tower had its own defence. What was the truth of all this? Was the Lombard Conteza involved? He had certainly described himself as a man of power, who could whistle up an army of retainers. A merchant prince with all kinds of resources available. A man who jokingly hinted that even someone such as himself could be a member of the Carbonari. The three men opposite him could easily enrich themselves. They could accrue enough wealth from this robbery to live like princes and ride in glory. The real loss, Athelstan ruefully reflected, would be suffered by the English Crown. Young Richard had lost another fortune, and would have to find another to replace what he had lost. Athelstan started as Cranston nudged him.

'My Lord Coroner?'

'Brother, I appreciate you are deep in thought,' Cranston tactfully replied. 'But what about this proclamation?' Athelstan picked up the scrap of parchment. He made out the crudely drawn gallows; the stick-like figure hanging from it. Beneath this rough etching was scrawled, 'Vengeance! The Upright Men and their Reapers never forget.' Athelstan wearily threw it back on the table. 'We all know,' he declared, 'that our hangmen were busy after the revolt. Men and women were executed the length and breadth of this city, as well as in Southwark and the shires around. According to this piece of parchment, the murders are revenge for such executions.'

'So it would seem.' Thibault struck the left side of his chest. 'One dagger thrust, a killing blow to the heart. I may suspect why they were killed but I cannot understand why their bodies were stripped.'

'It is curious,' Athelstan affirmed. 'The hangmen were not assaulted in the street. It would seem, according to the evidence, that they disappear, they are then murdered and their bodies tossed onto midden heaps. Master Thibault, I agree with you. Why are they stripped? Why are their bodies left in such filthy circumstances? And why this note about vengeance?'

'Is there more?' Cranston asked.

'Sir John,' Thibault replied, 'you know what we do. My chancery clerks will send you a schedule of any other information.' Thibault stared across at Athelstan. 'So, what do we have on the robbery?'

'We have, Master Thibault, the same questions that confronted us when we started. Who plundered the treasury? I cannot say. Signor Conteza, you might be correct. The Carbonari may well be responsible. It is quite possible that a coven of outlaws, lurking deep in London, somehow perpetrated this audacious robbery. However,' Athelstan held up a hand, 'we must first deal with those closest to the problem; those who were associated with the guarding of that treasury. Namely, your good selves, but also Beaumont and his four clerks.'

'You suspect them? Or some of them?' Gaunt retorted. 'They could be seized, despatched to the Tower for questioning . . .?'

'No no, my Lord,' Athelstan tartly replied. 'I need to interrogate these clerks in my own fashion. Brutal blows won't bring the truth. Silent logic will. Now, we have five clerks, yes? Each with his own residence, which, by the way, must be searched immediately. Master Thibault, as you suggest, they are possible suspects in this felony. I need to question them, and it would make my life, and theirs, much easier if they were confined comfortably in the one place. Moreover, if we are to investigate the murder of these hangmen, and I take it that we shall, then we must visit the Guild's quarters, namely The Hanging Tree, one of this city's more comfortable taverns.'

'I agree with Brother Athelstan,' Cranston declared. 'It would be best if Beaumont and his comrades were lodged in The Hanging Tree. I could issue writs of restraint, to confine them in one place, as well as a writ of purveyance to Mine Host of The Hanging Tree to provide them with every comfort at the Crown's expense.'

All agreed and the meeting ended soon afterwards. Gaunt beckoned Conteza and Thibault into the shadows at the end of the chamber, whilst Cranston and Athelstan left the Secret Chancery without further ado. For a while, they walked in silence, until Cranston grasped Athelstan's arm.

'Well, little friar, what do you make of all that?'

'Sir John, I make nothing out of nothing. We learned very little. This robbery is the work of sheer subterfuge and the most insidious cunning. We are, as ever, about to enter the meadows of murder. We are going to hunt the most subtle of killers, a true son of Cain, even though God has yet to brand him as such. To achieve that, God and His Grace the King need us. So come, my Lord Coroner, let us return to Flambard's Tower.' Athelstan paused and turned, wagging a finger in Cranston's face. 'Sir John, remember logic.'

'Brother Athelstan, I am all ears.'

'Listen, Sir John, Flambard's Tower wasn't attacked, it wasn't stormed, it was robbed! The answer to this mystery lies in that tower and what happened inside it. The truth will be dictated by what occurred and how it was arranged. So far, I haven't a clue, the slightest perception, but I think I am correct that Flambard's Tower knows the truth.' They moved on, bracing themselves against the freezing breeze. A river mist, a cloud of moving, icy grey, was wrapping itself around Westminster, so dense and thick that torches and candles were being lit all over the royal precincts.

Cranston and Athelstan reached Flambard's Tower. Flaxwith and his cohort were still on guard. The chief bailiff assured Cranston that the corpses had been removed, but everything else remained as it was behind closed doors. Cranston thanked him and took two of the primed lanternhorns, informing Flaxwith that he and his comrades were no longer needed. The bailiffs left the tower, walking as fast as they could through the gathering mist and aiming, like well-loosed arrow shafts, towards the warmth and comfort of The Inkpot and Pen, where they could satisfy their hunger and warm their blood. Athelstan watched them go, their merry voices trailing away, leaving a brooding stillness which pricked at Athelstan's soul. He crossed himself quickly and murmured a prayer against the trickery of Satan.

'What's the matter, Brother?' Cranston stamped his feet against the creeping cold. 'What is the matter, little friar? What gnaws at your soul? Come tell me?'

'Oh, my friend, just a feeling of evil. Some malevolent spirit hovers close by but . . .'

Athelstan pulled open the first door leading into the tower stairwell. For a while he scrutinized both locks, their keys and the edging along the door. 'Nothing,' he whispered. 'Nothing at all. So Sir John, let us climb.' Athelstan, grasping a lantern, led the way. Cranston followed more slowly, stopping now and again to catch his breath. Athelstan helped by pausing on each eighth step to examine the now loosened trip cords. 'A cunning device,' Athelstan declared as he firmly clenched the guide rope. 'How could anyone holding treasury bags go down those steps and remain undetected? Surely they would slip, trip and fall? Anyway let us proceed.'

They reached the top. Athelstan pushed open the door and they entered the murder chamber. Some candle flame still danced under their caps, while the mobile braziers glowed a dull red. Athelstan walked slowly around. He sensed the evil lurking there. An invisible presence, which hid from human view but lurked deep in the shadows, peering out, waiting for its moment. Athelstan continued his walk, drawing in what he could feel. This was a simple, stark chamber, yet it was also a place of hideous sin. Athelstan recalled his own words. The solution to these mysterious murders would lie in this tower. He and Cranston spent some time carefully examining each of the enclaves, as well as other items placed around the chamber, including the dead men's clothing, but their searches bore no fruit.

'There's nothing,' Athelstan exclaimed. 'Not one spark to cast light on these deep, murky mysteries.' Athelstan gestured around. 'This chamber has a fortified door and five windows, though these are filled with horn and securely barred. The only other aperture out of this room is the latrine, garderobe, whatever you call it.' Athelstan walked across and opened the door to the jakes closet. A simple whitewashed enclosure, it housed the bench with a turd hole in the middle and a lavarium which he'd glimpsed on his first visit. He pulled out the sack of plunging rods. Athelstan undid the bundle and, helped by Cranston, began to screw the rods together, before thrusting the lead rod, with a thick sponge fastened to it, down the turd hole, pushing it deeper and deeper until the sponge broke free at the end of the chute. 'There,' Athelstan gasped. 'Sir John, the cleansing rod went down without encountering any obstruction. However,' he sighed, 'a sponge on the end of a rod would slip through easily enough, but treasury bags bulging with hard coin,' he shook his head, 'that might be more difficult. So, Sir John, let's visit the cesspit.' Athelstan stood staring down at the floor.

'Brother?'

'I am going to leave the doors unlocked. Sir John, we are finished here – let the doors hang open. Who knows – perhaps our deadly assassin might come crawling back to this dreadful place – but come, we are done.'

They left the treasury and cautiously made their way down to the cellar. The door to it was bolted at top and bottom. Athelstan drew these and, holding the lanterns, they entered the cellar, an almost circular crypt with two stout, round pillars supporting the steep spiral staircase and treasury above. The air had a nasty reek to it. They cautiously made their way across to where Athelstan reckoned the cesspit stood. Cranston pointed at the goods stored there: sacks of oil, bags of charcoal, rolls of coarse matting, coils of rope and baskets of kindling. This was a storeroom which, Athelstan quickly realized, had no access to the treasury room above, except for the cesspit on the other side of the crypt. They reached this, a stark, simple affair, no more than a large iron hooped barrel standing on a plinth. Its covering lay on the ground beside it, with the end of the latrine chute only a few inches above the barrel. From what he could see, Athelstan realized the chute was a perfectly vertical hollow, hacked through the stone, which had then been smoothed to allow the filth to pass easily and swiftly down. The stench was horrific, the contents of the half-full barrel disgusting. Bowls of pinewood juice and the narrow air vents in the nearby wall did little to mitigate the horrid stink. Both coroner and friar swiftly examined the cesspit then moved away.

'Well,' Athelstan gasped, smoothing the sweat from his face. 'Our noble Regent demanded that we investigate this place, and so we have. Undoubtedly the latrine chute is a sheer vertical drop from the treasury chamber. However, for the life of me I cannot see how it was used in the robbery. The chute is nothing but a narrow, steep funnel. Bags of coin would easily become stuck, and I cannot imagine anyone fishing around in that barrel for their plunder. The cesspit is half full and not recently cleaned by the gong farmers or dung collectors.' Athelstan stood staring at the cess barrel. He turned and grinned at the coroner. 'I am, Sir John, a foolish friar.'

'I am sorry, Brother . . .?'

'The thief might not have dropped the sacks of coin down the chute, only the coins themselves. Yes yes!' Athelstan pointed at the barrel. 'I must think and reflect more deeply, Sir John. I am sure this chute – clear, smooth and totally vertical – was used in the robbery, and that plunging rod also served its purpose but, let me think, let me think.'

'You may well be right,' Cranston retorted, taking a generous sip from his wineskin before offering it to Athelstan, who gratefully gulped the rich Bordeaux. He handed it back and, pulling up the muffler on his robe, returned to the cess barrel. Grumbling under his breath, Cranston reluctantly followed. Athelstan, lifting the lantern, walked around, but then abruptly paused, shaking his head. 'There's nothing suspicious here.' He then tensed.

'Brother?'

'Sir John, listen! What is that noise?'

'Water dripping, I am sure.'

Athelstan startled when the door to the crypt, which they had left off the latch, was slammed shut and the outside bolts drawn across. Athelstan caught a glimpse of flame out of the corner of his eye. He turned. A fiery taper was being pushed through one of the vents; it flared as it hit the ground.

'Oil,' Athelstan shouted. 'Sir John, someone outside is pouring in oil.'

Cranston, despite his bulk, sprang towards the door, even as a sheet of flame leapt up like a demon from the oil now seeping in. More lighted tapers were pushed through. Cranston picked up a shovel and, braving the heat and flames, pounded at the door until it shook and cracked. At the same time, Athelstan used a basket of dust-encrusted rope matting to smother the fire and quell the flames. The fire persisted but then began to diminish. Cranston continued to fight against the danger and was able to withstand the puddles of flame, thanks to his thick, heavy boots. He pounded at the door, which abruptly swung open, and a cloaked, hooded figure stood in the entrance, shouting and beckoning them forward. Cranston helped Athelstan around the pools of fire and out into the freezing mist, still swirling in thick clouds; their rescuer pulled back his hood and lowered his visor.

'Flaxwith!' Cranston roared. 'Good man!' The coroner embraced his now highly embarrassed chief bailiff, whilst Athelstan quickly checked himself and the coroner. No real damage,' he breathed. 'God be thanked for that, and for you, Master Henry. But first, let us return to the crypt.' They did so. Flames still danced and flickered but the threatened inferno had been averted.

'I suspect our assassin intended to pour more oil through the vents and under the door, but your arrival forced him to flee, Flaxwith. Let's put the fire out.'

For a while they pounded at the small puddles of fire, using dust-covered items to shower the flames until they were reduced to thick wisps of black, stinking smoke. Cranston then sent Flaxwith to summon retainers from the palace, who would ensure the fire remained extinguished. The chief bailiff eventually returned with a cohort of labourers, who had been busy repairing a nearby well. They declared that they had smelt the smoke but dismissed it as someone burning refuse. Cranston depicted the fire as an accident, then he and Athelstan left the labourers to it, once again explaining to their leader that the fire must have been the result of some stupid mistake. They walked out of Flambard's Tower. Flaxwith, striding beside Sir John, explained how he'd simply returned to discover what the Lord High Coroner next intended.

'Thank God you did.'

'I heard your banging, Sir John, smelt burning and,' the chief bailiff shrugged, 'the Lord be thanked,' he muttered.

Cranston paused in the gateway leading into the tower bailey; he tapped Flaxwith on the chest. 'And you saw no one?'

'No one, Sir John.'

The coroner opened his purse and thrust two coins into Flaxwith's hand.

'Samson and your merry men will be waiting for you.' The coroner patted Flaxwith on the shoulder. 'And you are certain you didn't even catch a glimpse of our attacker?'

'As I said, Sir John, not a glimpse!'

'And there's been no other visitors to the treasure chamber?'

'None, Brother Athelstan.'

'Good, keep an eye on Flambard's, you'll find I have left the doors unlocked. We have seen what we need to.' Athelstan blessed Flaxwith. 'So go, my friend, and drink the finest ale that The Inkpot and Pen can provide.' Flaxwith promised he would and Cranston and Athelstan stood and watched him go.

'The assassin meant to burn us to death,' Athelstan declared. 'I suspect he was only beginning his mortal sin when Flaxwith arrived. That crypt is pure rock; it would have become as hot as any oven in Hell.' Cranston gently squeezed Athelstan's shoulder.

'And that's where we will send the perpetrator, Brother Athelstan.'

'Oh yes, Sir John, and his journey is about to begin.'

Athelstan recalled those words as he knelt in the nave of St Erconwald's, staring down at the corpse of Clement the Key-Master. The cadaver was gruesomely wounded, the garrotte scar around Clement's throat a deep, purple-red streak. Athelstan, crouching beside the corpse, could only murmur a verse from the '*De Profundis*', then returned to his scrutiny. Clement had been skilfully choked. All the available evidence suggested that Clement had been standing by one of the pillars when the assassin had struck. He'd slipped the noose over the Key-Master's head then expertly tightened it, twisting the small rod as easily as sliding a bolt into its clasp. Death would have been sudden enough. Clement would not have had much time, a matter of heartbeats to resist. However, that would have been futile, Clement swiftly collapsing as he slipped into death.

Athelstan stared around. Cresset torches now flared, their flames leaping like dancers in the ice-cold breeze, which seeped through the gaps, cracks and vents of this ancient church. Lanterns dully glowed whilst great tallow candles had also been lit and positioned around this place of slaughter. Beyond this circle of light were grouped Athelstan's parishioners: dark shrouded figures, hoods, cowls and capuchons pulled close. They stood silent witnesses as their beloved priest, the little olive-skinned Dominican, studied the corpse of a soul long gone to God.

Athelstan crossed himself and clambered to his feet. He certainly felt weary after his return from Westminster. He'd hardly disembarked at the stew steps, when the Hangman of Rochester, along with Crispin the Carpenter and Watkin the Dung Collector, had emerged from the dark to inform him about the murder.

'I hear them whispering, Father.' Thomas the Toad coughed as he edged into the pool of light around his priest. 'I hear them talking. They gossip and jibber in this corner or that. Sometimes they climb the pillars and sit on the rafters. But they always chatter.'

'In God's name who?' Watkin demanded, his voice hoarse and carrying.

'The dead,' Thomas declared.

'Never mind that!' Pike the Ditcher, his thin face all querulous, lifted his hands as he approached his priest. 'In God's name, Father,' he demanded, 'what do we do now?'

'You mean the dead,' Thomas the Toad declared. 'I'll tell them what to do. They'll listen to me.'

Athelstan sensed Thomas would not be silenced, and this would inevitably lead to a very fractious row, even if it were only to ease the tension.

'Before we ask the dead and have a bitter disagreement,' Athelstan's voice rang around the shadow-filled nave, 'can I ask what any of you know about this murder?'

'Father, I can tell you something.' Benedicta stepped forward, her face made even more beautiful by the dark blue, lace-fringed hood. She pointed at the corpse. 'Clement the Key-Master is a friend, a distant kinsman of Crispin's.'

Athelstan raised a hand for silence as the carpenter bustled forward. 'In a while, Crispin. Continue, Benedicta.'

'Father, it's cold. The dead do gather. I can see them now like a moving cloud.'

'Quiet!' Athelstan stilled both Thomas and the groans of the others. 'Benedicta, tell me what you know.'

'Clement arrived just after you left, Father. He was desperate to speak to you. I asked him if he wanted to wait in the priest's house but he said no. He was most reluctant to go anywhere, and that included The Piebald. So I offered him to stay in the church and he accepted. I informed him how the doors would be locked, though the postern gate in the main door could be opened from the inside so, if he did leave, he would not be able to return. If that did happen, he would have no other choice but to go to The Piebald. He said he would stay so I left.'

'Locking the church behind you?'

'Yes, Father. I thought all was well.'

'And so it should have been.' Athelstan smiled thinly. 'But then?'

'The day wore on. I could hear bells ringing for the different prayers. I thought it was time to check on our church and ensure all was well. I came through the Devil's door and immediately glimpsed a glow of light. It wasn't like now with the candles and the lanterns, there was just a flickering glow, only one tallow candle had been lit and placed close to the corpse. I hurried across and saw what you now see. Clement's corpse and the garrotte around his throat. I summoned Mauger the bell clerk—'

'And I said we should leave everything as it was,' the bell clerk interrupted. 'That we should lock the church and mount a guard until you returned.'

'Which I now have.' Athelstan smiled to hide his weariness.

'Oh my goodness,' Benedicta exclaimed. 'Father, forgive me. I forgot all about Blodwyn, our sanctuary man, Blodwyn the Blessed!'

'Oh yes.' Bladdersmiff the Beadle moved into the pool of light. 'Blodwyn was caught filching from the common oven.'

'He fled first to the priest's house where I was cleaning and tidying. Father, I apologize, but all the commotion—'

'No, don't worry!'

'Anyway, Father, I brought Blodwyn here. I let him creep in. I asked if he needed food. He said he had wine and some of the bread he'd stolen, so I left him in the sanctuary enclave behind the high altar and, to be truthful, totally forgot about him.'

'So where is he?' Watkin, leader of the parish council, now asserted himself. 'Stay here, Father. Comrades, let us search the church for this fugitive.'

Watkin's invitation was gleefully accepted by the rest, eagerly joining the hunt for the hapless Blodwyn. A little excitement to break up the monotony of the day. The parishioners hurried off into the darkness, leaving Benedicta and Athelstan to sit on a wall bench.

'You are well, beloved Benedicta?'

The widow woman laughed softly. 'I am well, Father, apart from these present troubles. Oh Father, we've heard stories about a great robbery at Westminster. Are they true?'

'Yes,' Athelstan wearily replied. 'They are true, Benedicta, a great treasure has been stolen. A veritable king's ransom; someone will die for that. Master Thibault, and my Lord of Gaunt are beside themselves with fury. You see, months ago, gold and silver were collected and taken to the smelting ovens at the Tower Mint.

The coins are fashioned, then taken to the Exchequer of Coin to be counted, weighed and checked. These coins were to repay the huge loans the Lombard Bankers have advanced to our young King. Well, in truth, to my Lord of Gaunt, though it was the King's name that went on the indenture. Now the gold and silver have gone, the English Crown will have to find fresh coin to pay its longstanding – and very heavy – debt to the Bardi.' Athelstan rubbed his face. 'Believe me, Benedicta, the storm is only beginning. I can sense Thibault's fear. People will seize on this and use it as a weapon against him. There is little more I can tell you about it. However, all is well here in our little kingdom?'

'Father, Bonaventure hunts. Hubert the hedgehog is firmly ensconced in his bed, whilst Philomel, your old warhorse, lies in his stable, his belly full, his poor head crammed with memories of more sterling days.'

Athelstan smiled, grasped the widow's hand and squeezed it. 'Benedicta, without you, God knows what I would do! However, for our present troubles? I doubt if my beloved parishioners will find Blodwyn here, whilst it's time I was gone. Tomorrow, immediately after the Jesus Mass, tell the hangman and Crispin to break fast with us.'

Athelstan made to get up when the postern in the main door was flung open. The figure who came striding through was cloaked and cowled, a swiftly moving shadow. Athelstan felt a spurt of fear, but relaxed when the man pulled back his hood to reveal a swarthy, sunburnt face.

'Michael the Painter,' Benedicta declared.

'Michael the Cypriot,' Athelstan retorted, clasping the man's hand.

Benedicta immediately began to ask about the Cypriot's wife and twin children. Athelstan sat down and stared at this most recent arrival in his parish. A refugee from Turkish oppression, Michael and his family had fled to London, and soon settled in St Erconwald's, where the Cypriot had established himself as a most reliable craftsman. 'A true fixer of things,' as Benedicta called him.

'Michael.' Athelstan sketched a hasty blessing. 'Have you come about your babies being baptized?'

'I have, Father.' Michael's accent was clipped but clear. He pointed up the nave. 'But I have also heard there has been a death?'

'A brutal murder,' Athelstan replied.

'God help us all,' the Cypriot retorted. 'May St Michael and all his angels set up camp around us. As for me, Father, I became curious about what I heard and saw. Anyway, as I approached the church, a stranger stopped me.'

'Who?'

'Father, he was a stranger, all muffled and visored against the cold. He handed me this.' Michael took a small sack from beneath his cloak. 'He said it was for you, Father.'

Athelstan grasped the sack and felt its contents. He knew what it was even before he undid the piece of dirty cord and shook the small pieces of charcoal into his hand.

'Father?'

'Nothing, Benedicta, nothing for a while.' Athelstan retied the small sack and thrust it into his pocket. He then rose and clasped both Benedicta and the Cypriot on the shoulder. 'Goodnight to you both.' He murmured. '*Pax et bonum*. Do not concern yourselves.'

'Nothing!' Norbert No-Nose, one of Pike the Ditcher's henchmen, shouted as he came out of the darkness. 'Nothing, Father,' he repeated. 'No sign of Blodwyn the Blessed.' Norbert's proclamation was echoed by other parishioners, who now gathered around their priest. Athelstan, hiding his tiredness, heard them out, satisfied that they had scoured the church and found no trace of Blodwyn.

'In which case,' Athelstan raised a hand, 'I give you all my most solemn blessing.'

'Truly solemn?' Ranulf the Ratcatcher exclaimed.

'Most solemn indeed.'

'In which case.' Ranulf knelt, placing the box containing his two ferrets, Audax and Ferox, on the paving beside him. The rest of his fellow parishioners followed suit, shuffling mud-caked boots and exclaiming at how cold the slabs were. Athelstan bestowed his blessing, wished them goodnight and left. He then paused and turned back.

'Benedicta, please make sure all candle flames are extinguished and the church is locked.'

'Of course, Father.'

Athelstan left and quickly strode through God's Acre. The darkness was truly freezing, closing about him like a shroud.

'Father,' a voice sang out. 'The dead are gathering. They ride the wisps of mist and want to gather for secret conclave.'

'Goodnight, Thomas the Toad,' Athelstan called back. 'Leave the dead – not to mention me – in peace.'

'God bless you, Father.'

Athelstan trudged on. He was becoming used to Thomas the Toad's proclamations and his insistence that he could talk to the dead, or rather that the dead spoke to him. He wondered why this eccentric little man hadn't joined the rest of his parishioners in the hunt for Blodwyn. But, there again, Thomas was a law unto himself. The friar reached the priest's house, unlatched the door and went in, securing it firmly behind him.

'This small cottage,' Athelstan whispered, 'is a gift from God and greatly comforts me.' He stared round and rubbed his hands. The fire had been built up. The bowl on the tripod above it was full of hot, steaming oatmeal. Fresh bread had been left in a linen cloth, along with small pots of honey and butter, whilst the floor and table had been scrubbed to perfection. Athelstan crossed himself, put down his satchel and went over to the lectern. He took the book resting there and sat down at the large kitchen table. He put his face in his hands, sighed, then rose to fetch a stoup of ale from the small buttery.

'So, friar,' he whispered to himself, 'calm yourself. Distract your mind from the cares of the day.'

He opened the psalter that Prior Anselm had loaned him from the great library of Blackfriars, the motherhouse of the Dominicans just across the Thames. Athelstan loved to leaf through this, examining the jewel-like miniature pictures, each a story in itself with its ornate script and mythical creatures. Athelstan turned to his favourite, where demon bats hung upside down from a vine tree. Each of the grapes contained a different face, be it pig, fox, rat or badger. Beneath the vine, horn-headed devils boiled a drunkard in a bubbling vat of scalding water. The picture overleaf depicted Murder. Athelstan liked nothing better than to study the intricate, highly coloured picture, where Murder was portrayed as a young, flaxen-haired lady of the court, in her brilliantly hued gown and demure white veil. At first glance, a vision of beauty, except for the dagger the woman concealed in one hand and a poisoned chalice in the other, the tainted wine bubbling around the goblet's jewel-encrusted rim.

The picture made Athelstan reflect on the day and his meeting with the Kingdom of Darkness which sheltered the murderers he was hunting. He put the book down, stared at the fire and recalled Flambard's Tower, that grim donjon with its specially fortified doors. In his mind's eye, Athelstan went through into the tower. He would ring the bell, and the one in the treasure chamber was supposed to peal a reply. Athelstan imagined going up that winding, steep, narrow staircase. He would have to carefully search for the trip cord stretched across each eighth step. At the top the door was locked. Nevertheless, the assassin went through. And then what? The chamber was guarded. Despencer and his four comrades were all mailed clerks, veterans of the battlefield. Nonetheless, each and every one of them had been cruelly garrotted without the slightest hint of any resistance, by men trained to sell their lives dearly. So how was it done? If the assassin had attacked one of the clerks, surely the others would have intervened? However, all five went as quietly into the dark as lambs to the slaughter, with no sign of any resistance or defence. Once the killing was over, the assassin . . . Athelstan glanced up, or was it more than one? Yet, surely, if that was the case, Despencer and his comrades would have disputed their entrance?

'Whatever,' Athelstan murmured. 'The assassin then plundered the treasure chamber and removed thousands of gold and silver coins. But how?' he asked himself. 'Not down those steep, sharp steps, surely?' He and Cranston had also examined the latrine, its privy hole and chute stretching down to that barrel, half full of stinking, putrid waste. Then there was the burnt charcoal left in the sacks. Was that a sneering, contemptuous gesture by the Carbonari? But why? Why bring themselves to the attention of everyone? Did they have some longstanding feud with the Bardi and the other Lombard banks? Was there in truth more than one assassin, a solitary robber? But, there again, that brought him back to the vexed question of how Despencer and his comrades were overcome. Athelstan shook his head. 'The gold and silver,' he whispered, 'would surely need more than one man to carry it away?'

Athelstan closed his eyes. Who could deploy, he wondered, an army of accomplices? One of the riffler chiefs of London? A gang leader? Yet, why stop there? Conteza was powerful and well supported but, there again, Athelstan grimaced, so is Master Thibault. Was the robbery and the horrid murders the result of some clever, subtle conspiracy? Was Master Thibault intent on filling the pockets and purses of himself as well as his Master Gaunt? Or did Conteza wish to steal the treasure hoard for himself and his bank, then insist that the English Crown honour its debt, so a fresh payment be made?

Athelstan's eyes grew heavy, but he started at the frantic scratching at the door. Athelstan rose and opened it. Bonaventure sped in like an arrow towards the fire. The great tomcat then stretched out, revelling in the warmth. Athelstan returned to his reflections. 'That thief, that murderous thief,' he exclaimed to a now curious Bonaventure, 'tried to kill me and Sir John in that crypt. He was almost caught in the act.' Athelstan paused. 'And yet, if he had been allowed to continue for even a few breaths . . .' Athelstan fell silent. The assassin had been unsuccessful, but he had, perhaps, destroyed evidence in that gloomy crypt. Athelstan prayed that was not the case because he had a growing certainty, despite all appearances to the contrary, that the crypt had definitely played an important part in the great robbery, though for the life of him he could not say how.

Had that same assassin, he wondered, actually crossed to Southwark to leave that bag of charcoal? But why? A warning? A threat? Was the murder in St Erconwald's connected in any way with those in the Exchequer of Coin at Westminster? Athelstan shifted and started in his chair, his eyes growing increasingly heavy. 'Enough is enough.' He whispered. Bonaventure had now leapt onto the table and was studying him curiously with his one good eye. 'Bonaventure,' Athelstan blessed his feline companion, 'the day is done, my Lord Cat, and so are we. Come, we are for the dark, my friend.'

PART THREE

'Some desire the gold their words do bring.'

Athelstan woke early the next morning after a deep, refreshing sleep. He washed, shaved, donned his robe and sandals and, with Bonaventure solemnly following, went down to the church to celebrate his Jesus Mass. In theory, Athelstan reflected, no services should be celebrated in St Erconwald's following the hideous murder the day before. However, as Athelstan confessed to Mauger whilst he vested for Mass, it would take weeks to deal with the archdeacon's chancery so he would reconsecrate the church himself. Athelstan then celebrated his Mass with the majority of his parishioners crowding beneath the rood screen. So many that the friar deeply suspected they had not come to greet the gospel, but to hear about the murder, their curiosity much sharper than any devotion. Once the Mass was finished, Athelstan, ignoring the questions of his parishioners, gave instructions to Mauger and hurried back to the priest's house, where Benedicta, Crispin and the Hangman of Rochester joined him for hot scones and a pot of morning ale from Merrylegs' pastry shop. Athelstan blessed the food before inviting his guests to eat and drink. They did so, Benedicta assuring her priest that Mauger would look after both sanctuary and sacristy, adding that Clement the Key-Master's corpse was now honourably ensconced in the parish death house.

'Where was he from?' Athelstan put down his pewter cup. 'He was a relative of yours, Crispin?'

'A distant kinsman, Father.'

'And what was he doing at St Erconwald's? I understand he came to visit me but why?' Crispin just grimaced, his thin, pasty face taut and anxious. He winked at the priest, before glancing at the others sitting around the table. 'Come Crispin,' Athelstan spread his hands, 'you know you can trust everyone seated here. Your relative has been brutally murdered. I want to discover the truth. I need to trap the perpetrator, so he is caught fast, judged and hanged.'

'Clement was a good man,' Crispin blurted out. 'He was kind, thoughtful and, above all, most skilled in his trade.'

'He was a locksmith?'

'More than that, Father, a true Key-Master.'

'We have heard stories about the great robbery at Westminster,' the hangman declared, 'of clerks being slaughtered, treasure stolen? Even about bags of spent charcoal being left as a mocking farewell?'

Athelstan smiled at this most skilled of artists. The hangman had a God-given talent, a lesson to Athelstan never to judge the man's soul by the hangman's troubled past and eerie looks. The executioner now sat combing his long, straw-coloured hair with his fingers, his snow-white peaked face cleanly shaven, which emphasized even more his blood-red lips.

'Father, you are staring at me?'

'My apologies, I am letting my mind drift. Yes, you're correct, bags of charcoal were left by the robbers.'

'How is it that such detail is now well known?' Benedicta asked.

'Oh, that's the deliberate intention of Master Thibault. He has proclaimed what happened in the hope – vain, I think – that someone will come forward to provide information and so receive a reward.'

'Thibault would probably torture anyone who did,' Crispin retorted, 'then hang them out of hand.'

Athelstan laughingly agreed before asking Crispin to continue telling them what he knew about Clement.

'Your kinsman was no parishioner here,' Athelstan declared. 'Perhaps I may have glimpsed him when he came across on a visit.'

'True, Father, Clement owned a narrow tenement in New Fish Yard.'

'Ah yes,' Athelstan declared. 'That's near Bridge Street, so it must be within walking distance of The Hanging Tree.'

'You know that?' Crispin asked.

'Well, everyone knows The Hanging Tree,' Benedicta retorted.

'Yes they do, and Sir John and I have business there but, for the moment, Crispin, let's hear what you have to say.' The friar mockingly beat his breast. 'And I'll try not to interrupt.'

'Clement lived in New Fish Yard; however, years earlier, he had a splendid mansion in Cheapside. He was a wealthy, well-placed member of the Guild. And then disaster struck, swift as an arrow from a bow.' Crispin paused, staring into the tankard he clenched. 'Strange,' he continued. 'These stories about the great robbery at Westminster. Father, you do realize it was our Clement who fashioned the locks and keys for the two fortified doors in the treasury? Oh yes.' Crispin nodded at Athelstan's quickening interest. 'Clement the Key-Master was responsible for them. They were to be a work of art, the legacy of a great craftsman.'

'I'll remember that.' The friar waved a hand. 'And so, the threads are becoming even more entwined. Tell me, when did this all happen?'

'Some eight years ago, just before the old King's death. Anyway, at the time, Clement had sworn a great oath that all casts, workings, drawings – indeed anything and everything connected with those locks and keys – were to be utterly destroyed. If you wish, Father, make enquiries; it's a common enough practice in the construction of a fortified area.'

'I am sure it is, so what happened?'

'Clement made a very foolish mistake. He kept the schedule of documents for the royal works: drawings, sketches, as well as bits and pieces associated with the locks and keys. Someone secretly accused him of trying to fashion extra keys. They must have laid this information before the Secret Chancery. Clement's house, shop and foundry were raided by royal serjeants led by Master Thibault. They seized the schedule, and anything associated with the fashioning of the keys and locks. Clement was threatened with being arraigned before King's Bench on a charge of treason and other dreadful felonies. However, the proof was not sufficient, the truth hard to establish, whilst Clement's good character and excellent service saved him from any physical punishment.'

'And what did Clement plead?'

'Father, he simply maintained he had made a dreadful mistake. He certainly had,' Crispin added fiercely, 'and he paid for it. He was dismissed from the Guild, exiled from its councils, and rejected by both prince and prelate. Nobody wanted to do business with him. He was reduced to begging for work. In a word, Clement's life was utterly ruined.'

'Good Lord,' the hangman breathed, 'poor man!'

'Poor man indeed!' Crispin continued heatedly. 'Matters went from bad to worse. Clement's wife Anna contracted a bloody flux and died of a wasting disease. Clement suffered the same.' Crispin rubbed his stomach. 'Some malignant humour of the belly. Tragedy too for his own beloved son, Columba. He married Isabella Fleming, the only daughter of Simon Fleming, City Hangman and Master of the Guild of Hangmen, as well as being Mine Host of The Hanging Tree tavern on Bridge Street. The marriage was not the happiest, it had its problems, and then disaster struck again; Columba simply disappeared.'

'When?'

'About three years ago.'

'Why?'

'Father, we don't know. A sturdy young man, devoted to his father, Columba just disappeared. Vanished like mist on a summer's morning.'

'And his effects?'

'Oh, some of these were missing, but it appeared that Columba had apparently packed a fardel and left for pastures new. Oh, by the way, Father,' Crispin scratched the side of his head, 'I have yet to search Clement's clothing, but I did visit his tenement across the river. I found nothing of note. Clement certainly died a poor man.'

'But what was the reason for his son's disappearance?' Benedicta asked.

'Surely some reason was given? Or even later the true cause established?' Athelstan intervened.

'That's possible, Father. Clement always believed that Thibault's raid of his house and workplace was due to information secretly being laid against him in the Court of the Secret Chancery. At first Crispin thought it might be a rival who had betrayed him. However, when Columba disappeared, Clement began to wonder if it was his son.'

'Surely not?'

'Father, Columba was a merry soul who, on occasion, liked nothing more than revelling in the taproom of The Hanging Tree. Perhaps he said something he shouldn't have, let slip information about his father's work and, unwittingly, revealed what Thibault's minions later discovered. Whatever, Columba disappeared with a few paltry possessions. He made no farewell and has made no attempt to return. Nor did he communicate with his beloved father. No real reason was ever given for his disappearance. Clement was heartbroken, a mere shadow of his former self, until a few weeks ago. Clement started to visit me again. He used to in years gone by, but the tragedies he suffered drove a wedge between Clement and all those who cared for him. By then Clement was certainly ill, but I glimpsed a fresh determination. He declared he had reflected on his litany of troubles and reached certain conclusions.' Crispin supped greedily from his tankard.

Athelstan repressed an abrupt chill of fear. Deep in his heart, he sensed he had reached another gateway into the meadows of murder. Was Crispin hinting that some evil, long and lasting, had devastated Clement, his family, indeed his entire world?

'I tried to talk to him.' Crispin put the tankard down. 'But Clement's mind was like dice tumbling in a cup. He would say things but not explain. Hint but never make clear.'

'Such as?'

'Clement began to believe something dreadful had happened to his son. How someone, he didn't say who, had deeply blighted his life and of all those he loved. Moreover, in the last few weeks when he was talking about Columba, he would make the same mysterious remark. How his son would never have left without "The Walsingham".'

'"The Walsingham"?' Athelstan exclaimed. 'What did Columba have to do with that great shrine to the Virgin Mary?'

'Columba nourished a deep devotion to Our Lady of Walsingham, but I could never make Clement explain his remark. Instead, Clement maintained he needed to speak to someone he could trust. Some priest who would hear his confession and listen to what he had discovered. I pointed out that London was full of priests who would shrive him at the mercy pew, but Clement just shook his head. To be honest, Father, Clement was a city dweller where churches stand at every corner. I never thought of you till I met Clement one night at The Hanging Tree.'

'He went there often?'

'Recently very often. You see Isabella, his daughter-in-law, had received a decree giving her freedom to remarry, which she duly did to Robert Penon, who now manages her father's tavern. They cared for Clement, said he was always welcome there.'

'And Clement's search for a priest?'

'One night I was talking about the parish, and I suddenly thought of you.'

'That's kind of you,' Athelstan teased.

'Father, you have enough troubles. In truth, I was praising you. Clement became interested. He had visited St Erconwald's before, though he had very little to do with our church. Once I had mentioned you, I brought him here so he could see you. I urged him to meet you. At first he was reluctant, but eventually he agreed. However, he insisted on making the journey by himself. Of course, I offered to help but he was adamant. He insisted on coming here alone as he did yesterday. I had no choice but to leave him to it.'

'He arrived just after you left, Father.' Benedicta replied to Athelstan's questioning look.

'Tell me again,' Athelstan replied. 'It is very important. As far as we know, you were the last person Clement spoke to before he was murdered. So, tell me again and include every detail!'

'Clement said that he needed to see you urgently on a most important matter. I said he could stay elsewhere, be it at The Piebald or with me at the priest's house. I pointed out that the church was to be locked. He seemed gentle enough, Father, a good man. I'd glimpsed him before with Crispin. Ah well. He was determined to stay in the church, so I let him. I felt he might need to pray or meditate. I gave him some ale and scones. I then explained that I was locking the church but, if he had to leave, the postern in the main door opened outwards. However, once through, and it had shut behind him, he would not be able to re-enter. Clement seemed distracted, but he appeared happy enough with what I told him.'

'And he said nothing about the reason for his visit?'

'Only to see you.'

'And Blodwyn?'

'Oh Father, he crept into the parish like a spider, sometime around the Gabriel bell. He had eluded his pursuers, darting into God's Acre and disturbing me in your house. He claimed sanctuary, adding that he was being pursued by the market beadles. From what I can gather, Blodwyn regards such pursuits as an occupational hazard.'

'True,' the hangman intervened. 'Blodwyn is a notorious felon, nothing serious. He just roams both the City and Southwark, garbed in his ragged scarlet jerkin, ripe and ready for mischief. I know a little about him. Blodwyn is sometimes hired as part of the hangman's escort. He sits in the death cart and helps secure prisoners until they are turned off the ladder.'

'I brought him in here,' Benedicta declared. 'I threw one of Philomel's blankets around him, took him back through God's Acre, opened the postern in the main door and thrust him through. I think he had a wineskin with him and some of the bread he had stolen. I just regarded him for what he was – totally hapless.'

'Yes, yes,' Athelstan murmured absent-mindedly, staring down at the table top. He reflected how, in the pursuit of an assassin across the meadows of murder, the twisting paths of other mysterious deaths often crossed the very one he was hastening down. The same was true here. Clement the Key-Master had fashioned those locks and keys, the ones he had examined in Flambard's Tower. Was there a connection here? Had Clement, either then or now, been involved in some plot to plunder the treasury? Or had he just made a stupid mistake and paid a terrible price? In addition, who had betrayed him and given the information to the Secret Chancery? Were there other keys? Yet that would be almost impossible.

'Lord save us,' he breathed. 'Well Benedicta, is there anything else?'

She shook her head.

'And so we come to the murder.' Athelstan abruptly rose and grabbed his cloak slung across his chancery chair. 'Come,' he urged. 'Let us play our own murderous masque.' His companions, startled by their priest, hurriedly rose and followed him out of the house and down to the church. Once inside, Athelstan locked the corpse door and asked the hangman to check that all the other doors were locked. He then gathered his parishioners around the pillar where Clement's corpse had been found.

'Let us pretend.' Athelstan's voice echoed hollowly through the nave, a place of flitting shadows broken only by the dancing pools of light from the tapers and candles glowing in the Lady Chapel. For a moment, Athelstan wondered if Clement's spirit still hovered close. Some theologians argued that after death souls became deeply disturbed, especially if they had been abruptly thrust into the dark. So anxious, so frightened, they hovered close to the place of their death. Was Clement here, watching from behind the veil? And would he remain close until the confusion dissipated and his assassin was brought to judgement?

'Father, you brought us here.'

'My apologies to all,' Athelstan retorted. 'Now look, Crispin, you pretend to be Blodwyn, go into the sanctuary enclave.' The friar grinned. 'Though I cannot give you a bulging wineskin to drown your sorrows like the one carried by our unexpected guest.' Crispin nodded and walked away, up the sanctuary steps, through the rood screen and into the darkness around the high altar.

'Benedicta, you simply watch what happens. Giles,' Athelstan turned to the hangman, 'you are the assassin and I'm your victim so, I'll stand facing the pillar. Right, let us begin.'

Benedicta walked away. Athelstan turned his back. He was about to say he was ready when the garrotte string looped over his head, drawing tight around his throat. Athelstan panicked, lashing out, before the cord slackened. Athelstan, gasping for breath, just slumped down to rest against the pillar. He stared unbelievingly at the hangman squatting before him.

'So swift,' Athelstan gasped. 'I never heard, saw or felt anything till that cord . . .'

'Quick and quiet, Father. Once that noose is tightened, there's really very little chance. A few heartbeats and you'll soon be a member of the heavenly choir.'

'I understand that,' Athelstan retorted. 'But why not the knife or the crossbow?'

'A bolt from an arbalest could miss or fail to kill. A dagger thrust is not so certain. There's always the danger of the blade slipping or its point hitting something hard, a medal or a belt buckle. No,' the hangman's snow-white face creased into an icy smile, 'the garrotte is swift, no more than a few gasping breaths. I can do this easy.' He added, 'But not the knife, the sickening thrust . . .'

'Very well.' Athelstan clambered to his feet. 'Our assassin has killed Clement; why, we don't know. Nevertheless, the deed is done and he must flee. But how could he, from a locked church?'

'The postern in the main door?'

'No, Benedicta, that would take him out onto the concourse.

He could easily be seen. Many of our parishioners assemble there; people are constantly crossing to and fro, at least until the Compline bell. Then there's the bailiffs who pursued Blodwyn; a character we must return to. And so,' Athelstan joined his hands as if in prayer, 'murder is committed, the perpetrator escapes. But how? I can provide one solution. Benedicta, you returned to the church and discovered the corpse? Please,' he smiled, 'repeat exactly what you did yesterday when you came in here to find poor Clement.'

Benedicta hurried off, leaving the church through the Devil's door. A short while later she returned through the corpse door, flinging it open and hurrying across to where Athelstan and the hangman stood. She paused, all breathless, and pointed to the base of the pillar.

'Clement was lying there.'

'So, as soon as you entered the church, you crossed immediately to here.'

'Yes Father, I did.'

'Why?' Athelstan demanded. 'Why should you hurry through a darkening church?' Athelstan closed his eyes, opened them and smiled. 'Very, very clever,' he declared. 'You came hurrying across because of the lighted tallow candle, yes? The church was cloaked in darkness, so you were curious about a glow of light where, in fact, there shouldn't have been one.'

'That's true, Father. I opened the door. I came in and glimpsed the dancing light. Of course, I was curious at a single tallow candle burning next to a pillar.'

'Yes, my dear Benedicta, that's logical. Our killer must have taken that candle from the sacristy and,' Athelstan emphasized his words, 'if he went there, Blodwyn must have glimpsed him. Or he Blodwyn . . .' Athelstan led them up the sanctuary steps and across into the sacristy. He then turned and went out again. Crispin, peering around the altar, clambered to his feet.

'I understand what you are doing, Father,' he called out. 'There's a very good chance Blodwyn and the killer met.'

'Could Blodwyn be the killer?' the hangman asked. 'I mean, he is a man associated with death. He knows something about nooses and knots. He could fashion a garrotte and use it as skilfully as anyone else.'

'I doubt it,' Athelstan replied. 'Blodwyn fled here seeking sanctuary.'

'He may have stolen the bread simply as a pretext for entering St Erconwald's and slaughtering Clement.'

Athelstan shook his head. 'My friend,' he declared, 'why should Blodwyn kill Clement?'

'Still a possibility,' the hangman retorted. 'After all, Blodwyn has fled. Why?'

Athelstan nodded in agreement. 'Giles, you are correct: it's a possibility, but let's continue. What we do know is that the assassin played a clever trick. Once he had murdered Clement, the assassin hid in the darkness, waiting for Benedicta to return. We all concede that when you opened the door, Benedicta, you were going to hurry over to discover why a light is glowing near that pillar. You leave the door off the latch and the assassin simply slips out into the dark.'

'And Blodwyn followed him.'

'Possible. But why?' Athelstan tapped a sandalled foot against the freezing flagstone. 'Why did Blodwyn flee sanctuary? After all, he was the one who sought it. He certainly risked capture, so why? As you pointed out, Giles, he was alone in the church with Clement and he disappeared after that poor man's death. He could be the assassin, though I doubt it very much. So what other explanation is there for Blodwyn's disappearance? Did he see something which truly frightened him? In addition, one further question. Blodwyn was alone in this church with Clement, I concede that. But who else knew the Key-Master was coming here, apart from you, Crispin?' The carpenter simply shrugged and shook his head.

'And one final question; why was the small bag of charcoal given to me? You've all heard the stories about the great robbery at Westminster.' A murmur of agreement greeted his question. 'Does that strange gift mean there's a further link between the robbery and Clement's murder?'

'Further?' the hangman demanded.

'Well, we now know the story about Clement and the keys to the locks on the royal treasury. I just wonder if it is all linked in a chain of events, which stretches from the darkness and disappears into the darkness. Why did Clement cross the Thames on a freezing January day? Anyway . . .' Athelstan paused as the corpse door was flung open and Tiptoft, Cranston's messenger, garbed in his usual Lincoln green, strode into the church. Tiptoft's sharp, pasty face was even more so, his spiked red hair gleaming with nard.

'Sir John?'

'Of course, Brother Athelstan. He urgently seeks your counsel. He waits for you at The Hanging Tree. I am to accompany you there.'

'I am sure you are.' Athelstan sketched a blessing in the air. 'Benedicta, Crispin, our church is now in your care. Giles.' He beckoned at the hangman. 'Please come with us. Tiptoft, you hasten ahead and tell Sir John that I follow close behind.'

Within the hour, Athelstan and the hangman left St Erconwald's, going down the narrow alleyway which housed Merrylegs' pastry shop and The Piebald tavern. The latter was crammed with customers, people pushing through to buy Joscelyn's ale and listen to Watkin. The dung collector was now regaling customers with the story of 'the horrid murders carried out at both St Erconwald's and the King's own palace at Westminster'. Watkin had set himself up as a teller of tales, and one without the slightest regard for the truth. Athelstan, who paused for a while to listen, groaned inwardly at the dung collector's lurid account. Watkin had embellished his story with all kinds of horrors, be it dark spirits crawling along the church walls, or the living dead who scampered up the tower and played host to the sinister lords of the air. Athelstan realized it would be futile to intervene. The parishioners would listen to him but then pester Athelstan for what he knew. In truth, Watkin and Joscelyn were like Herod and Pilate: they had formed an unholy alliance. Watkin would spin the tale, Joscelyn would sell the ale, and both would divide the profits. Athelstan, cloaked and cowled, forced his way past.

They reached the approaches to what Athelstan always called 'the descent into Hell'. The friar truly feared London Bridge, and the causeway onto it was just as frightening. Athelstan wryly believed that the visions of Hell captured by artists such as the hangman paled in comparison to this antechamber of Hades. Athelstan had read the accounts of the great Celtic saints who experienced visions of Satan's empire, and the friar firmly believed that the approaches to London Bridge were in full accord with such dire descriptions. All kinds of people surged backwards and forwards, a swirling sea of colour, sound and smells. Progress was slow. He and the hangman had to pause as a group of Smithfield grooms tried to calm a horse. The animal had broken free, desperate to escape from the severed head of a pig carried on a platter by a butcher's boy. Once the horse was settled, the crowd moved on, taking Athelstan and his companion with them. They pushed through groups both boisterous and belligerent. Eventually, they reached the execution yard; the slaughter ground of Southwark. Peace-breakers and night-walkers were being fastened in the different pillories and stocks, to be held fast by neck, wrist or ankle. One prisoner was screaming as his ears were nailed to a board. Another stridently cursed the bailiffs who branded his cheek with a bloody 'F' for 'Forgery'. The line of gallows stretching down to the bridge were festooned with the cadavers of river pirates convicted by the morning courts and immediately despatched to judgement. Kinspeople of the hanged thronged beneath the dangling legs, eager to seize the corpses once they were cut down, as well as to protect the cold flesh from warlocks. These sorcerers swarmed about, eager to pluck the dead and use such ghastly morsels during their gruesome midnight rites.

A short distance away, Friars of the Sack gathered to sing hymns; songs of mourning as well as the psalms for the dead. The friars had to compete against the clamour from troubadours, minstrels, tale-tellers and the heralds of the alleyways. Makeshift stalls had been set up to sell drink and food, all of questionable origin. Nevertheless, the pasty pages and hotpot girls did a thriving trade. Both the hangman and Athelstan kept their purses close against the naps, foists and pocket-pickers who infested the area, searching for victims. These squires of the sewer were most skilled at avoiding the attention of the bailiffs and beadles who were busy around the scaffolds and pillories. A cohort of dwarfs, all dressed in the same livery, performed a drunken dance to the tune of reedy pipes, flutes, and the hollow beat of a tambour.

The hangman sensed Athelstan's unease and kept close to the friar, helping him through the crowd as they moved onto the bridge. Athelstan always felt highly nervous once this happened. To all appearances, the thoroughfare was like any city street, with buildings on either side, whilst the usual stench and noise permeated the salty air. At times, however, the bridge would shudder and shift. Gulls, screaming piercingly, stooped low, dark shapes fluttering like lost souls, desperate to break free. Now and again all this noise would fade, then the clatter of the windmills, as well as the surge of the river against the starlings below, would be a sharp reminder of where he was, crossing a piece of wood between heaven and earth.

They passed Becket's chapel, built in the centre of the bridge. Choirboys, under their master from St Paul's, stood on the steps leading up to the small church. They were carolling a hymn to the saintly, martyred archbishop. Behind them, Robert Burdon, the diminutive keeper of the bridge, as well as conservator of the severed heads impaled on its spikes, was busy at his work. Dressed in his usual blood-red taffeta, Burdon had washed, pickled and tarred a number of severed heads. He was busy combing the hair on these gruesome remains, so a Friar of the Sack could bless them when they were arranged along a table just outside the church. Athelstan crossed himself whilst the hangman murmured his own prayer.

They moved on and at last they were across. The city side of the bridge was much more orderly, despite the long line of carts and sumpter ponies taking provisions to the Tower. The great fortress reared up against the sky: 'The House of Blood, the Home of the Red Slayer', as Sir John described this majestic yet sombre building, brooding over the city. Athelstan, threading his ave beads, followed his companion into Bridge Street, which abruptly turned and twisted away from the shadow of the Tower. On a corner deep in the ward, and in its own ground, stood The Hanging Tree. A quite magnificent hostelry, with its cobbled yard and lofty stone-porticoed entrance. The gateway was dominated by a garish yet eye-catching sign of a majestic elm with bodies hanging from its branches. The tavern was certainly busy, tinkers, chapmen and local residents gathering in the taproom. Athelstan followed his companion in, then stopped and stared around in amazement. The taproom was spacious and lofty, with meats, cheeses and other foods hanging from the painted beams to be cured by the heat and smoke from the fire roaring in the deep, hollow hearth. Athelstan, however, was distracted by the taproom's macabre furnishings, its blatant display of all the devices used at a hanging: the knife, the noose, the manacles, the hood and the execution shift, a thin, threadbare garment. Such items dominated one wall. On the other were different masks donned by the hangmen and their assistants. Some of these were a blood-scarlet, others displayed the faces of a dog, monkey or rat. The crowning glory of this blood-chilling display was a scaffold post, built into the far wall opposite the hearth, the execution branch jutting out, with a noose hanging from a hook at the far end.

'In heaven's name,' Athelstan breathed.

'Quite a sight, yes Father?'

Athelstan gazed around at the different customers, eating and drinking so merrily amidst such sinister furnishings. 'This room,' the friar murmured, 'certainly makes you reflect on the Last Four Things.'

'Father?'

'Heaven, Hell, Death and Judgement.'

'Can I help you?'

Athelstan and the hangman turned as Mine Host, covered from chin to ankle by a snow-white apron, stood, arms folded, staring at them. Beside him a bold-faced woman, a blue veil pushed back on her red hair, a green and gold demi apron round her slim waist. The taverner peered closer.

'Why,' he exclaimed, 'the Hangman of Rochester. It's a long time since we met my friend.' He clasped the hangman's hand, then Athelstan's. 'I am Henry Penon, owner of this tavern. This is my wife Isabella, whilst you must be the illustrious Brother Athelstan?'

'Not so illustrious now. Just cold, tired and—'

'Eager to meet Sir John Cranston, the Lord High Coroner?'

'The same,' Athelstan retorted.

'He is upstairs in a private chamber, breaking his fast on a dish of venison, stewed and garnished—'

'And he's waiting for us,' Athelstan intervened. 'And Sir John does not like to wait, so you'd best show us up.'

Cranston had been given a most comfortable chamber, rope matting on the floor, the plastered wall covered with gaily painted cloths. The coroner was sitting at a table close to the unshuttered window, the empty platter pushed away. Sir John, cradling his miraculous wineskin, was watching the busy stable yard below. He rose and greeted Athelstan with a tight hug, clasped the hangman's hand and ordered Mine Host, who was hovering at the door, to bring up morning ales as well as a dish of buttered manchet and two more chairs for his visitors. Once they had settled, Athelstan gave Cranston a brief description of Clement the Key-Master's murder at St Erconwald's.

'So,' the coroner murmured, sitting back in his chair, eyes half closed. 'There appears to be some sort of link between that murder and affairs at Westminster. But why should someone murder Clement and why now? Oh, by the way . . .' Cranston waved a warning finger at the hangman. 'What you learn here is not for the taproom at The Piebald.'

'Of course, Sir John.'

'Then, sir, before I impart my news to Brother Athelstan, tell us what you know about the Guild of Hangmen and The Hanging Tree.'

'In truth, Sir John, I have little to do with the guild.' The hangman shrugged. 'I am regarded as a newcomer.' He smiled bleakly. 'As an apprentice.'

'Aye, and the best I have ever seen,' Cranston retorted. 'So why is that? Why do they dismiss you as an upstart?'

'Oh, the guild meet here. This is their house, their home. Always has been, their place of gathering. You've seen the taproom downstairs, Sir John. They'll welcome me here, but I am not allowed to participate in their affairs. Thanks to you, Sir John, the sheriffs hire me, provide me with good work, but that does not make me too popular with the guild. You see, I am of recent origins. I did not cross the Narrow Seas to fight for the King in Normandy or anywhere else. Now the guild,' he hurried on, 'was founded or commissioned by royal charter, drawn up and issued during the old King's wars in France. Edward wanted a cohort of hangmen to deal out punishments decreed by the marshals of the royal array, both during the fighting and in the subsequent peace. Most of the hangmen, if not all, were from London. They became busy enough. The old King and the Black Prince, his eldest son, were as ruthless as ravenous dogs. If they decreed peace, they meant peace. So if anyone broke into a church, harmed a woman or stole a cup, they'd hang. The hangmen also stood in the battle line, so they were given the right to keep plunder, as long as they paid the usual percentage to the Crown.'

'And how many members?'

'At the time, about fifty.' He paused as Cranston whistled under his breath.

'And now?'

'Death and disease have culled the cohort. I would say about twenty, even less.'

'And they have also been culled by murder.'

'Six,' the hangman replied. 'At least six.'

'True,' Cranston declared. 'Master Thibault sent me a schedule of information; nothing much. Six hangmen found dead, stabbed through the heart, their naked corpses tossed into a lay stall or cesspit. A notice pinned to their cold dead flesh proclaiming the word 'Vengeance' under a crudely drawn gibbet. The message would have us believe the murder was the work of the Upright Men or the Reapers, leaders of the Great Revolt.'

'Anything else?' Athelstan asked.

'According to the Master of Secret's schedule,' Cranston replied, 'that scrap of parchment was found on the corpse of the most recent victim, about three days ago. The cadaver still lies in the Chapel of the Hanged at Newgate.' Cranston drew a deep breath. 'Brother Athelstan, whether you like it or not, we have to visit that House of Iron.'

'From what I know,' the hangman moved a wisp of corn-coloured hair from his face, 'matters have progressed very slowly. There is very little urgency to discover why these men have been murdered.'

'Of course, of course,' Cranston murmured. 'That's the way of the world! Hangmen are not Lords of the Soil but their servants. Nevertheless, the Guild has a royal charter. Hangmen, as you know my friends, are officials of the Crown. Some of these old veterans appealed to our young King, who passed the petition to investigate to the Guildhall, who gave it to the sheriffs, who handed it back to the Guildhall, who sent it back to Westminster.'

Athelstan laughed softly at the coroner's sardonic tone. For a while, all three sat in silence, sipping their morning ale.

'So!' Athelstan put down his tankard. 'Six hangmen have been stabbed. The Guild meet here, yes?'

Cranston nodded his agreement.

'And the present Master of the Guild is Mine Host at The Hanging Tree. Yes?'

'Correct.'

'Very well, Sir John, I suspect you have other business with me, but let's strike whilst the iron is hot. We must question Master Henry and his wife.'

'My friend,' Cranston pointed at the Hangmen of Rochester, 'I would be grateful if you would deliver our summons then stay in the taproom below.'

A short while later, the taverner and his wife came into the chamber. They both sat together on the edge of the bed. Athelstan moved his chair to face them.

'You, Master Henry,' he began, 'are Mine Host and Magister of the Guild of Hangmen?'

'Yes.'

'And you are married to Isabella here, widow of Columba, a locksmith who mysteriously disappeared some years ago, the daughter-in-law, or former daughter-in-law, of Clement the Key-Master. You know he has been murdered? Garrotted in my church, St Erconwald's in Southwark?'

'Yes, we heard the news from Master Tiptoft, as well as proclamations by the street heralds. Such news,' the taverner added, 'travels swifter than the wind in London.'

'It certainly does.' Athelstan crossed himself. 'God rest poor Clement. However, I must be blunt. You do not appear to be surprised, shocked or grieving at Clement's murder.' He stared at Isabella.

'Brother Athelstan, of course I am sad that he was murdered. I am truly sorry he has died, but Clement and I were never very close; that's the way life's path twists and turns.' Athelstan held Isabella's gaze. She smiled and glanced away. Sometimes, Athelstan reflected, you can catch the essence of a soul, and this was no different. Isabella was strong-willed, forthright and highly intelligent. She glanced back. 'Tell me,' Athelstan demanded, 'about the path you and Columba took.'

'It started so well. We exchanged our vows at the church door. I expected we would live a comfortable, well-ordered life. After all, he was a skilled craftsman and I was the daughter of the taverner of this prosperous hostelry. However, Brother, like everything under the sun, it began to crumble. Columba was a member of the Guild of Locksmiths, very much in the shadow of his illustrious father, Clement the Key-Master, who was favoured and patronized by all the great and good. And then,' her voice faltered, 'it all fell away. Clement fashioned special keys and locks for the royal treasury. He was supposed to destroy all plans, designs, casts, and anything else to do with his work.' She waved a hand. 'You know the story. Clement's wealthy Cheapside mansion and workshop were raided. Evidence was found that he had not destroyed what he should have done. Some say he was fortunate in escaping with life and limb. However, he was disgraced; dismissed from both the Guild and the service of the Crown.' She smiled thinly. 'If a star falls, Brother Athelstan, you of all people know it drags other stars with it. Columba too was disgraced, cut off, excommunicated.' Isabella shook her head. 'A shadow of a man; then one morning, about three years ago on Spy Wednesday during Holy Week, Columba just disappeared.' Isabella snapped her fingers. 'As swift and as silent as a fading wisp of smoke. He took a few possessions,' she fought to keep her voice steady, 'and he was gone like dust in the wind. So no, I do not grieve, Brother Athelstan. Columba blighted my life; he made a very selfish decision and deserted me.' She stretched out to grasp her husband's hand. 'Henry and I became firm friends. I obtained a decree from the archdeacon's court,' she smiled, 'and so we were married. Henry and I have worked together to make The Hanging Tree a very successful hostelry.'

'And Clement the Key-Master?'

'A mere ghost in our lives. He would drift in and out of here. Sometimes he would drown his sorrows as he talked about the old times.'

'But he changed, didn't he?' Cranston, who had sat listening, eyes half closed, now asserted himself.

'I am sorry, Sir John, what do you mean?'

'Well, according to his good friend Crispin the Carpenter – you know of him, yes?'

'Yes, a distant kinsman of Clement.'

'He would meet Clement here to sup and eat.'

'Yes, he did.'

'Now Crispin,' Athelstan declared, 'maintains Clement became deeply troubled about what happened.'

'I am sorry, Brother, I don't follow you. Clement was always troubled about what had happened to him.'

'No, more recently.'

'In what way?' Isabella's question was sharp.

'Mistress, we don't really know,' Athelstan replied. 'In brief, Clement began to believe that something dreadful had befallen his son. He maintained that he had not disappeared but was probably taken from you. Now recently Clement informed Crispin that Columba would never leave without the Walsingham. Do you know what that is? What did he mean?'

'Columba had a special devotion to Our Lady of Walsingham in Norfolk. On one occasion, just after our marriage, Columba visited the shrine. Perhaps he brought back a medallion or some other pilgrim badge. Apart from that, I cannot say.'

'You were married to Columba when Clement fell from grace?'

'Oh yes.'

'Do you know why Clement insisted on keeping items he had sworn to destroy?'

'No, Brother,' Mine Host and his wife chorused together.

'And in his last days,' Athelstan insisted, 'it would appear that Clement came to believe that the dire events which had befallen him were not as they would appear.'

'In what way?'

'I cannot say. Except for his agitation, his desire to see me, and the references to the Walsingham.'

'Father,' Isabella leaned forward, 'we know Clement was agitated. Only a few days ago, he met Crispin here. They ate and drank and conversed in whispers.'

'About what?'

'Brother, I don't know.'

'Did he work?'

'Sir John,' Mine Host replied, 'Clement was regarded as you would a leper. We tried to help; we offered warm lodgings, which he took now and again, as well as food and drink.'

'But did he work?'

'Sir John, he did minor repairs for those who could not afford a locksmith. Of course, we also asked for his help here with our locks and doors, particularly in our cellars. They are cavernous, we keep our ales and wines secure.'

'And that sudden, abrupt raid on Clement's house and workshop?' Cranston sipped from his ale. 'Somebody must have laid information against him. Do you have any suspicions?'

'Sir John, Clement had his opponents, rivals in the Guild, people jealous of him.' Isabella rubbed her face, her long white fingers splayed. 'Whatever, a true dish of troubles was served. A potage highly bitter to the taste. One thing after another. Clement's wife, Anna, died of a bloody flux, whilst tension between father and son ran deep. Clement wondered if Columba had opened his mouth in our taproom below . . .'

'What do you mean?'

'Brother Athelstan, father and son frequented the tavern. Don't forget, I also work here.' She half smiled. 'I am an accomplished cook and chief lady of the buttery. Anyway, Clement and Columba often came here.'

'So you're saying that, under the influence of drink, Columba, or even Clement, could have unwittingly revealed that some items for those locks and keys were still extant.'

'Perhaps. Both men could sink deep in their cups. God only knows what they muttered about.'

'Did either man ever,' Athelstan paused, 'and I mean ever, discuss those keys with you or, to your knowledge, anyone else?'

'Never.'

'At the end of the day,' Mine Host spoke up, 'we do not know who actually caused the fall. After it, Clement and his son became shadow-dwellers. The only singular event over the last few weeks was that Clement was obviously agitated, but that was only something I glimpsed. He never confided in me or Isabella.'

'Did you know he was coming to see me?'

'No.' Isabella shook her head. 'Clement wandered wherever he wished. He was harmless enough.'

'Apparently not so,' Cranston snapped. 'Somebody deliberately and maliciously pursued him, then murdered him in a most cruel way. So who? The great Cicero maintained that, with any murder, you should start with the question '*Cui Bono?*' – who profits? So who would profit from Clement's death, eh?'

'Well certainly not us,' Isabella snorted. 'I truly do not know.'

'And you've nothing else to add? Nothing you can say which might help resolve this mystery?'

'God save us, Brother, but we cannot.'

'So let us move on,' Cranston declared briskly. 'The Clerks of the Light from Westminster under Magister Beaumont . . .'

'They are to lodge here.' Mine Host smiled as he preened himself. 'Master Thibault has chosen this hostelry for their confinement. They are to be provided with every comfort, but must stay here. I understand they will eventually be joined by four Tower archers.' Mine Host rubbed his hands in gleeful appreciation at the great profits to be made.

'This hostelry was chosen for another reason,' Athelstan remarked. 'It is the Livery House for the Guild of Hangmen.'

'Oh yes, and has been for years.'

'And you know the Hangman of Rochester?'

'Of course, he awaits below.'

'Fetch him up,' Cranston ordered, tapping the ale jug, 'and bring another of these.'

Once the hangman was seated and the ale served, Athelstan pointed at Mine Host. 'Tell us about the Guild. Swiftly now.' The taverner hastened to obey. He hastily explained how the Guild was formed by the Crown during the war across the Narrow Seas. How the Guild had its own house and its own treasure, the profits of plunder now safely entrusted to a Cheapside banker.

'Stop there,' Athelstan intervened. 'So the hangmen brought their plunder and created a common purse?'

'True, Brother. The bankers make a swift account and disburse monies to each guild member twice a year, at Michaelmas and midsummer, around the feast of the Birth of John the Baptist.'

'And the amounts distributed are drawn on this communal purse, which is augmented by any interest accrued, so every hangman receives payment from this common source?'

'Not me,' the Hangman of Rochester declared. Athelstan caught the tinge of bitterness in his companion's voice.

'My friend,' Mine Host chided, 'you were not with us in France and you're only an apprentice in our Guild. Even though,' the taverner added in a rush, eager to answer any protest, 'you are most skilled in your art. Membership of the inner court of hangmen,' the taverner now turned to Athelstan, 'is dependent on how long you have served your apprenticeship, as well as military service abroad.'

'And when a hangman dies?'

'His portion is kept by the common purse. No heir can claim it.'

'And how many full guildsmen form the inner court?'

'About twenty. We serve the gallows and gibbets of London, as well as those within a day's ride of the city gates.'

'You recruit new members?'

'Very rarely.' Mine Host pulled a face. 'We were very busy after the revolt. Now that's crushed, and since the King's peace was enforced, business has declined.'

'And you gather here for your guild meetings, banquets, festivities, pageants and the honouring of your patron saints?'

'Of course.' Mine Host put his hands up. 'The Hanging Tree is a true home for all our comrades. We brew our own ale and buy the best Bordeaux in Dowgate. We are a band—'

'And these murders?' Cranston intervened.

'About six in number,' the taverner retorted.

'What happened?'

'Brother Athelstan, what happened is what is proclaimed by the street heralds. They in turn learn it from those who discovered the corpse of a city hangman, stripped naked, stabbed to the heart and tossed on a midden heap.'

'Completely stripped?'

'Of everything, Brother Athelstan.'

'I believe the most recent victim now lies coffined in the Chapel of the Hanged at Newgate. I need to view the body.' The coroner jabbed a finger at the taverner. 'You have omitted one important detail. A message was left scrawled on a dirty piece of parchment: "Vengeance", and the crude depiction of a gallows. However, apart from that, there's no other evidence to suggest who is responsible, or why and how the murder was committed.' The coroner drummed his thick fingers against the blackjack. 'Of course, the message proclaims that this vengeance is the work of the Upright Men and their henchmen the Reapers – but most of them are dead, and I believe, along with many others, that the message is only a pretence used by the assassin.'

'But surely,' Mine Host retorted, 'the culprits are obvious. The hangmen have enemies; those involved in the revolt who still survive nourish a deep hatred for us.'

'I don't think it is as simple as that.' The friar sipped from his own tankard. 'As Sir John has said, that's all a pretence.

Nevertheless, I am truly mystified. All the victims were hangmen – sturdy, tough characters like yourself, Master Henry; former soldiers who've stood in the battle line. Men skilled and experienced in every kind of dagger play. Yet they were all slaughtered. And, where did this happen? How were they knifed through the heart, stripped, carted through the streets, and dumped on a lay stall for all to view? Yet no one saw or heard anything untoward regarding the disappearance and murderous deaths of these seasoned veterans.'

'A true mystery,' Cranston declared. 'Neither the Crown nor the Guildhall have acquired any evidence to solve these murders. Death was silent. No hue and cry raised. No clothing or any of their possessions ever found. No indication of where they died. No report or sign of any struggle. According to all the information collected, these men disappeared from house, home and hearth, only to be found sprawled naked on a shit heap with a mortal wound to the heart.'

'I still believe we hangmen have our enemies,' Mine Host replied. 'We played an important part in the campaign to root out and punish the leaders of the revolt.'

'So did many others,' Cranston countered, 'including myself. I executed Tyler. So why the hangmen?'

'By the way,' Athelstan moved to ease the cramp in his neck, 'you have heard of Blodwyn?'

'Oh Blodwyn.' The taverner laughed. 'We all know Blodwyn, light of finger, which makes him a notorious foist, but also skilled in tying knots to hold a prisoner fast.'

'He took sanctuary in St Erconwald's,' Athelstan declared, 'and has now vanished. I understand he used to dance attendance on the execution carts. I just wonder if he has fled to the Guild.'

'Not to my knowledge, Brother.'

'Ah well.' Athelstan rose and stretched. 'Sir John, are we finished here?'

'For the moment,' the coroner retorted.

'Fine, in which case,' Athelstan declared, 'we are done.' He thanked both the taverner and his wife, then stood by the door, listening to their footsteps fade along the gallery.

'Brother, do you still need me?'

'Yes, I do Giles.' Athelstan crossed and patted the hangman on the shoulder. 'I want you to frequent this tavern. Sit in that macabre taproom. See what you can discover about Mine Host and his lovely wife, the hidden life of this place, the business of the Guild and, above all, anything which might explain the murder of these hangmen. Oh yes, and five royal clerks will also be taking up residence here, if they haven't already. Keep a close eye on them.'

'They are from the treasury at Westminster?'

'They certainly are!' Athelstan declared. 'See what you can find out about them.'

'You will receive help and support.' Cranston laughed. 'No less a person than Master Culpeper will be joining you. Oh yes,' Cranston tapped the side of his nose, 'Master Culpeper has one God-given talent. He can crawl through the narrowest gap. He is a self-proclaimed master of the shadows. Master Culpeper will keep a sharp eye out for villainy around this hostelry. You know him by sight. Once Culpeper takes up residence here,' Cranston declared, 'you can leave.'

The hangman said he would do his best and hurried from the chamber. Cranston nodded at Athelstan and went across to stare through the window, gazing down at the stable yard, now busy and noisy as a stream of customers flocked in to eat and drink once the angelus bells had ceased their tolling. Athelstan sat on the edge of the bed, sifting his ave beads through mittened fingers. He let his mind float as he recalled that eerie treasury chamber, those five clerks strangled in their chairs and a king's ransom completely taken. Stolen, moved from that chamber without any sign of who had perpetrated such a crime or how. Athelstan wetted his lips. Mysterious disappearances seemed to be the order of the day. Crispin's son Columba, Blodwyn the Blessed. Athelstan gazed at a noose fastened to the wall beneath a crucifix. And what was the truth, he wondered, behind the murder of at least six hangmen? Was it the work of the Upright Men, the few surviving leaders of the Great Revolt who now call themselves the Reapers, or was it their street warriors, the Earthworms? Had they seized each of those hangmen, struck them through the heart, stripped their corpses and disposed of them as you would a piece of rubbish. Athelstan shook his head. 'No no,' he whispered. 'The Great Revolt is well and truly crushed!' Athelstan was certain that the murder of the hangmen had nothing to do with that bloody, turbulent time.

He wondered yet again why they had been murdered in such a way, and how. The hangmen would not give up their lives easily. They would resist, fight back, cry 'Harrow!' and seek assistance from others. Athelstan crossed himself as he quietly conceded that the murders he confronted were baffling in the extreme. He closed his eyes and invoked the '*Veni Creator Spiritus*', asking for the help of the Holy Spirit. He reached the verse 'If you take your grace away, nothing good in me will stay' when he startled, opening his eyes as the chamber door was flung open and Tiptoft, all cloaked and hooded against the cold, strode dramatically into the room.

'Sir John, Brother Athelstan. Lord Thibault and Signor Conteza await you in the Keeper's Hall at Newgate. Galliard the Goldsmith is also in attendance. Apparently coins from the robbery have appeared in his shop.'

'Yes, yes,' Cranston retorted, 'I heard rumours about that earlier.' He winked at the friar. 'Brother Athelstan, my apologies, I did not tell you. However, as you will soon discover, the city is rife with all kinds of rumours about the robbery.' He turned back to Tiptoft. 'I suppose they have more details, fresh information.'

'If you say so, Sir John.'

'Then let us not keep such illustrious men waiting. Tiptoft, as fast as you can to the Guildhall. Tell Simon the Scrivener and Osbert my clerk where I shall go now and where I can be found later.'

'The Lamb of God?'

'Most intuitive of messengers. You are correct; no lesser a place than the Lord High Coroner's personal chapel.'

Tiptoft hastened away, clattering down the stairs. Cranston stood, head cocked, listening to him go.

'Why Newgate, Sir John? You mentioned a corpse in its chapel.'

'Ah well, my little monk.'

'Friar.'

'And one beloved of God,' Cranston answered. 'I told Thibault I'd be going there and, if he wanted to see me, we could meet in Newgate. The prison is nearer than Westminster, and a safer place than the palace offices, a royal residence with a thousand eyes and a thousand ears. As I said, we also have business in Newgate.

First, that hangman's corpse, and secondly the immediate release of Culpeper. I have already sent orders for him to be scrubbed, shaved and suitably dressed. So, my little friar, let us visit that House of Iron and see what business has to be done.'

They left the chamber, going down into the taproom, now emptying as the traders hurried back to their shops and stalls after a brief repast. The Hangman of Rochester was sitting disconsolately in a window seat across the taproom. Master Beaumont and his clerks, who must have arrived shortly after Athelstan did, now sat hunched over a table with an array of almost empty platters. Athelstan sketched a blessing towards the hangman and the clerks, then followed Cranston out into the busy streets. Athelstan felt slightly guilty at not giving the clerks a more fulsome greeting, but what was there to say? No new evidence had been discovered, and Athelstan had yet to impose logic on the turbulent slayings in that treasury chamber.

'Sufficient for the hour is business enough,' he whispered, making sure the strap of his chancery satchel was firmly secured. Clutching the bag in one hand, his ave beads in the other, Athelstan followed Sir John as the coroner cut through the noisy, smelly throng.

Citizens of every kind now flooded the streets to buy or sell. A mass of shifting colour, the chatter of the crowds was almost drowned by the clatter of wheels, the clanging of metal and the constant braying of horns. Beggars in rags whined as they rattled their clacking dishes to the left and right. Other citizens of the night, the dark-dwellers and street-stalkers, prowled like hungry cats, sharp eyed, keen witted, and ready to pounce on the unprotected purse or open basket. Men-at-arms swaggered by, raucous after the ale they had drunk. One of these had decided to relieve himself in public above the sewer running down the centre of the street. He immediately incurred the wrath of city bailiffs and beadles; a fight seemed imminent. Cranston roared at the jostling men to observe and keep the King's peace before striding on.

Athelstan doggedly followed, reciting his aves, now and again sketching a blessing to the few who greeted him. Cranston, however, was well known, and the usual good-natured taunting and name-calling echoed across the streets. The coroner seemed to know the name of every caller and bellowed back a suitable reply. They dodged carts, horses, sumpter ponies, and wheelbarrows crammed with every type of merchandise, not to mention the occasional corpse being hurried to some city church for hasty burial. Athelstan wryly noticed how such handcarts and barrows, covered with dirty cloth, embroidered with a crudely drawn cross, were given wide berth by the citizens who usually wouldn't concede an inch. The living were certainly busy, but so were the dead. The bellmen pushed their way through the crowd, ringing their bells before proclaiming a litany of names. The criers pleaded for prayers for all those good citizens who had died during the night and were now bound for burial. On one occasion Cranston had to pause because of a jostling mass of citizens eager to view *The Dark Night of the Soul*. This masque was being played out on a make-shift stage by mummers garbed in black, their gowns decorated with a drawing of a skeleton. Athelstan idly wondered if such a troupe could be hired for St Erconwald's. He was going to stop and ask the cost, but the coroner abruptly turned and thrust a pomander into his hand.

'Satan's Tits, little friar, cover your nose and mouth. It's slaughter day at the fleshers', whilst Newgate will be stinking worse than any sewer.'

They walked on, crossing the meat market where blood-drenched butchers chopped and hacked the carcasses of rabbit, deer, duck and chicken. The smell was foul, the very air blood-tinged, the ground underfoot swilling with the torn-out guts and innards of the slaughtered. Ragged children scrambled around on their knees to collect these juicy morsels in a sack and so take them home to be cooked over a fire in some dirty cellar or shabby tenement.

Cranston surged on, and at last they reached the great concourse stretching in front of the grim and ghostly towers of Newgate. The prison was a black-stoned edifice with iron-barred windows and metal-studded gates. This notorious House of Iron overlooked the great punishment yard of London, a stretch of cobbled ground where the stocks, pillories and whipping posts reared up like black and ugly shadows against the light. The sheriff's men had filled these, fastening their prisoners by neck, wrist or ankle. The punishment benches were full, so a group of roisterers had been made to sit in the fetid water of a long and quite deep horse trough. The cries and moans of those imprisoned in the freezing water were piteous.

'Sir John, for mercy's sake,' Athelstan hissed. 'In God's name, show some clemency.' The coroner, however, seemed unaware of his surroundings or Athelstan's plea. He continued on to the main gate and, using the summoner, a large piece of iron carved in the shape of a skull, banged hard time and again. He then turned and walked over to a group of bailiffs and ordered them to release the now sober night-walkers freezing in the horse trough. He strode back to rejoin Athelstan just as the postern opened and a keeper beckoned them inside. Athelstan accompanied Cranston into the stygian bowels of Newgate. If the approaches to London Bridge were a descent into Hell, Athelstan now felt he was entering the very heart of Satan's empire.

Newgate reeked of evil as well as filth. The prison had been built like a maze, a veritable warren of narrow, twisting paths. The thick dirt on the walls and floor glistened like water in the light of spluttering torches. Athelstan described it as the sweat of human souls. Newgate was damp and icy cold to its very marrow. Along the maze of needle-thin runnels were the cells, nothing more than hutches, sealed by heavy iron-plated doors. Rats and every type of vermin crawled or scrabbled across the floor. Newgate truly was a mansion of nightmares, of leaping flame and constant noise. Sir John maintained that this was where Satan heard his vespers. Screams, shouts and curses echoed eerily yet constantly to the banging of doors and the clash of steel. Athelstan kept his head down. He did not wish to glimpse the frenetic eyes peering through the grilles on the doors on either side. Nor would he look at the open enclaves they passed where the severed heads and torn limbs of traitors were being parboiled and tarred before being displayed above the gates of London and elsewhere. Athelstan heaved a sigh of relief as they cleared the devil's warren. They climbed steep steps and crossed the deserted press yard into the Keeper's Hall. Thibault sat at the head of a long, scrubbed table, Conteza on his left and a frightened-looking merchant to his right who, Athelstan believed, must be Galliard the Goldsmith. Thibault testily waved Cranston and Athelstan to chairs as he rapped his fingers against the table top.

'Time passes, the candle burns,' he exclaimed. 'Gentlemen, we have pressing business. We cannot delay. We must not waste time. We must be like a hawk on the wing, ready to plunge. Keen of mind and sharp of wit.'

'Which is why I take a drink of the best Bordeaux,' Cranston retorted, plucking out the miraculous wineskin for a generous mouthful. He then offered it to Athelstan, who shook his head. Cranston thrust the stopper back and pointed at Galliard. 'Do you have the coins?'

'I do,' Thibault retorted. 'We must be swift. The Lady Grace awaits me.'

Thibault pushed the two coins across the table to Cranston. The coroner picked both up and examined them carefully before handing them to Athelstan, who closely scrutinized the two pieces of gold.

'Superb!' he exclaimed, weighing them in his hand. 'Quite distinctive.'

'Tell them.' Thibault pointed at Galliard. 'Tell them exactly what happened.'

'Early this morning, I was at my stall in front of my shop. Two foreigners, hooded and visored, approached me. They handed me those two pieces and asked me to trade them in for used coin.'

'Definitely foreign?'

'Certainly, my Lord Coroner.' Galliard pointed across the table at Conteza. 'From the little I could see, they were Italian; they certainly had the accent.'

'Carbonari,' Conteza spat out. 'Carbonari, I am sure.'

'Continue,' Thibault rasped, glancing away. 'This is a dire place and, as I said, I want to be gone.' Athelstan followed Thibault's gaze and, for the first time, noticed the strange-looking hangings which occupied most of the soaring, shadowy walls of this bleak hall.

'The Tyburn Tapestries,' Cranston whispered in Athelstan's ear. 'The Keeper of Newgate is given a portion of every condemned prisoner's clothing. He has the different items sewn together and—'

'Furnishes his hall with such filth,' Thibault snapped. 'Let's leave that. Galliard, continue.'

'The men who approached me asked me to weigh the gold coins and to make an exchange. They were nervous, in a hurry. The news about the great robbery at Westminster was only just becoming known, though bailiffs and beadles were already busy searching for the very coins I had been handed. I took the gold pieces into my shop but, when I returned to my stall, one of the apprentices declared that the strangers had hurried away. A short while later, the market searchers appeared. They seized the coins and mounted guard outside my shop until Master Thibault despatched archers to bring me here.' Galliard spread his hands. 'I can tell you no more. I have done no wrong.'

'True, true,' Thibault replied. 'We now know the stolen treasure must be somewhere in this city.'

'We also know,' Conteza intervened, 'that the Carbonari are responsible. They must be.'

'So where do we begin our search?' Athelstan demanded. 'Is there a ward in London which houses these Carbonari?'

'Not so much the Carbonari, but certainly those who come from Italian cities such as Venice, Florence, Pisa and so on. They can be found along Lombard Street.' Conteza held up his hand as if taking an oath. 'Rest assured, Brother Athelstan, Sir John, we also have our own searchers who are the most diligent and skilled hunters.'

'The robbers certainly moved swiftly,' Athelstan declared. 'The coins were stolen last night or early this morning.'

'Rather stupid,' Galliard declared. 'They must know a search is on.'

'Do you know something?' Athelstan retorted. 'I believe they were testing the water but, for the life of me, I can't see why.'

'What do you mean?'

'Well,' Athelstan replied slowly, 'we have robbers who plunder the royal treasury; they seize freshly minted coins, most singular in their appearance. Anybody and everybody who sees those coins will regard them as quite distinctive. To put it bluntly, to try and trade these pieces is a very stupid thing to do. Your account, Master Galliard, proves it. Master Thibault, Signor Conteza, what happened to Galliard doesn't make sense.'

'I agree,' Cranston observed. 'Whatever they intended this morning at Galliard's stall, the robbers are not going to trade these coins in this kingdom. You know that, Master Thibault, it's too dangerous. They'll ship them abroad, smuggle them across the Narrow Seas, then we'll see them, what?' Cranston pulled a face. 'In about six months' time, though by then it will be too late.'

'If your logic is correct . . .' Thibault snapped as he got to his feet, Conteza following suit.'

'Master Thibault, my logic is correct. The robbers will hoard the treasure and somewhere, sometime soon, they will ship it abroad.'

'And that,' Thibault pointed at Athelstan, 'must not happen.'

PART FOUR

'I preach most often on that well-known vice, my very own sharp avarice.'

Thibault and Conteza left the hall. Cranston waited for them to go before summoning the keeper to take them to the Chapel of the Hanged. The fat, red-faced official, mumbling under his breath, led them out of the hall. They went down a narrow stone gallery which led into what Athelstan considered the bleakest, most uncomfortable chapel he had ever visited. The Chapel of the Hanged was as stark as any barn and contained very little except for a simple altar with benches laid out before it. On a table just beneath the altar lay an open coffin containing, so the keeper lugubriously declared 'the mortal remains of one Matthew Slyman, late hangman in Farringdon Ward'. Cranston demanded that the large squat tallow candles around the coffin be lit. The keeper hurriedly produced a tinder and, after a great deal of cursing, the candles flared into life. The keeper then left, but not before Cranston ordered him to arrange for the prisoner known as Culpeper to be in attendance outside once they were finished with Master Slyman. The keeper hurried out leaving the coroner and friar to scrutinize the greyish-white, scabrous corpse. They stood either side of the arrow chest.

'In life Slyman was ugly, in death he truly is.'

Athelstan heartily agreed. Slyman was thin-ribbed, lean-shanked, his head balding except for a few strands or tufts of dirty white hair. His skeletal face was quite hideous, with its sunken cheeks, gaping mouth and half-closed, heavy-lidded dead eyes.

'Stabbed,' Cranston murmured, tapping the left side of Slyman's chest. 'Stabbed by a knife which dealt a wound direct to the heart. Death must have occurred in a few breaths. But how? How did Slyman's assassin draw so close? When? Where? Why? How?'

'And why strip the corpse?' Athelstan asked.

'I wager Slyman's clothing didn't amount to much, so it certainly wasn't robbery. Or was the killer just intent on humiliating his victim in death as he had in life. What do you think, friar?'

'All things are possible,' Athelstan replied, trying to control his revulsion as he examined the corpse more closely. With Sir John's help, he turned the dead body over, searching for any sign of a fresh wound or proof of binding or ligature.

'Thank God,' Athelstan murmured. 'Both corpse and coffin have been drenched in pinewood juice. I just wonder . . .'

'What?'

'If the corpses of the murdered hangmen were stripped and tossed onto a midden heap to hide something.'

'Such as what, little friar? What was the assassin trying to hide?'

'Oh, where they were killed.' Athelstan made a face. 'Just a thought. Anyway,' Athelstan blessed the corpse, 'Master Slyman, rest in peace.'

They replaced the lid on the arrow chest. Athelstan recited the '*De Profundis*' followed by a requiem. He'd hardly finished when there was a loud rapping and the door was flung open. A thin, bouncy-haired man in ill-fitting clothing, was dragged into the chapel by a surly faced turnkey. The jailer pushed the man towards Sir John, nodded at the coroner and left, slamming the door behind him.

'Good morrow, Master Culpeper,' Cranston declared.

'Oh, Sir John.' The prisoner sank to his knees, hands clasped. 'I thank God for your mercy, illustrious coroner. I will pray for you, your family . . .'

'Enough,' the coroner barked. 'Get to your feet. I see you have been washed, scrubbed and clothed.'

Culpeper plucked at his tattered jerkin.

'Thank you, Sir John, and thank you to slippery Simon.'

'I have heard of him; a foist with nimble fingers.'

'Nimble no longer, Sir John. Hanged this morning over Tyburn stream.' Culpeper scrambled to his feet. 'The keeper gave me Simon's effects; he doesn't need them any more. A loose fit, eh Sir John?'

'Shut up.'

'Yes, my Lord Coroner.'

'Now my friend.' Cranston abruptly lurched forward, grabbing Culpeper by the shoulder and drawing him close.

'My Lord Coroner, Brother Athelstan.' Culpeper turned pleadingly to the friar. 'Mercy. Mercy!'

'You'll be shown mercy when you have done what I ask.' Cranston loosened his grip. 'Don't even think of fleeing, my arm is very long.'

'Well known to all, Sir John.'

'So don't forget it. Now listen, I know there's not a door, window or any man-made aperture you can't get through. Brother Athelstan here will tell you what we want you to do, as well as the story preceding it.'

'I can guess, Sir John. The great robbery at Westminster? It's being gossiped about even in the death house.'

'Precisely, but Brother Athelstan will give you the facts. You will reflect on these whilst you lodge at The Hanging Tree.'

'The Hanging Tree?'

'Yes, my friend. Good board and warm lodgings paid by the Guildhall and delivered through the courtesy of no lesser person than myself.' Cranston searched beneath his cloak. He drew out a small purse and thrust it into Culpeper's dirty hand. 'As I said, you can take the coin and scurry away. If you do, don't worry, I will still catch you, then I'll hang you myself.'

'Sir John, the thought would never cross my mind.'

'Really?' Cranston smiled. 'Well, first keep a sharp eye on the doings in that tavern, and in particular the five clerks who lodge there; Clerks of the Light who discovered the horrid murder and treasonable pillaging of the Exchequer of Coin.'

'What do I look for?'

'Anything out of the ordinary. Anything that may be of interest to our investigation. You may even visit Westminster. You may even see where the hideous crimes were perpetrated. However, that's for the future. Now, my little friend, I will fall silent whilst Brother Athelstan accurately describes the murderous mystery and mayhem which now confronts us. Listen and listen well. Master Culpeper, you are not what you seem. You act as timid as a hare yet you have the cunning and stamina of a fox.'

'In which case,' Athelstan intervened, 'you might have made a good friar. But, let me begin . . .'

* * *

The Hangman of Rochester was also reflecting on murder as he stared around the taproom of The Hanging Tree. The tavern was almost empty. Tradespeople and their customers had flocked back to sell, buy or trade before the market horns brayed and the beacon lights flared in the steeples of London's churches. The hangman had attended meetings of the Guild here in this same taproom. However, despite his macabre popularity with the sheriffs, and aldermen, the Hangman of Rochester was viewed as a mere apprentice by his colleagues. Not that the hangman cared. He had learned that the Guild finances were greatly depleted, and the work being farmed out had drastically fallen. The great revolt had been crushed and the commissions of jail delivery had emptied the prison cages throughout the city and beyond. The hangman promised himself he would inform Athelstan about these developments as soon as he could. In the meantime . . . The hangman stared across the taproom at the five Clerks of the Light, who sat around a table whispering heatedly amongst themselves. The hangman had risen and crossed over, as if curious about one of the artefacts nailed to the wall. However, as soon as he drew near, the clerks fell silent and remained so until he moved out of earshot. The hangman had returned to his table to become lost in his own deep dark reverie. He felt uncomfortable; there was something about this tavern which repelled him. Oh, Mine Host and his wife were friendly enough; nevertheless, an eerie cloud of foreboding hung around this hostelry.

He glanced across at the far wall, which was covered with velvet, as black and soft as sin, a former pall used to cover corpses after they had been cut down from the gibbet. He narrowed his eyes as he stared at the pall. Did little demon dwarfs creep in and out of it? Or was that just the cloth rippling in the draughts which cut across this taproom? Were the dead assembling around him, that ghostly congregation of those he had hanged? He was certain they were visiting him. They always did. He had confessed as much to Brother Athelstan. The dead would gather to stare at him. The hangman would recognize their faces in the fold of a piece of drapery, the carving on a chair, or even in the tangled weeds of gorse across God's Acre in St Erconwald's. They followed him to his little narrow house off Pig's Alley in Southwark. They'd gather in the corner and scrabble like mice as they murmured to each other. Only one such ghost truly frightened him, the old crone he'd hanged after she'd been convicted of killing a child. The hangman swiftly crossed himself. He would wake and she would be there hovering above him, her face coloured like a fungus, a leprous white and grey, her hard black eyes shimmering, her bloodless lips parted in a display of sharp yellow teeth like those of a cat.

The hangman heard a door slam. He broke from his reverie and stared around in astonishment. The taproom had fallen chillingly silent. Mine Host, his wife and their household now clustered around the main buttery table. They almost clung to each other, gaping at the black-garbed strangers, hooded and visored, armed with small arbalests. These sinister visitors had apparently slipped into the tavern when the hangman was deep in his reverie and they now controlled the entire taproom. All the doors were closed and guarded.

The hangman stared around. He reckoned there must be at least ten of these nightmare newcomers. Well organized, they'd apparently struck at a time when the tavern would be empty. Only a few startled customers sat around the tables, whilst Mine Host, his wife and household had been pulled in to cower before the threat. The hangman licked dry lips and wished he'd had a fresh blackjack available. These visitors, garbed like night wraiths, were truly menacing. They seemed so silent – watchful and dangerous in the extreme. They had closed the tavern, but for why? The leader of the coven, standing in the centre of the taproom, abruptly turned and pointed his arbalest at the clerks grouped around their table.

'You,' he rasped, his accent strong and throaty. 'Come, come!' he ordered. 'Stand up.'

The clerks apparently did not move swiftly enough, so the leader raised his crossbow and a bolt whirled over their heads to smash into the wall behind them. The clerks hurried out into the middle of the taproom. The leader ordered them to kneel, which they hastily did. He then walked up and down either side of them. He abruptly paused and demanded their names. The leader listened carefully then called one out.

'Luke Whitby, stand.' The young, fair-haired, anxious-faced clerk clambered to his feet. He stood swaying as the leader walked behind him.

The hangman caught his breath. He suspected what was going to happen, just watching the leader of the night wraith insert another bolt into the groove of his arbalest. The hangman moved his hand and tapped the hilt of his dagger, yet he knew it was futile, what could he do? The sinister group now controlled this tavern and the hangman was certain their visit would end in bloodshed.

The leader abruptly turned, staring across, as if he knew the hangman was readying himself. The black-garbed figure walked slowly towards him. The hangman gripped the handle of his dagger, concealed beneath his loosely clasped cloak. The leader stopped and leaned slightly forward.

'Good day, my friend.'

'You are not my friend.'

'Today I am, and you shall deliver a message for me to fat Jack Cranston. I recognize you as the Hangman of Rochester. You must know our corpulent coroner. Anyway, tell that bulk of lard and his ferreting friar to leave the Carbonari alone. They have not and, if they continue their interference, others will certainly die.'

The dreadful apparition then spun on his heel and walked back. He stopped in front of Whitby, raised the arbalest, and released the catch. The bolt burst into Whitby's head, sending the clerk staggering back, his face all torn and rent, the blood gushing out like wine through a crack. At first, there was silence. Then Mine Host's wife gave a long, deep moan, almost drowned by the screams of fear from the young scullions. The killer walked across to the buttery table, grasped a ladle, banging it up and down until he had silence. He beckoned Mine Host's wife over and she edged across. The leader roughly seized her and dragged her closer, even as one of his companions stepped warningly in front of her husband, who made as if to intervene. The other four clerks still knelt, hands clasped, heads down.

'You stay like that, clerks,' the leader taunted. 'In fact all of you, on your knees.' Mine Host and his minions hastened to comply.

'Stay where you are,' the leader ordered. 'Do not move. Do not call out. Do not cry "Harrow" and so raise the hue and cry. If you obey me, this buxom lady remains safe.' He pointed across to the hangman, who had not moved but crouched, ready to spring.

'Tell fat Jack . . .' The leader broke off. He stepped over Whitby's corpse, almost swimming in a widening pool of blood, and crossed to a brazier, its charcoal all spent, nothing more than greyish-white dust. The leader dug a leather-gauntleted hand into the brazier. He drew out a handful of spent charcoal and let it crumble from his hand. '*Sic transit gloria mundi*,' he mocked. 'Thus passes the glory of the world. So remind fat Cranston that he is dust and into dust he shall return.' The leader smacked his hands together to clear the remaining dirt. 'He and his feckless friar, if they continue to interfere, will certainly turn to dust long before they expected.' He lifted a warning hand. 'They must leave the Carbonari alone.'

Cranston and Athelstan sat in the buttery of The Hanging Tree, a snug, comfortable chamber with a fire roaring in its stone-flagged hearth, the air perfumed with fragrance from the herbs sprinkled across the logs. The coroner pushed away the platter of chicken roasted in a spicy sauce and sipped appreciatively at the ale specially brewed by Mine Host. Cranston leaned back in his chair, staring at Beaumont and his companions. The clerks huddled together, still shocked by the vicious killing of their comrade. They had described what happened and delivered the messages left by the leader of those assassins. They all now stared plaintively at Athelstan, as if the friar could dispel the hideous shadow which had enveloped them.

Sir John and Athelstan had been briefly informed of what had occurred at the tavern by the Hangman of Rochester, who had hurried to The Lamb of God. He had delivered his message before announcing he was returning to Southwark. Cranston agreed, adding that Culpeper would continue the watch at the tavern, which would now be protected by four Tower archers. Both Cranston and Athelstan had then left Cheapside and arrived at The Hanging Tree to discover Mine Host, his wife and household as terrified as the four clerks cowering in their chamber. Athelstan had eventually established exactly what had happened, though he could find no reason for it.

'They murdered Whitby,' he declared, 'as retribution for our investigation into the Carbonari who possibly,' the friar spread his hands, 'I repeat possibly, might be responsible for the robbery at Westminster, though we have no hard evidence to prove they were. Nothing to form a lasting indictment. So we return to the question, why? Why the outrage here? Do they really think the Crown, not to mention Master Thibault, will gently concede to their murderous demands and fade away like smoke on the wind?' Athelstan shook his head. 'Oh no,' he pointed at the clerks, 'can any of you suggest the real reason for this outrage? The brutal murder of your comrade?' Silence greeted his questions. Athelstan tapped the table. 'I shall suggest one solution. Let us ignore the reason proclaimed and concentrate on the strong possibility that one of you,' Athelstan shrugged, 'or more, saw or heard something which could loosen the tangle of lies and deception surrounding the robbery at Westminster. You were the first to enter that chamber once the assassin had left, to climb those stairs, to open the door, to scrutinize the treasure chest. Assassins make mistakes. They think they have everything under control, but then one slip, one petty mistake and their well-laid plans begin to crumble.' Athelstan paused. 'Everyone is a suspect.' He breathed. 'You know your chamber will be searched. Enquiries made. Investigations carried out, but it's only to discover the truth behind all of this.'

'So did you?' Cranston demanded. 'Did any of you see or glimpse anything amiss or out of the ordinary?' Again, silence. Athelstan let it deepen to make the clerks even more nervous. The friar secretly prayed that one of these men could help.

'Whitby has been murdered,' Athelstan declared. 'Sir John has demanded a small company of Tower archers set up camp both within and without this tavern. Nevertheless, you, as must I, appreciate the real threat, which has been posed because of our investigation. According to the evidence, Whitby died because we wish to discover the truth. Such a threat will not recede. Consequently, I ask you to reflect on the events that morning when you first entered the treasury. Search for something amiss, however small.'

'Whitby did,' Calpurne retorted, fingers going to his lips.

'Yes he did.' The sharp-faced Crossley agreed.

Calpurne glanced around at his companions.

'Whitby made a remark that "our plainchant was sorely disturbed".'

'What did he mean by that?'

'I don't know, Brother Athelstan. Perhaps,' Calpurne pulled a face, 'he was referring to what we discovered in the treasure house.'

'I think he was,' Crossley spoke up. 'I remember him repeating that phrase whilst we were waiting to travel here. Do you remember? In the antechamber at Flambard's Tower. He made the same remark about plainchant, and I don't think he was referring to the choirs of Westminster.'

'Then what, Master Crossley?'

'Perhaps the horarium or routine of us clerks.'

The others murmured their agreement and Athelstan stifled a small murmur of pleasure. He was certain, though, without any sturdy evidence, that Whitby's remark was significant. But how and why? Above all, Athelstan stared down at the table top, was Whitby's death just the murderous chance of fickle fortune? Or did the Carbonari discover, God knows how, that Whitby held information about them, highly injurious information, which provoked his dreadful murder?

'Brother?'

Athelstan broke from his meditations.

'Are we finished here?' Cranston asked.

'For the time being, Sir John, but,' Athelstan scraped his chair back and rose to his feet, 'my learned clerks, be most careful. Stay here and stay close to each other for, I assure you, that poor Whitby's murder may not be the last . . .'

Brother Athelstan sat before the dying coals of fire deep in the hearth of the priest's house. He and Cranston had parted company at The Hanging Tree. The coroner wanted to escort Athelstan across London Bridge but the friar was obdurate.

'Hasten home, Sir John, we have done enough for the day. The clerks are now protected at The Hanging Tree. Flaxwith's merry men guard the treasure house, two of these have alerted the sheriffs about Blodwyn, whom I am keen to meet. He may know a great deal about the murder of that Key-Master in my church. However, we have done all that we can. So yes, Sir John, we have finished for the day.'

Cranston reluctantly agreed, but only after he'd hired two dwarfs, professional torch-bearers and guides who rejoiced in the names of Cosmas and Damien, to guide the friar across the bridge to the very door of his house.

Athelstan shifted on the stool, hands outstretched, eager to embrace the warmth. He had arrived home safe enough, recited the Divine Office and, as he did, wondered again about the murdered Whitby's enigmatic remark about the 'plainchant being sorely disturbed' on the morning they discovered the robbery. Athelstan picked up his beaker of fresh water and sipped carefully. His eyes grew heavy then he started at a sharp knock on the door. Athelstan picked up a fire tong.

'Who's there?' he called.

'Father, it's Crispin. I have something for you.'

Athelstan rose, opened the door and ushered the carpenter into the kitchen. He offered Crispin a blackjack of ale, but the carpenter just shook his head as he pushed into the deep pocket of his threadbare woollen robe and drew out a polished oaken carving, which he thrust into Athelstan's hands. The carving was robust yet delicate. An accurate miniature replica of the famous statue of Our Lady of Walsingham. The statuette depicted the Virgin Mary crowned, clothed and enthroned as a queen. The Infant Christ nestled in her left arm, whilst Mary's right hand held a sceptre, a long lily wand. The wood was of the highest quality, the polish a work of skill, with great attention to detail, be it the fold of a robe or the infant Christ's outstretched arm. The carving was about three inches high and the same across. Athelstan weighed it carefully in his hand before turning it to examine the base.

'It's sticky,' he murmured. 'The base has been drenched by glue or some other substance. Anyway, what's the meaning of this?'

'Father, we found that on poor Clement, wrapped in a linen cloth in a deep pocket of his jerkin.'

Athelstan again raised the statuette and peered more closely.

'Beautiful,' he murmured, 'most exquisite. Can I keep it for a while?'

'Of course, Father. Do you think that the statuette has anything to do with Clement's claim that Columba would never have left without the Walsingham? Was that a reference to this relic, this pilgrim's statuette?'

'Perhaps, perhaps.' Athelstan leaned back in his chair, listening to the sounds of the night, made more uncanny by the mournful hoot of an owl perched in an old sycamore tree close to the house. 'Strange,' he mused. 'Here we are, Crispin, cloaked by the night. Oh, by the way, talking about the night, did you make close enquiry about our mysterious guest Blodwyn?'

'I certainly did, Father, that too is a mystery. Bladdersmith alerted all the beadles and bailiffs but no one, Father, and I mean no one – in the parish or beyond – has seen our blessed Blodwyn.'

'No one?' Athelstan replied. 'You mean to say that Blodwyn, with his tattered scarlet jerkin and bright blond hair, was never glimpsed? He'd be more apparent than a flame in the dark!' He smiled at Crispin. 'As I said, my good friend, we sit here cloaked by the night but the mysteries which confront us are even darker.' He held up the statuette. 'But I thank you for this.' He leaned over and patted the carpenter on the knee. 'Crispin, remember, the dead do talk. Perhaps you were meant to find this statuette. You are correct, it must have something to do with the mystery surrounding Clement and Columba. Anyway . . .' Athelstan sketched a blessing in the air. The carpenter thanked him and left. Athelstan returned to his stool beside the fire, staring into its fiery embers. He glanced down at the statuette lying in his lap. 'One more twist to the mystery,' he murmured.

The Fisher of Men was also confronting a mystery. Once darkness had fallen, this eerily black-garbed official of the city had begun what he called his 'nightly harvest'. He had ordered his majestic, freshly painted war barge away from its moorings along the deserted, derelict quayside just past La Reole. The Fisher's high-prowed, lofty-sterned craft was a truly fearful sight to many who traded and journeyed along the turbulent Thames. The Fisher of Men hunted corpses. The mortal remains of those unfortunates who'd slipped and drowned or, more commonly, been brutally murdered, their corpses committed to the deep, where their killers hoped they would remain 'till the Final Resurrection'. Of course, the river always gave up its dead; gruesome grisly bundles of mouldering flesh and tattered clothes. The Fisher of Men would hook or net these in for display at The Chapel of the Drowned Men, a large renovated warehouse which fronted the deserted quay-side. A proclamation on the door of this chapel proclaimed the different charges for corpses, depending on their age, sex and cause of death. The Fisher harvested the river for these macabre prizes. The Guildhall, advised by Sir John Cranston, fully supported a service, which removed one further responsibility from themselves. The council did not care a whit about who the Fisher was or where he had come from. He cleaned the river of corpses, and that was enough for them.

On that particular night the Fisher, hooded and visored, smiled to himself, as he often did when his mind journeyed back into the past. Fortune had been good since his return from Outremer. The curious gossiped about his origins but the Fisher ignored this. He was now settled in his comfortable mansion and this barge was all that he really needed. Well, apart from his acolytes.

The Fisher walked down the plank separating the oarsmen on either side. All of these were grotesques, men shunned by their fellows because of their physical appearance, yet the Fisher valued them. Be it Eel-Slayer, his leading oarsman, or Soulsham his tiller guide and, above all, Icthus. The Fisher peered through the dark at his henchman, who now stood on the prow, staring into the inky darkness, impervious to the bitter, freezing river breeze. Icthus was a human fish, hairless, even his eyelids. The young man's face was like that of a cod with its snub nose and protuberant mouth. Nevertheless, Icthus was truly invaluable. He could slip through the water like a porpoise and swim as swift and strong as any silver salmon. He was also of very keen sight and, in his usual sibilant whisper, had just informed the Fisher that something was about to happen close to the far bank. If Icthus said that, the Fisher believed him.

They had taken up position and the Fisher was waiting. So far, the harvest had been poor, with one singular exception. They had left the quayside to scour the water past Dowgate when they had fished a corpse from the Thames. A plump, blond-haired young man, completely naked, his face all frightful due to the garrotte tied like a vice around his throat. The dancing, fitful light of the barge's lanterns provided enough glow for the Fisher to recognize Blodwyn the Blessed, the sanctuary man who had fled St Erconwald's after a gruesome murder perpetrated there.

The Fisher had dealings with so many of the dark-dwellers that he knew them by name, face and reputation, Blodwyn included. Moreover, the bailiffs, street heralds and tale-tellers had spread the news about the horrible murder at St Erconwald's. How no less a person than Sir John Cranston was involved, and he now wished to speak to Blodwyn about the sacrilegious slaying. Blodwyn's description had been proclaimed in every detail across London Bridge. The Fisher smiled to himself. Of course, there would be a reward for catching Blodwyn, but who would murder such a hapless felon? And why? What had he done? Was Blodwyn's death connected to the murder in St Erconwald's? Or, more importantly, to the plundering of the treasure house, of a value worth more than a king's ransom?

The news of the robbery had swept the city swifter than smoke. The gangs, the rifflers, the utlegati and all the dark-dwellers had become sharply alert, like some ravenous wolf pack sniffing the air. Every outlaw in London, all those who lived in the twilight, were desperate to discover where the treasure might be. There were rumours that some of the coins had been used earlier in the day, which only sharpened appetites. The Fisher always listened to the chatter and gossip of the river people, whilst his own coven of grotesques busily ferreted out all the news. A gull screamed, flying low above him. The Fisher shook the damp from his robe then glanced around. His crew now rested, wrapped like little slugs in the thick military cloaks the Fisher had bought them. He heard a cough and glanced up. Icthus, silent as a ghost, now stood before him.

'Master.' Icthus's voice was no more than whisper.

'What is it, my friend?'

'Barges, concealed along the far side. They watch the sandbanks, they are waiting for something. I was right, master. I have not failed you.'

'Yes, you were right, and you never fail me, my friend. Oh yes . . .' The Fisher murmured to himself. Icthus had alerted him earlier that something quite out of the ordinary was happening in or around the treacherous sandbanks; the Fisher had decided to stay and see what happened. Most of the lights on his barge had been doused as he hid in the deep, tree-shadowed inlet where he could watch without being seen. The only light flaring up over the river were the great beacon fires burning lustily along the sandbanks. A tangle of wood, tar and pitch; a slow-burning pyre to warn craft that they were fast approaching a most treacherous part of the river. The tongues of flames leapt up and down like tormented dancers casting flitting shadows, as well as illuminating the corpses of river pirates, hanged on a riverside scaffold, before being impaled on stakes along the sandbanks; a brutal warning to all pirates who prowled the Thames. The Fisher could not see beyond these dire beacons, but Icthus did.

'Barges,' the Fisher's henchman whispered. 'Full of men. They're waiting, master, but for what?' Icthus paused. 'Ah, I think it comes.'

The Fisher strained his eyes, peering through the dark, trying not to be distracted by the shifting blur of the river. Then he glimpsed it! The mast, stern and prow of a small, fat-bellied cog.

'It's the *Serafino*!' Icthus exclaimed. 'Owned by the Genoese, Genova.'

The Fisher knew all about that cog and its master, a bold smuggler who traded whatever he could steal and filch from the London markets. The *Serafino* did not really concern the Fisher. Genova was probably doing what he was best at: smuggling. But why were these barges lying off the sandbanks? The *Serafino*'s hold was probably crammed with different items, but not of the type to attract a fleet of river pirates, and that's what was happening. A horde of outlaws was waiting to ambush this hapless cog. The *Serafino* meanwhile was closing fast, totally unaware of any danger. The Fisher knew he could do nothing. The *Serafino* would follow the usual routine of any boat approaching the sandbanks, its sail would be reefed and the cog would slow down to less than a walking pace, so as to carefully navigate this deeply treacherous stretch of water. The Fisher was relieved he had sheltered so deep in the darkness. He had no other choice but to wait and watch.

'So it begins,' Icthus softly sang out, pointing to the fire arrows searing through the darkness. More shafts were loosed. Some missed, others hit their target, and the shadowy outline of the *Serafino* became illuminated as the fire greedily caught hold of dry sail and cordage. A sudden fountain of flame abruptly sparked the night.

'They've hit a pot of oil or tar,' the Fisher exclaimed. 'God help those poor souls, sent to judgement through fire and water.'

The Fisher crossed himself as he watched the flaming cog bright against the darkness. The pirates now closed with the *Serafino*. They would board, slaughter any soul alive, plunder the hold, then vanish into the night. The Fisher prayed for forgiveness as he drew comfort that now there would certainly be more corpses to harvest. He went to stand by the taffrail. One of his acolytes brought across a goblet of the finest Bordeaux. The Fisher took this and sipped as he stared across the river. He would wait. Icthus's eyesight never failed. At last his henchman, standing high in the prow, threw his arms in the air and gave a long, noisy sigh.

'Master,' he called. 'It is finished. Only the corpses.'

The Fisher rapped out orders. The crew were roused and, with Icthus softly chanting directions, its oars flashing up and down, the Fisher's craft swept out of the inlet. Battling the cross-currents, the massive barge veered to port, turning to find the channel through the sandbanks. They followed the same route as the ill-fated *Serafino*, then heaved to, yards from the blazing stern of the doomed cog.

'No closer,' Icthus whispered hoarsely. 'Let me see.' He pulled off his linen shift and loincloth and slipped like an otter into the water. Icthus swam towards the burning wreck then turned, grasping a corpse, which he pushed back towards the death barge, where the crew pulled it aboard. Icthus then returned to his macabre fishing, and seven more corpses were brought in. 'There's another, I think he may be alive,' he shouted up to his master. 'But he is some distance away. I will try to bring him back.' Icthus disappeared into the freezing darkness. The Fisher stared around. Lanterns had been lit, warming pots fired, the crew all excited at such a rich harvest. A resounding crack echoed through the darkness. The *Serafino*'s mast crumpled, the fire now abated as the river water greedily poured over the stricken cog.

'So sudden,' the Fisher whispered. But that was war along the river: a brutal assault, followed by boarding, the execution of the crew and the swift plundering of the hold. Life was cruel along the Thames. 'Dog eat dog' was a common expression, but it was also a true reflection of the bloody mayhem which raged along both banks.

'Here he is,' Icthus called. Members of the crew hurried across to starboard and lifted the body out of the water with a net. They pulled this in, then left the grey-bearded victim spread-eagled out between the rowing benches. The Fisher knelt beside the wounded man. He lightly pressed a gauntleted finger against the blood-bubbling neck wound, and stared pityingly down at the survivor's bruised face.

'My friend,' he leaned closer, 'make your peace with God because God knows there is little we can do for you.'

'Why?' The man coughed. 'Why?'

'Why indeed,' the Fisher replied. 'But man has been wicked since God was a boy.'

'Why?' The man gasped. 'Why did they think we had the treasure?' He coughed bloody phlegm. 'They asked the master that. Poor Genova didn't know what they were talking about.'

'Treasure?' The Fisher leaned closer. 'What treasure?'

'The gold. The Westminster gold.' The man gabbled. 'They thought we had it.'

Athelstan stared pityingly at the corpses in the Chapel of the Drowned Men which fronted the quayside where the Fisher of Men plied his trade. All of the slain displayed nasty cuts and slashes to the neck or chest, wounds inflicted by arrow, sword or knife. The flesh of most of the corpses was scorched and burned, be it the hair and scalp or the black sockets where their eyes had turned to water. The Fisher, walking behind Athelstan and Cranston, described what they had witnessed the night before. How he believed it was very important, which explained his haste. At first light, even before the sacred bells had rung out to drive away the nightmare demons, the Fisher had despatched urgent messages to Cranston and Athelstan that he needed to meet them without delay. Cranston had been plucked from the Guildhall, Athelstan from his parish church to witness the true ferocity of that deadly ambush along the river. The *Serafino* wasn't even worth being viewed, a collection of black scorched timbers being pushed backwards and forwards by the river, its crew no more than cold slabs on the mortuary tables.

'I am sure they will have kin to collect them,' the Fisher declared mournfully. 'We've alerted the river reeves and water bailiffs . . .'

'Those who are not collected,' Cranston declared, opening his purse and putting a silver coin on the table, 'those who have no kin or have kin who don't care, give them honourable burial in St

Mary's atte Bowe. The Haceldema, its Field of Blood, the burial plot for the unknown and the unloved will welcome them.'

'God have mercy on their souls,' Athelstan whispered. He reached the end of the line of mortuary tables and administered a blessing followed by a recitation of the '*De Profundis*': 'Out of the depths do I cry to thee, O Lord.' Athelstan chanted the verses, the refrain being taken up by the Fisher and his retinue, now clustered in the doorway; a mournful solemn chant as it rose and fell. Once finished, the Fisher plucked at Athelstan's sleeve and led both him and the coroner across to a table against the far wall. He removed the linen shroud and gestured at the naked corpse sprawled there. Athelstan took one look at the matted blond hair and the fat face now contorted by swift, brutal death. 'Blodwyn the Blessed,' he murmured. 'God save you. Look, Sir John, strangled like a Newgate chicken.' The dead felon's face was truly horrid. A strange purple hue blotted the skin, the nose had been nibbled by some river animal, whilst the swollen tongue was thrust out between slightly rolled-back, rotting lips.

'The garrotte,' Cranston observed, 'deals a sordid killing blow.' The coroner abruptly covered his mouth and nose against a waft of stinking air. Athelstan turned and gratefully accepted the pomander the Fisher thrust into his hand.

'Where did you find him?'

'Off Dowgate Sir John, floating amongst the reeds, as naked as the day he was born.'

'Ah well.' Cranston stamped his feet, took a gulp from the miraculous wineskin, then thrust it back beneath his cloak. 'My friend.' The coroner extended a bow to the Fisher. 'My thanks. Athelstan, it's time we adjourned to my chapel.'

They left the quayside, but not before Cranston summoned his messenger, Tiptoft, who had accompanied him across. He tapped his faithful shadow on the shoulder.

'Go to The Hanging Tree, collect that minion of midnight, Master Culpeper, and take him to the treasure house at Westminster, where Flaxwith will lead him through what happened.' Cranston heaved a weary sigh. 'Perhaps that snooper will see things we did not.' Cranston glanced back at the Chapel of the Drowned Men. 'Once you have delivered Culpeper,' he continued, 'go into Whitefriars. Enter the Halls of Night and inform the Lords of

Misrule that Sir John Cranston, Lord High Coroner of London, wishes to have words with them.'

Cranston and Athelstan continued walking up into the waking city. The streets were still fairly deserted, though the houses, shops and booths on either side were preparing for a new day's business. Window casements were flung open. Jake jars, piss pots and other baskets of filthy refuse were being emptied, with a cry to any passer-by to be careful. The air reeked of different smells, be it the foul stench of the cesspits or the occasional sweet fragrance from the pastry shops, taverns and alehouses. The noise was beginning to grow as the city prepared for the day. Knights on horseback, their destriers brilliantly caparisoned, made their way towards the tilt yard at Smithfield. These armoured men, dangerous in their pride and honour, slouched on their high horned saddles, their liveried shields and pennants paraded by squires walking before them. Dogs, freshly released, barked and howled as they scuttled backwards and forwards, noses snouting for any possible food. One of these mongrels had been caught beneath the wheels of a cart, its strident screams only silenced by a passing archer who cut its throat. On the corner of one street a pile of scaffolding had collapsed; one of the workmen lay pinned beneath a heavy bar, his chest crushed, his mouth all bloodied. He could only chatter in agony as a passing priest shrived and comforted him for death. The Proclaimers of Purgatory, the Heralds of the Grave and the Masters of the Mortuaries were out reciting the names of those who had died during the night. They rang their bells and beat their drums as they asked for all faithful Christians to pause and pray for the souls of the faithfully departed. A few citizens did, most were too busy preparing for the day. Bailiffs and beadles paraded a long line of night-walkers, now much sobered, as they were forced to carry slopping buckets of refuse on their way down to the stocks and pillories close to the Standard in Cheapside.

At last, they reached the entrance to the great marketplace and its place of punishment. Athelstan tried not to look at the corpses, necks all awry, faces twisted and tortured, who had been executed on a mobile gallows. Athelstan recalled The Hanging Tree and wondered if Culpeper had, amongst other things, learnt anything fresh about that tavern and the Guild it housed. They reached the great thoroughfare of Cheapside, its gaily coloured stalls almost ready for business. The traders of everything from glass goblets to rare and precious silk stood eagerly about. They waited for the bells after the Jesus Mass, and the braying market horns, which would signal the start of a new day's business.

Cranston shouldered his way through the gathering throng, pushing away the mummers, acrobats and wandering tale-tellers, all eager for a coin in return for their fables. As he approached his favourite tavern, Cranston was accosted by those two shadows who constantly lurked near the coroner's haven of delight. This morning was no different. Leif, the one-legged beggar, and Rawbum his confederate, emerged from the mouth of a runnel shouting benedictions on Sir John and everything in his codpiece. They kept proclaiming the greatness of Sir John until the exasperated coroner silenced them with a twirling coin. Once safely inside The Lamb of God, Mine Hostess, pink-cheeked and merry-eyed, ushered both men into the tavern's comfortable snug solar and Sir John's favourite cushioned window seat. She then served them rich tankards of morning ale, brewed in her own buttery, along with a platter of freshly baked bread and strips of the crispiest pork, cooked in a mustard and honey sauce. Both coroner and friar eagerly broke their fast. Sir John finished by taking a generous mouthful from the miraculous wineskin and beamed expansively at Athelstan.

'Very good, little friar, let us confront the mysteries.'

'Sir John, thank you. I have broken my fast and I now feel a better man, though perhaps not a better friar. But listen, a number of mysteries confront us. A real challenge to our wits. We are not yet sure whether they are all connected, though they may well be. First, we have the murder of Clement the Key-Master, a skilled craftsman who fell into disgrace. We know the reasons for that, so there is no need to repeat them, except to note that the special doors to the treasure chamber at Westminster also play a part in Clement's life and, perhaps, in his death.'

'I agree,' Cranston replied. 'I do wonder who gave the Crown the information about what Clement had done or failed to do.'

'A possible source for such information,' Athelstan declared, 'might be Columba, Clement's beloved son. Wittingly or not, Columba might have revealed what could be found in his father's house and workshop. Anyway, the same Columba married Isabella, now the beloved wife of the taverner of The Hanging Tree. God knows what her first marriage was like or what happened between man and wife. Columba became unhappy, then he vanished from the face of God's earth. Nobody knows where he could be or why he should disappear so mysteriously. Clement is heartbroken, his wife dies, he retreats into the shadows a broken man. Isabella, his former daughter-in-law, is not so accepting. She continues with her life and gains licence from the archdeacon to marry our taverner. The licence was probably granted on the grounds that Columba was dead and so life surges on.' Athelstan sipped from his tankard. 'Nothing really changes until recently. At the very most, a few weeks ago. According to Crispin, Clement emerged from the shadows. He is now deeply concerned about the truth behind his son's disappearance. He speculates on the possibilities, whatever they might be. Above all, he makes elliptical reference to how his son would have never left home and hearth without what he calls "The Walsingham". Now,' Athelstan opened his chancery satchel and drew out the polished statuette, 'Clement had this on him when he died.'

'"The Walsingham",' Cranston breathed. 'A beautiful statuette! Well carved and costly: the sort of item which can only be bought at the shrine itself. But what's this?' Cranston had already discovered the thick stickiness on the base of the statuette.

'Sir John, that also intrigues me. I don't know what it is. However, to press on. Clement came to believe something dreadful had happened to his son. He sought advice from his friend and distant kinsman Crispin, who urged Clement to come and see me. Now, someone, and we don't know who, wanted to stop this. We must ask who actually knew Clement was crossing the Thames to visit me? However, on reflection, Crispin, or indeed anyone else, could have made a slip. Or there again, the assassin may have kept Clement under close watch. Whatever, the killer bided his time and chose his moment to strike. He entered my church, murdered Clement, then fled.' Athelstan paused, chewing on the corner of his lip. 'And so we come to another murder, probably connected with that of Clement's. The brutal death of Blodwyn the Blessed. I think I now know how Blodwyn escaped and I also suspect the true reason for his murder.'

'Brother?'

'For the time being, Sir John, that will have to wait. We now pass on to the murdered hangmen. Such killings go back some months?'

'So it would seem!'

'They were first abducted?'

'That's what Master Thibault's schedule of information suggests. Each victim disappeared for a few days, only to be found, as we did Slyman, naked, knifed to the heart, and tossed on a midden heap or in some stinking lay stall. They were all members of the Guild.'

'And what do we know about that?'

'I've made enquiries,' Cranston replied. 'Not as prosperous as it once was. The plunder taken from France has certainly diminished, whilst the profits accrued by the hangings which followed the Great Revolt have also severely dissipated.'

'Let us go back to the important question,' Athelstan declared. 'Why has someone taken to killing London's hangmen? According to the meagre evidence on those scraps of parchment, such murders are the work of the Reapers, a few surviving rebel captains now soul-bent on wreaking revenge for their loss.' Athelstan shook his head. 'I don't think so. The revolt is dead. Those pathetic proclamations a mere cover for something else, though what I don't know. Except, I just wonder . . .'

'What?'

'Why the corpses are stripped? Why wreak such humiliation on a dead man! And how were these former soldiers stabbed, without there being any trace on their corpses of a struggle or even token resistance?'

'I agree, little friar. The idea of vengeance for the revolt is nonsense. The hangmen were merely officials who carried out sentence. Why choose them? Why not the justices, sheriffs and bailiffs? Why not the jailers of Newgate or the Fleet?'

Athelstan toasted Cranston with his tankard.

'And now we come to the rarest of mysteries, the fount and origin of so much violence. The devil's own work.'

'The robbery at Westminster?'

'Oh yes, and what do we have here, my Lord Coroner? On that fateful morning, Beaumont and the Clerks of the Light gathered for a day's work. As usual, Magister Beaumont had collected those precious keys from Master Thibault. The abbey bells tolled for Prime, and so it begins . . .'

'And, at that moment in time, nothing is amiss.'

'Correct, Sir John, nothing! Beaumont opens the first door into the stairwell, his clerks follow him in. The bell is sounded three times in honour of the Trinity but the bell from the treasure chamber does not reply.' Athelstan swilled the dregs of his ale around his blackjack. 'The bell is rung,' he murmured, 'but there was no reply. Is that what Whitby meant by the "plainchant being sorely disturbed"? The regular routine violated. Perhaps, but at that moment Beaumont and his colleagues could do nothing about it. To continue. Beaumont leads them up that steep spiral staircase. The Magister goes first, carefully removing the trip cords, which are still stretched tight across each eighth step. They reach the door to the treasure chamber. Perhaps they expected it to be open but, whatever, Beaumont unlocks it and they enter a place of slaughter. Despencer and his four clerks, each in their enclaves, have been cruelly garrotted. The treasure is gone yet there is no sign, no indication, about how such a bulky and heavy hoard was taken away. We have examined the treasure chamber. Its doors and windows are most secure. The only gap in its defences is that jakes chute which runs down to hang above the cess barrel. There was no sign of violence, the food and wine, or what remains, have been tested and, I understand, found to be wholesome?'

'True,' the coroner murmured. 'That's what Flaxwith reported. All the food and drink from that chamber was mixed together and spread out on a platter. Apparently the rats made a feast of it and remained none the worse!'

'I thought as much. So, my Lord Coroner, how did the assassin manage to get in and out through those specially locked doors? How did he, she or they escape the trip cords? How could the assassin slaughter five vigorous mailed clerks? How did he remove such a heavy treasure?' Athelstan sighed noisily. 'One thing we do know, or rather suspect, the assassin worked under the cover of night and the deep darkness which shrouds that tower. Now remember, in the main we talk of one assassin, but there must have been more, surely. I mean . . .' Athelstan paused at a rap at the door and Mine Hostess, pink-cheeked and all a-flutter, tripped in.

'Sir John,' she proclaimed breathlessly. 'My apologies but there is a stranger.' She beckoned back towards the taproom. 'Sir John, a true stranger. He calls himself All Hallows.'

'Oh yes.' Cranston rose, seized his hostess and kissed her warmly on each cheek. 'All Hallows, the official emissary of the Lords of Misrule in the Halls of Night! My dear, do usher him in.'

Mine Hostess, now even more pink-cheeked, bustled out. Cranston retook his seat. There was a gentle knock on the door and a grey-garbed, grey-haired, grey-faced little man slipped into the solar. At first Athelstan thought their visitor was a cleric, priest or monk, but then he noticed the warbelt strapped around the man's waist and the heavy boots on his feet. He bowed to both Cranston and Athelstan, then took the stool Sir John pulled across for him.

'Greetings Sir John. Brother Athelstan. *Pax et bonum*. My masters sent me to help if I can.' All Hallow's doughy face creased into a forced smile.

'The robbery at Westminster,' Cranston declared.

All Hallows joined his hands as if in prayer. 'Nothing to do with us.'

'And the attack on the *Serafino*. The total destruction of a cog and its crew. Wanton murder, wanton robbery, wanton wickedness.'

'Sir John, Master Micklegate—'

'Micklegate!' Cranston snapped. 'What has that miscreant, that notorious housebreaker got to do with anything? Lodged in Newgate, he has been condemned to hang and will soon join the choir invisible. Ahh,' Cranston grinned. 'I follow your logic. A pardon free and full so Micklegate can dine with you rather than the devils in hell. Though,' Cranston added ruefully, 'there's little, if any, difference between the two.'

'Now, now Sir John!'

'Now, now nothing. Tell me,' Cranston jabbed a stubby finger at their visitor, 'the robbery at Westminster, were the Lords of Misrule involved?'

'No no, Your Worship.'

'Shut up.'

'Yes, Sir John.'

'Were the lords involved in any way?'

'Of course not.' All Hallows almost spat the words out. 'No

they, we, were not. We only heard about it afterwards. None of us knew. Sir John, the Lords of Misrule will swear to that. We had nothing to do with the plundering. Indeed, Sir John, we are as perplexed as you are.'

'I am not perplexed.'

'My apologies, Sir John, but we certainly are. We have scoured the city, yet we hear no gossip or chatter. Nobody knows anything.'

'Yet the attack on the *Serafino*?'

'The Lords of the River, Sir John: that's their fief, not ours.'

'But why the attack?' Athelstan insisted. 'We have learnt from the Fisher of Men how one of the survivors, before he died of his wounds, claimed the assailants were hoping to seize the stolen treasure.'

All Hallows expression changed, a cunning, knowing look in his deep-set eyes.'

'Help us,' Cranston declared. 'Help us, All Hallows, and Micklegate will join you before the Compline bell tomorrow. We need information. Of course, I didn't expect you to put your hands up and admit to the robbery, but just watching you is answer enough. I am convinced the Lords of Misrule were not involved in the murderous mayhem at Westminster, but you can still help us.' All Hallows, hands in his lap, nodded as he rocked backwards and forwards. He glanced swiftly at Cranston.

'Micklegate walks?'

'He is free as a bird. So—'

'Brother Athelstan, Sir John think, reflect, follow my logic. More than one person must have been involved in that robbery. The treasure is very heavy. How was it transported away so quickly? More importantly,' All Hallows gabbled, wiping the spit from his lips, 'those coins cannot be traded here or anywhere in this kingdom. Those responsible must get it out as swiftly as possible without being caught. Those who stole the treasure know that if captured, they would not only lose the treasure but suffer the most hideous punishment for treason. They must be very careful, prudent.'

'Of course,' Cranston breathed. 'Trying to smuggle it through a port, be it London, Dover or anywhere else would be extremely dangerous. Master Thibault's searchers are crawling over the ports and harbours like fleas on a turd.'

'Very perceptive, Sir John. The treasure has to be smuggled

out. Now as for the *Serafino*, its owner Genova is – or should I say was – an accomplished smuggler. Moreover, the *Serafino* slips in and out of London.'

'The ideal master, cog and crew for such an enterprise.'

'Again, Sir John, most perceptive. The Lords of the River must have been watching the *Serafino* and gambled on it containing the treasure.'

'Yet what proof did they have that Genova and his cog held such a prize?'

'Sir John, what if the Lords of the River were given false information?'

'Why?'

'Oh I know,' Athelstan retorted. 'Or at least I suspect. Those responsible were simply deepening the confusion, spreading the mystery.'

'I would agree,' All Hallows murmured.

Athelstan leaned forward and touched their visitor on the back of his hand.

'Many men have died since this mystery began. Is there anything you can tell us which could help solve this mystery?'

All Hallows just shook his head.

'Brother Athelstan,' he declared, 'remember to whom you are talking. I belong to and represent a Guild of Thieves. If I had my way, if I thought I could do it, I would have stolen that treasure.'

'But the killings?' Athelstan retorted. 'The wanton slaying of men like Genova and his hapless crew.' All Hallows simply looked away.

'There are two further items,' Athelstan declared. 'First the deaths – or rather the murders – of London hangmen?'

All Hallows pulled a face and shook his head. 'Of course we know about them. We openly rejoice at the death of those who despatched so many of our brotherhood into the dark. But we are not responsible, nor do we even suspect who might be responsible.' All Hallows waved a black-gloved hand. 'Oh, I've heard about the message left pinned on each corpse. The word "Vengeance" and the crudely drawn gibbet. However, as you know, that's arrant nonsense. The Great Revolt is truly quashed and those responsible despatched for judgement.' He smiled at Athelstan. 'And the second item, Brother?'

'The Carbonari, the charcoal burners. A gang of thieves who hail from the Italian states. Are they active in London?'

'If they are, we don't know. Oh, we have heard stories about the charcoal burners, rumours that they were responsible for the great robbery but,' All Hallows spread his hands, 'in our eyes the Carbonari are what they claim to be, dust on the breeze. If they are in London, they are truly well hidden. They do not cross us in any way, so we would view them as we would any other gang who does not threaten us. However, if we did discover that they were definitely responsible for the robbery, matters would change soon enough.' All Hallows rose. 'Sir John, Brother Athelstan, can I go?'

'Oh we are finished,' Cranston replied. 'Give my regards to the Lords of Misrule. Tell them Micklegate will be released, but that both he and they will never be far from my thoughts.'

All Hallows slipped silently from the solar. Athelstan and Cranston sat in silence for a while, then the friar gave a deep sigh and got to his feet.

'You are leaving, Brother? Let me accompany you.'

'God be with you, Sir John, but no. I will be safe enough, whilst the Lady Maude and your poppets must now be yearning to see you . . .'

PART FIVE

'How can I gain men's goods and gold?'

Athelstan sat dozing before the fire in the priest's house. He'd returned to St Erconwald's at least three hours ago, if he correctly recalled what ring the flame on the hour candle had reached. The parish lay very quiet. Benedicta and Mauger had seen to both church and house. They had assured their priest that all was as calm as it appeared. No disputes had arisen. Most of his parishioners had finished early as dusk descended, eager to join each other in The Piebald tavern, to drink and carouse until the curfew bells tolled and the beacon lights flared in the steeples.

It had been a cold, hard day. The ground underfoot, as Benedicta declared, was iron hard, difficult to dig, as Watkin, Pike and the rest hacked out a grave for the mortal remains of Clement the Key-Master. Crispin had made it very clear that his kinsman would prefer to wait for the Final Resurrection in St Erconwald's, rather than some city graveyard. Moreover, the carpenter had added, if Clement stayed close to where he had been murdered, then he could invoke the Lords of Light. He could also plead with the angels to guard, protect and help his spirit accept the anguish of death. Moreover, the presence of the corpse of a murder victim added strength to efforts to discover the victim's killer and bring him or her to judgement. Indeed, as the carpenter had lectured his fellow parishioners, he could remember his grandfather once telling him that if an inquisition into a murder took place in the presence of the corpse, then it might be easier to establish who was responsible. Each of the suspects would be asked to place their hand on the murder victim's head and some sign would be given if the guilty person did that. A wound would start to bleed, or a touch cause the corpse to tremble. Athelstan heard this out and closed his eyes, sighing with relief. Some of his parishioners certainly believed in the old ways, which were often gruesome and, on many occasions, invoked magic forbidden by the church. Benedicta assured him, however, that everything was in order: Clement's corpse lay shrouded ready for Christian burial.

Once he had finished his business in the church, the friar had gone straight to the priest's house to eat and drink a little. Afterwards he stood at the lectern and recited the hours of Vespers and Compline, finishing with a requiem for all the victims of murder he was investigating. Athelstan leaned down and scratched Bonaventure's one and only ear until the great tomcat stretched and purred with pleasure.

'All is well, Bonaventure. You are fed and warm, Philomel snores in his stable and dreams of glorious charges. Hubert the hedgehog is lost in his winter's sleep. My church and house lie secure so why, Bonaventure, do I feel restless? Why do I believe there is a shadow behind me just out of sight?'

As if in answer, the breeze outside gathered its strength and an owl hooted in protest, its chilling warning echoing through the dark. Athelstan drew himself up in his chair. In a word, he sensed danger. Some lurking hidden menace had fastened on to his spirit and he could not shake it off; an unnamed fear plagued his soul. He had left Sir John in the city but only after the coroner had his way and hired the two dwarfs, the sturdy link men Cosmas and Damien, to escort Athelstan down to London Bridge and across into Southwark. As the friar and his escort strode up the alleyway, past The Piebald, Athelstan had felt a prickle of fear, as if icy-cold fingers had pressed the nape of his neck, running down between his shoulder blades. He asked his guides to stop and turned, staring back up the runnel, but there was nothing except the light shimmering in the puddles. Eventually he reached his church, thanked his escort, and became immersed in all the petty business of the parish. Yet he still felt restless. Wary, as if some malignancy was silently stalking him. He glanced over his shoulder at the door; it was locked and bolted. Athelstan, still agitated, returned to his reflections. He thought of Blodwyn the Blessed and smiled to himself.

'At least,' he whispered to the ever-attentive cat, 'I have resolved that mystery. I cannot sleep so, Bonaventure, let us hear the chimes of midnight.' He got to his feet, fastened his cloak about him, grabbed the small arbalest from its hook on the wall, unlocked the door and left, Bonaventure padding soft as a ghost beside him.

Athelstan stared across God's Acre, a truly desolate place, with its ancient yew trees and the sprouting, frozen gorse pointing up like fingers against the gloaming. He caught the sliver of light from the shutters across the window of what he called the House of the Faithful Departed. 'Good,' Athelstan breathed, 'so you too watch the midnight hour.' He followed the winding beaten path and hammered on the door. 'Thomas,' he shouted. 'Thomas, this is your priest.' Bolts were hastily drawn, a key turned and the door swung open. Thomas the Toad stared blearily at the friar.

'Father . . .?'

'Can I come in, Thomas, thank you.' Athelstan brushed by his reluctant host and strode into the square chamber. The air smelt sweet, with the fragrance of some herbs strewn on the fire flickering in the hearth. Athelstan gazed round. Comfortable lodgings with its sparse furniture, scrubbed paved floor and, to his right, a row of small cages containing Thomas's parishioners, or disciples, as Athelstan called them: toads of every kind, size and colour. Thomas hastened to pull up a second stool before the hearth. He then lit a lanternhorn and placed this between himself and the friar. Once settled, he picked up the bowl of potage he'd been eating.

'Father,' he murmured, 'do you want some, or perhaps a stoup of ale?'

Athelstan shook his head and stared around at the croaking disciples in their cages. The toads, now disturbed, increased their noise, as if some infernal chorus was greeting Athelstan's arrival.

'Father,' Thomas gestured towards the cages, 'I can stop them.'

'I don't want you to stop them, Thomas. Nor do I want anything to eat or drink. I have come for the truth. Oh, by the way, just in case you don't already know: Blodwyn the Blessed is now truly blessed. I hope he is in heaven.'

Thomas just gaped.

'Blodwyn is dead, murdered!'

Thomas nearly dropped the bowl he was cradling.

'Oh yes,' Athelstan continued, 'poor Blodwyn was garrotted and his corpse stripped before being thrown into the Thames off Dowgate.'

'God save him, God rest him,' Thomas stuttered, now looking

even more like the creatures he fostered. 'Father, what has this to do—'

'To do with you?' Athelstan finished the sentence, turning to confront the keeper.

'Father—'

'Don't Father me, Thomas! Blodwyn escaped from sanctuary in my church. Now, with his blond hair and blood-red jerkin, Blodwyn would find it very difficult to hide, particularly when every beadle and bailiff between here and beyond were scouring the crowds for him. Of course, Blodwyn knew that so, fast as a whippet, running at a crouch, he crossed God's Acre and knocked on your door. You took him in.' Athelstan jabbed a finger, trying to hide his pity for this poor frog-faced recluse. 'Don't lie, Thomas, I have been very good to you and,' Athelstan nodded towards the cages where the toads were now croaking merrily, 'your disciples. So Thomas, the truth. Do you know something? I wondered why you were wandering the church and cemetery that night, loudly proclaiming how the dead were speaking to you. You were trying to distract us, weren't you? Thomas the chatterer, lost in his own world. Certainly the one parishioner who would know nothing about what was happening. Well, of course you did, because you were responsible for a great deal of that confusion. You knew Blodwyn had escaped and you also knew where he was hiding. So?'

'It is as you say, Father. There was a great deal of clamour over the murder. I decided to go out, I was greatly afeared and . . .'

'Well?' Athelstan insisted.

'Blodwyn knocked on my door. I let him in. He begged me to hide him and, if I did, he would share his new-found wealth with me.'

'What wealth?'

'Listen, Father, Blodwyn begged for my help, gabbling about a reward. Anyway, to cut my tale, I hid him, not that anyone came searching. I just had to wait for a while. Once it grew quiet and the church emptied, Blodwyn told me how he'd seen the killer, Clement's murderer. He'd glimpsed his face and recognized him immediately.'

'Who?'

'Ah Father, Blodwyn wouldn't say, but he claimed the killer

had a well-known face. Blodwyn then added that he was going across the river to confront the sinner. He'd make him pay dearly for Blodwyn's silence. Again I pressed him on who the murderer might be, but Blodwyn simply tapped the side of his nose and said we would all be very rich.'

'So it was somebody wealthy?'

'Must have been. Anyway, Blodwyn then asked for the loan of a cloak and hood. I gave him both and he left saying he would return. He pointed out that I was now part of the conspiracy because I had sheltered him, a fugitive from sanctuary. He said that if he were captured, I would be in trouble as well. I knew what he was saying. He was telling me to keep my mouth shut.'

'Clever Blodwyn.'

'Too clever by half, Father. Whoever he met murdered him.'

'So it would seem.' Athelstan turned back to the fire. 'Who could it be, Thomas?' He whispered. Both men were suddenly startled by a banging on the door followed by a cry: 'Brother Athelstan! Thomas!'

The friar rose and crossed to open it, Thomas trailing behind him. Athelstan half turned the lock then paused. 'Whoever called out,' he glanced back at Thomas, 'knew I had come here. I thought I was being watched, stalked.' He hastily locked the door then stepped back, as his would-be assailants hammered on both door and window shutter. Athelstan heard crossbow bolts slam into both. Thomas began to wail. The friar stood staring at the fire as he recalled why Thomas had been given this dwelling.

'The horn!' Athelstan shouted. 'Thomas, get me the horn.' The toad man scampered off towards a chest beneath the bed loft. He threw back the lid, croaking like his disciples as he fished among the contents. He shouted with glee, holding up the hunting horn.

'For God's sake, Thomas, blow!'

The toad man did but his mouth was too full of spit. Athelstan grabbed the horn and blew as hard as he could; a long, braying wail, repeated time and again. He just prayed that parishioners, such as Cecily the Courtesan or her sister Clarissa, who might be plying their trade in or near God's Acre, would hear the alarm being raised. Perhaps, despite the late hour, someone crossing the concourse or going down the alley to The Piebald might be alerted.

Athelstan blew again then paused. The attackers outside had

fallen silent. Athelstan strained his hearing and prayed hasty thanks as he heard a faint shout which grew stronger as the ancient hue and cry were raised to yells of 'Harrow! Harrow!' Athelstan wiped the sweat from the palm of his hands. At last the shouts echoed from outside. He recognized Watkin's booming voice, followed by Benedicta's pleas for Thomas to open the door. The toad man did so, and Athelstan swept out into the freezing night to greet his semi-circle of parishioners. Athelstan, patting Benedicta on the shoulder, loudly assuring the rest that all was well. How his attackers were probably a band of wandering outlaws or peace-breakers. In truth, Athelstan had no doubt that the attack, like that at Westminster, was because of his investigations into the robbery: a murderous attempt to silence him. Athelstan, however, maintained a brave face. He praised Thomas the Toad as a hero, but then whispered to Benedicta that someone must train the little man in the use of the horn.

'That's why he lives here,' Athelstan declared. 'To raise the alarm if God's Acre becomes the meeting ground for the warlocks who plague the area. Now Benedicta, see me back to my house and, I pray, a good night's sleep.'

'And did you get a good night's sleep?' Cranston asked as he and Athelstan made their way up through the yawning Lion Gate of the Tower of London.

'I did, Sir John. Then I rose early to celebrate Clement's requiem Mass, as well as to see to his burial in God's Acre.' Athelstan laughed abruptly. 'Nor did he go alone! Two of Thomas's toads expired, probably frightened to death! Anyway, I blessed and buried them in the joyful hope of the Final Resurrection.'

'Do you think there will be toads in heaven?'

'If you want there to be.' Athelstan nudged the coroner. 'Along with miraculous wineskins. However, Sir John, we are now in the Tower. Be careful, we are entering a lion's den in more ways than one. Do you know why we have been summoned?'

'I suspect why, little friar, but,' Cranston gestured at the soldiers and clerks just inside the gateway, 'you are correct, the Tower has many eyes as well as ears.'

They lapsed into silence. Both Coroner and Friar made their way deeper into that Iron House of War which, as Athelstan once said, constantly reeked of the sooty stink of Satan. The great fortress was certainly busy, bustling with armaments and men of war. Sherwood archers manned the wall walks and parapets. Knights in half armour guarded the entrances to different towers. The gulleys and runnels which wound through the fortress were as busy as any Cheapside alleyway. Smoke billowed from the open fires of the many communal kitchens which served the Tower people. In fact, the fortress was a small town in itself; it was also a place for dark designs and bloody punishments. Severed heads, spiked and poled, decorated the walls and different gateways. Cranston and Athelstan passed shadow-filled enclaves, where felons stood pinned in the stocks, whilst Athelstan almost gagged as a cartload of severed, blood-soaked limbs trundled down to a gate close to the river. At last, they reached the green field and cobbled yard, which circled the soaring White Tower. Children played on the mangonels, catapults, battering rams and other machinery of war. Women clustered around the great well, busy washing and laundering. Others queued for dough from the communal kitchens. The air was sweet with the scent of soap and freshly baked bread. Soldiers lounged, waiting for orders. A group of verderers were busy gutting a deer and hog on a huge spit, its charcoal and wood being vigorously fanned into flame.

The coroner despatched one of the knights guarding the main entrance to the White Tower to inform someone that they had arrived. In the meantime, they had nothing to do but sit on a bench and wait. Athelstan glanced up at the clear blue sky and quietly prayed for the day to remain bright and not too cold. He'd informed Cranston about the attack the previous evening, as well as what Thomas the Toad had said but, as the coroner had enigmatically replied, such matters would have to wait for a while. Murder had to give way to majesty. John of Gaunt and his Master of Secrets needed urgent words with them.

Athelstan rose to stretch his limbs and strode casually over to the washerwomen, busy with their heap of soiled clothes and blankets. The women reminded Athelstan of his own parents, who always loved washdays. The sight sparked sweet memories, and Athelstan recalled how his mother would constantly deride any ale or beer stain as the worst to clean away. She would lecture Athelstan on how such stains became almost ingrained in anything, be it cloth, parchment or wood, its stickiness almost impossible to eradicate. Athelstan broke from his daydreaming when one of the women called out to him. He delivered the sought-after blessing and asked them a few questions. He then returned to sit by the coroner, who was slouched on the bench half asleep, impervious to the glossy black ravens pecking the ground around him.

'Sir John . . . Sir John.' The friar glanced up. The household knight had returned.

'Sir John, my Lords await you.' The knight took them into the White Tower, up some steps and into the small council chamber next to the royal Chapel of St John. Gaunt and Thibault were waiting, seated at the top of a highly polished table. Both men greeted them in a lacklustre fashion. Thibault gestured them to sit on the chairs to Gaunt's left. Once seated, the self-styled Regent leaned back in his chair and nodded at his Master of Secrets.

'Tell them,' he grunted. 'Tell them what we face.'

'My Lord of Gaunt and I,' Thibault smiled icily, 'now confront a veritable sea of troubles.'

'Over the robbery at Westminster?'

'In a word, yes. The Commons, together with those Lords who are not so friendly to my master as they should be, are hinting – nay, even loudly proclaiming – that my Lord of Gaunt and I are responsible.'

'Nonsense.'

'Nonsense indeed, Sir John. They've already submitted the lesser charge that the robbery was at least caused by our incompetence.' Thibault waved a hand. 'They claim there should have been more guards and a closer watch. They cannot see why an army didn't encamp around Flambard's Tower.'

'There is some truth in that,' Cranston observed tartly. The coroner drummed his fingers on the table top. 'I have also heard rumours that the Speaker of the Commons and others want a clear explanation on certain matters.'

'And they will get it,' Thibault snapped. 'They forget the robbery was carried out through great deceit and cunning, not force which could have easily been resisted. We, my Lord of Gaunt and I, firmly believe that the fewer people close or near to that treasure house, the better. Soldiers, particularly at night, are not the most vigilant, whilst in some cases bribery can open many doors.'

Athelstan glanced at the crucifix nailed to the wall. He was pleased this issue had been raised, and in the way it had. After all, why hadn't there been a military guard, some sort of presence?

'Master Thibault, I hear what you say about soldiers or archers,' Athelstan retorted, 'but I still wonder why there wasn't a better guard around Flambard's Tower?'

Thibault put his face in his hands, let them fall away, and glanced at the Regent who nodded imperceptibly. Athelstan, closely watching both men, suspected what was going to be said.

'Yes, yes . . .' Thibault moved restlessly in his chair.

'There was a guard, wasn't there?' the friar demanded. 'A mailed presence close to that door leading to the stairwell. There is an antechamber, a waiting room where the clerks would assemble; that was occupied, yes?'

'There was someone there,' Thibault replied. 'In fact, two guards: my henchman Albinus and his companion Wolfrich. They were not on permanent watch but returned at the end of each quarter, every fourth ring on the hour candle, to ensure all was well. On the night of the robbery they did so, four times at the agreed hour.' Thibault shrugged and glanced away. 'They neither saw nor heard anything untoward.'

Cranston whistled under his breath and leaned back on his chair. 'I see,' he replied slowly, 'where this path could be leading.'

'Sir John?'

'The Commons might chatter about incompetence, but they could raise the stakes—'

'And accuse us of theft, murder and treason,' Gaunt interjected.

'In a word, yes my Lord.'

'Yes my Lord,' Gaunt mimicked. 'And, believe me, Cranston, there's enough amongst the Lords, never mind the Commons, who would love to impeach me of high treason.'

'Proof would be sparse.'

'Who cares?' Thibault scoffed. 'Dirt would be flung and some of it would stick fast.'

'True.' Cranston fought to keep the glee out of his voice, very mindful of Athelstan pressing one sandalled foot on the toe of the coroner's boot. 'They would impeach,' Cranston continued, 'or at least try to exclude you from high office.'

'And the evidence mounts,' Athelstan intervened, eager to

prevent Cranston from showing even a trace of his deep distaste for this precious pair.

'What evidence?'

'Master Thibault,' Athelstan emphasized his points on his fingers. 'Firstly, Beaumont and the others were your appointment. Secondly, you were responsible for the workings and the security of the treasure chamber. Thirdly, on the night of the robbery, you held the other set of keys. Fourthly, you were also responsible for the external guard: Albinus and Wolfrich are your retainers, trusted henchmen.'

Thibault, face now all weary, nodded in agreement at Athelstan's assertions.

'My Lord,' the friar declared, turning to Gaunt, 'I merely spell out what your opponents would certainly organize into an indictment to be laid before both Commons and Lords.'

'So what do you suggest?' Gaunt replied, playing with the rings on his fingers, which dazzled as they caught the light.

'My Lord, I confess we are making little progress. Indeed,' Athelstan tapped the table top, 'we must question both Albinus and Wolfrich. It's a pity,' Athelstan added, 'that we were not informed about them earlier. Sirs, both my Lord Coroner and myself have been attacked. I deeply suspect that these murderous assaults are connected with the present business. We need to know everything. I understand,' Athelstan raised a hand as he kept his voice placatory, 'the presence of Albinus and Wolfrich. Nevertheless, their very involvement makes your custody of the treasure chamber highly suspect. Everything you planned and plotted could not protect the King's gold, and that's the way people will read it. So, is there anything else?'

Both men shook their heads and Athelstan, despite his deep distrust of Gaunt and his henchman, believed they were telling the truth. He could also sense their mounting panic. The Crown had lost a treasure hoard, and the Commons and Lords would be only too eager to wreak retribution.

'Sir John,' Athelstan turned to the coroner, 'we should question Albinus and Wolfrich as a matter of urgency.'

'I agree,' the coroner replied. 'Master Thibault?'

'They are here, Sir John. I will have them brought up.'

A short while later, a Tower archer ushered both henchmen into the chamber. They bowed towards Gaunt, then took seats opposite Athelstan, who smiled bleakly across at Albinus. He had met this henchman before; a retainer fanatically loyal to Thibault. A strange, eerie character with the most sinister reputation. Albinus was a dagger man who had served in France, where he had become a '*peritus*' – an expert – in siege craft, especially the construction of mines and the use of black powder to bring down even the strongest wall. Albinus glared back across the table: his snow-white hair framed a face of the same hue, with pink-rimmed, glassy light-blue eyes and thick lips, so deeply red that Athelstan wondered if they were carmined. Wolfrich and Albinus were garbed in Thibault's favourite livery colours of green and black. Ostensibly a court retainer, Wolfrich looked what he truly was, a riffler, a street fighter, his puffy face with its broken nose and protuberant chin reminding Athelstan of a fighting mastiff.

Thibault haltingly broke the silence and briefly summarized what he had told Cranston and Athelstan earlier. Once he had finished, Thibault nodded at Athelstan to question his henchman. The friar simply shook his head.

'Brother Athelstan?'

'Enough is enough is enough,' the friar whispered. 'This mystery is hidden deep in a web of lies and the most malicious trickery.' Athelstan pointed across at the hour candle under its cap on an iron stand. 'My Lord of Gaunt, it is not yet noon. I want – I need – to revisit the treasure chamber at Westminster. I also demand to have everyone there. Beaumont and his clerks as well as your two henchmen. This is a murderous masque, a true mystery play, and we have to study it carefully. My Lord, I beg you.'

'I have the power,' Cranston declared, taking a generous gulp from the miraculous wineskin, 'to sit as a justiciar. I can convene a court of Oyer et Terminer.' Cranston pushed the stopper back into the wineskin and beamed around. 'I do so now. At what hour, Brother, do you want the court to meet?'

'Nones.'

'Then Nones it is,' the coroner declared. 'Three hours after noon, we meet in the treasure chamber at Westminster.'

Culpeper the sneak thief squatted on the floor of his garret, the topmost chamber in The Hanging Tree tavern. Culpeper chewed on a sore gum, licking the open cut as he felt the tender scar around his throat. Culpeper was bored. He had been out to Westminster and, with Flaxwith hovering close and the bailiff's mastiff even closer, the sneak thief had examined the two doors, their locks, as well as the windows and jakes hole. Culpeper, a defrocked cleric, who had definitely seen better days, had written down his conclusions and hidden them away. Now he had been summoned to meet Athelstan and the Lord High Coroner at Westminster. What he had discovered, what he would propose would wait until then. Culpeper was more intrigued with this tavern, with its gruesome memorabilia decorating the taproom walls. Culpeper was also fascinated by the hostelry's winding passageways and galleries. He had even been down to the cellar, that long dark tunnel reeking of spilled wine, ale and beer. He'd passed the great barrels and tuns ranging either side. A dark, grim place with the occasional cresset torch spluttering to extinction. Well, at least there had been something to do and he was pleased at Cranston's summons. In a word, Culpeper was at a loss about where to turn next. He had tried to approach the four clerks but, since the brutal murder of one of their number, they had, apart from their Magister, become as cowed as rabbits beneath the shadow of a hawk. He had tried to engage with them, particularly their leader Beaumont, only to be coldly rebuffed. Culpeper sighed and pulled himself up. He was wondering if he should go down to the taproom when there was a sharp knock on the door . . .

Athelstan quietly wondered where Culpeper might be lurking. The sneak thief had been ordered to present himself at Westminster. Everyone else had obeyed Cranston's summons, and they now sat around the table in a bleak, whitewashed council chamber only a short walk from Flambard's Tower. Once Cranston and Athelstan had arrived, Flaxwith and his bailiffs, who had set up camp in a row of derelict outhouses close to the tower, had solemnly assured the coroner that all was well. Nothing untoward had occurred. No attempt by anyone to enter the treasure chamber.

'Oh we had our visitors, some palace servants and other long-nosed pryers,' Flaxwith declared. 'But we shooed them away as you would a flock of geese. Nothing, Sir John,' the bailiff continued, 'and I repeat nothing untoward has occurred.'

Flaxwith and his comitatus now stood on guard outside the council chamber and in the yard below. Cranston, acting with great speed, had organized his court of Oyer et Terminer. The Regent, of course, had excused himself. Thibault and his two henchmen had just arrived, followed by Beaumont and his three clerks, along with Conteza and Genaro, the Lombard's sallow-faced henchman. Once everyone took their seats, the coroner rapped the table, proclaimed who he was and why they were here. He then gestured at Athelstan to begin his questioning.

'We are here for the truth,' the friar declared in a ringing voice. 'Now, on that fateful night at about six in the evening, you Master Beaumont, Magister of the Clerks of the Light, finished your work and handed matters over to Despencer and his coterie, yes?'

'Yes, everything was as normal, wasn't it?' Beaumont, who seemed highly nervous, turned beseechingly to his companions, who loudly agreed.

'So you left the treasure chamber and went down those steps? You, Master Beaumont, going last so you could fix the trip cords across every eighth one. You reached the bottom step and followed your comrades out, locking the bottom door?' Again Beaumont stuttered his agreement. The clerk seemed highly nervous and Conteza, sitting further down the table, laughingly murmured something in Italian. Athelstan ignored this and continued with his interrogation. 'Now, on the question of keys. Each Magister held four keys to the four locks, two for the bottom door and two for the top, giving access to the treasure chamber?'

Everyone agreed. Athelstan pointed at Thibault. 'You held these two sets of keys? Each Magister would collect his set just before their horarium began, then return it as soon as he had finished?'

'Yes, and that is what happened at the time of the great robbery.'

'No other copies of these keys exist?'

'No, none at all, and they never leave my custody. Indeed,' Thibault added, 'they were the work of a skilled craftsman, almost impossible to replicate. Rest assured, Brother Athelstan, the keys to those four locks were most securely held.'

'On that matter,' Cranston declared, 'we have further mystery. The keys were the work of Clement, a high-ranking member of the Guild. He fashioned the locks, he was supposed to destroy all memoranda and anything to do with it, but he did not.'

'Yes yes. I remember that.'

'How did you get to know?' Athelstan demanded. 'Who actually informed you that Clement had not carried out your orders to destroy all casts, drawings and workings for these four locks and their keys?'

Thibault, eyes closed, scratched his brow.

'You're correct,' he murmured. 'When the news of the great robbery broke, I did think of Clement. I went back to scrutinize the record – writs issued, memoranda drafted – but in truth there was nothing. Clement simply made a hideous mistake and paid dearly for it.'

'But you raided his house and shop?'

'Of course, Brother Athelstan. I had to find out if the information provided was correct.'

'And who supplied this information?'

'A scribbled note, Brother, a few words, poorly scrawled on manuscript which had seen better days. At any other time, on any other matter, I might have ignored it, but I could not tolerate any chance that the work done might in the future be undone. So we raided Clement's house and workshop. We discovered that Clement had not kept his word: what he had sworn to do; what he had been ordered to do by both the Crown and myself.'

'And that message?'

'Oh, it's now gone.'

'Do you have any idea who wrote it?'

'Brother Athelstan, Clement was a member of the Guild, highly respected as a most skilled craftsman. Moreover Clement had just finished a unique work on behalf of the Crown.'

'You're saying it might have been jealousy?'

'I suspect it was. From what we learnt, Clement and his son were very proud of what they had achieved, both as a family and as locksmiths. Perhaps they said things they shouldn't have.'

'Very well,' Athelstan murmured. 'And so we now move to the very heart of this mystery. On that fateful occasion, Beaumont, you finished for the day. You go home, you sleep and, early the next morning, return to your duties?'

Beaumont coughed, then nodded as he cleared his throat. 'I remember that morning well, it was my birthday.' Beaumont shrugged. 'The day did not go as I had planned.'

'Now.' Athelstan pointed across the table at Thibault's henchman. 'You also had a presence in Flambard's. Beaumont collects the keys ready for a day's work as you finish your nightly duties?'

'That's true.' Albinus's voice was slightly slurred, and Athelstan suspected the henchman had drunk deep and well. 'We visited the tower at each quarter of the night and continued to do so until the bells rang for Prime.'

'And where would you go, what would you do? How did you actually perform your duties?'

'Wolfrich and I were armed. We carried a lanternhorn. We would come to the antechamber and peer through the eyelet in the door leading into the tower stairwell. We would then shelter in the antechamber for a while before returning to the main building. Brother Athelstan, as I have informed Lord Thibault, we made four such visits during the night, the last one just before dawn. Each visit followed the same routine. We saw or heard nothing to alarm us, nothing to indicate what had happened. Isn't that correct?' Albinus turned to Wolfrich who, eyes glaring at Athelstan, nodded his agreement.

Athelstan sensed Wolfrich's deep hostility. He'd encountered such enmity before from dagger men: misfits who fear neither God nor man, and seem to nourish a special hatred for any priest. Athelstan wondered if Wolfrich was one of these? More to the point, had Wolfrich and his comrade been involved in the robbery? They had certainly failed to prevent it. However, was this simply due to the robbers being more skilled, whilst Albinus and Wolfrich had probably not taken their duties seriously enough? Typical soldiers, they couldn't see the need for such vigilance over a treasure hidden deep in that formidable tower protected by five mailed clerks.

'So,' Cranston declared, 'the next morning Prime is rung and you, Master Beaumont, assemble where?'

'In the antechamber. I open the door to the tower stairwell. I unlock the door to the steps and we carefully climb. On my way up I removed the trip cords and—'

'No. No.' Crossley broke in. 'That's what Whitby was referring to when he said there was something sorely amiss with our plain-chant that morning. Do you remember, he was referring to the bell? You, Magister, pulled the warning bell three times in honour of the Trinity but there was no reply. Despencer should have replied.'

'So that was the first sign,' Athelstan demanded, 'that all was not well? Continue.'

'We climbed up the steps,' Beaumont declared. 'The trip ropes were still in place, pulled tight and taut. Of course, on the way up I released them. I expected the door at the top to be unlocked,' he continued in a rush, 'but it wasn't. I opened it . . .' He sighed noisily and shrugged. 'The rest is as you know.'

Athelstan curtly thanked the clerks then pointed down the table at Conteza.

'Signor,' he asked, 'do you have anything to add to all this?'

'Such as?'

'Anything at all.'

The banker simply pulled a face.

'The Carbonari,' Cranston barked, 'have you discovered anything?'

'Nothing,' Conteza's henchman Genaro retorted.

'Nothing at all,' Conteza confirmed. 'We have questioned our household. Sir John, Master Thibault, you are welcome to do the same, as well as search our properties, our warehouses, ships and galleys: we certainly have. However, we've discovered little about the Carbonari's involvement in the crime or the whereabouts of the treasure.'

Athelstan murmured his thanks, then whispered to Cranston that he'd heard enough and they needed to visit Flambard's Tower. The coroner agreed and loudly declared the commission was adjourned. Cranston and Athelstan made their farewells and, escorted by Flaxwith and his bailiffs, visited the antechamber, a stark, empty room which told them nothing. Athelstan crossed to the door leading to the tower. It hung open and was empty except for the cobwebs, which spanned the corners like little nets. He closed the door and peered through the eyelet. The bars of this aperture were well spaced, so Athelstan had a good view of the stairwell, as well as the fortified door sealing off the steps. Athelstan tried to imagine the night of the robbery. Albinus and Wolfrich would have come here. They'd have been tired, and cold. They would stare through this grille, noticing nothing untoward, either here, or anywhere around Flambard's Tower. 'And yet,' the friar whispered to himself, 'there must be mistakes. All sinners make them and, God willing, I shall seize on these.

'Athelstan,' Cranston murmured, 'you are talking to yourself.'

'No, Sir John, I am talking to the angels. Now we must wait for their reply. But, whilst we do, let us discover what is happening at The Hanging Tree.'

Cranston and Athelstan left the royal precincts, hurrying across the darkening abbey grounds, down to King's Steps. Athelstan strode along the narrow quayside and crowed with delight as he found what he was searching for: his loyal parishioner Moleskin, 'Captain', as Moleskin constantly proclaimed, 'of the sturdiest barge on the river. Safer than Noah's Ark', or so its captain trumpeted, 'and even more reliable than St Peter's Barque.' Athelstan called his parishioner across and, a short while later, with Cranston and Athelstan sitting in the canopied stern, Moleskin's barge pulled away from King's Steps, heading like an arrow along the river bank to Queenshithe.

Athelstan made himself comfortable on the cushioned bench. Cranston dozed beside him. The cold was intense, the river turbulent. Athelstan glimpsed the warning beacons flaring on other craft, whilst horns brayed constantly as boats counselled each other to be vigilant and watchful. The darkness was closing in. The river had a force of its own, pushing and shoving the barge as if fighting the oarsmen who struggled to keep it on track. Now and again, a gull would fly perilously close above them, its shrieks a haunting sound above the clatter of the river.

At last they reached Queenshithe. Moleskin shouted at the tiller man and six rowers to swing the barge carefully to starboard. On the prow, Moleskin's eldest son, Mouseskin, blew lustily on a horn and vigorously rang a handbell as a thick river mist was now forming to cut off sight and sound. Leaning forward, Athelstan asked Moleskin about the *Ludovico*. The bargeman pointed to a magnificent two-masted cog with a high fortified stern and long jutting prow, which stood berthed at the quayside, well protected by the galleys moored alongside it.

'Do you think it's ready for sea?'

'God knows,' Moleskin replied, 'and I don't really care! Why the interest, Brother?'

'Nothing,' Athelstan murmured. 'Except, Moleskin, you go up

and down this river more often than a gull. Have you noticed anything unusual?' The barge master pulled back his hood, wiped the spray from his face and gave a gap-tooth smile.

'I know why you are asking, Brother.'

'Then bloody well tell us!' Cranston demanded, shaking himself awake.

'The robbery?' Athelstan declared.

'Oh of course! We've heard all about that and the doings at St Erconwald's. But I'll tell you this Brother, Sir John. I have noticed nothing untoward yet; though you may not think it, the river does have eyes and ears. So let me tell you. The Lords of the River, and those who lead the gangs of rifflers, believe that the treasure will be taken out of the kingdom and that it will happen here. I know that, you know that, and they know that. So Brother, true I have seen nothing amiss; however, I've certainly sensed it. People are watching for any sign, any indication that the treasure is on the move.'

'You've heard what happened to the *Serafino*?'

'Yes, Brother, I have, and that proves my point. Now, let me bring you safely in.'

They disembarked on the quayside. Athelstan, shivering and eager for warmth, watched curiously, as Cranston had a hurried, whispered conversation with Moleskin, who in turn shouted at his crew to wait. The barge master, grasping the coins Sir John had pushed into his hand, then scurried off into the darkness.

'Sir John?'

'Never mind, my little friar, what Moleskin said is the truth. Anyway, devil's tits,' the coroner stamped his feet, 'let's go to The Hanging Tree?'

'Of course, Sir John, we must have urgent words with Squire Culpeper, not to mention some food and drink for the inner man.'

Cranston needed no further encouragement, but left the quayside as swift as any lurcher striding up the dark, dank alleyways, with Athelstan hurrying behind him.

The streets and runnels were now emptying of traders and their customers. This was the hour of the bat, the dawning of the dusk, the hour of the dark-dwellers to crawl from their holes and dens for another night's hunting. However, the night still had to settle, whilst the mist boiling along the runnels kept the shadow people, as well as the righteous, off the streets. People wanted to be home so the day's business was drawing swiftly to a close. Stalls were being taken down. Shops boarded. Flaring lanterns placed on hooks by the doors of most dwellings. A soul-crier, armed with a hand-bell, recited the list of those who had died that day, proclaiming their names as well as the cause of death, be it of a malady, a fall or some bloody affray. Athelstan recalled seeing such criers earlier in the day and, indeed, during most of his recent visits to the city. He wondered why, then realized that they were fast approaching the season of Lent, where the church invited the faithful to remember those in purgatory and to free such souls through almsgiving, prayer and fasting. The criers were reminding people of their sacred duty, and Athelstan secretly promised himself that he would make his own dear parishioners remember theirs.

'Brother?' Athelstan startled and realized he had stopped on a corner. So lost in his own thoughts, he had allowed a line of hooded Friars of the Sack to come between him and the coroner. Athelstan smiled, raised a hand, and pushed his way through to join Sir John. They walked on.

Athelstan paused to bless bailiffs and beadles, shepherding peace-breakers down for a night in the stocks. Tavern doors opened and shut in a glow of warmth, light and fragrant clouds of cooking from their kitchens. Athelstan savoured the sweet odours, only to gag as a dung collector's cart abruptly toppled over, tipping its horrid mess into the street before them. They got past this, rounded a corner, and almost collided with a cohort of mummers. All masked and costumed, the players were parading along the street under a banner inscribed with the name 'Uffizi' in blood-red letters. From the shouts and cries exchanged between these mummers and Sir John, Athelstan deduced that the actors were a travelling Italian troupe with licence to perform in the city. The friar, dutifully following behind the coroner, wondered if the elusive Carbonari might be hiding amongst such a group. Or, might the Carbonari be members of the crew of the *Ludovico* he had glimpsed at Queenshithe? Athelstan was still speculating on this when Cranston abruptly stopped, turned and pulled the friar close.

'Athelstan,' he hissed, 'I asked how you were, you never replied. Are you praying?'

'In a way yes, Sir John.' Athelstan looked around, then stared up at the garish sign proclaiming The Hanging Tree tavern. 'Oh sweet Lord,' he murmured, 'so we're here!'

'Yes we are, little friar, so let us warm our bellies and slake our thirst.'

They entered the taproom, which was slowly filling as travellers and workers gathered to celebrate the end of another day's work. Mine Host and his wife Isabella, garbed in long snow-white aprons, welcomed them, gesturing at the array of foods laid out along the great buttery table.

'Some ale,' Cranston ordered. 'Manchet loaves and some of the pork roasting so fragrantly on the spit.'

Both the taverner and his wife hastily agreed. Cranston and Athelstan were led over to a clean scrubbed table with cushioned chairs, small glowing braziers and warming pots. Both men made themselves comfortable, though the friar noticed how Cranston kept looking towards the door. But then, Sir John had his ways . . .! The food and ale were served. Cranston and Athelstan ate in silence, revelling in the warmth, as well as in the taste of strong ale and crisp pork. Once they had finished and the platters had been removed, Cranston leaned across the table.

'No sight or sound of Squire Culpeper.'

'No, Sir John.'

'By the way, what were you thinking about outside?'

'Oh, the Italian mummers made me reflect on our opponents, the almost invisible Carbonari. Strange,' Athelstan mused, 'I understand their attack on both you and me.' He shrugged. 'I don't agree with them, but I recognize we are their enemy. We are hunting them and it's a hunt to the death. However, there are other incidents which I can't understand.'

'What others?'

'Well, those two Carbonari who tried to trade gold coins with Galliard the Goldsmith? Why did they do something like that so soon after the robbery? Sir John, it is bizarre. Why just two coins? Why the haste? Weren't they aware of the dangers?'

'Perhaps they were taking a risk, a dangerous one, in order to discover if the authorities had learnt about the robbery and, as you put it, were already on the hunt.'

'Yes, that's a logical possibility, though a strange one. Nevertheless, they were really risking a lot. Secondly, there's the attack on Beaumont and his comrades here in The Hanging Tree.' Athelstan stared around. 'Oh, by the way, where are the clerks?'

Cranston summoned Mine Host and put the same question to him. The taverner pointed across to the staircase.

'They're in Beaumont's chamber. The clerk said they were tired of customers staring at them, even trying to eavesdrop. Master Culpeper attempted the same.'

'So the clerks demanded to be fed there?'

'Yes, Brother Athelstan.'

'And Master Culpeper?'

'Sir John, I saw him go upstairs earlier this afternoon but since then nothing.'

'Is he too dining alone?'

'I don't know, Sir John. Do you want me to look for him?'

'Yes,' Athelstan declared. 'We need urgent words with our friend.'

The taverner promised he would conduct his own search and left. Cranston watched him go then turned back to Athelstan.

'You were saying, Brother?'

'Yes, I cannot really understand the attack here. On reflection, I suggest it was ill thought out. I mean, why kill one of the clerks? The robbery was done. The damage inflicted immense, and our cohort of clerks were hardly heroes of the hour. Now, correct me if I am wrong but, according to what we have learnt, the assassins, the Carbonari, came in here. They ordered the clerks to kneel, which they did, then they asked for names, which were duly given.'

'And they executed Whitby.'

'Why him, Sir John? Did it have anything to do with that same clerk's comment about the first sign that something was wrong in the treasury was Despencer's failure to acknowledge the signal sent by Beaumont? How the bell was rung three times by the Clerks of the Light but they received no reply? Is this what Whitby meant by their plainchant being sorely disturbed that morning, a reference to the usual procedures not being observed? Was Whitby's execution therefore just an act of random, cruel violence to keep the clerk silent? Was it a warning to us? Or was Whitby's murder . . .' Athelstan broke off at Cranston's exclamation. The friar turned. A stranger had entered the tavern. He raised a hand, bellowed Cranston's name, then swaggered across to embrace the coroner. They hugged like two bears before Cranston introduced Sir Edmund Kyrie, Admiral of the King's Fleet from the mouth of the Thames to the north. Kyrie was as large and as bulky as the coroner, a sharp-faced man, his head completely shaven, which emphasized his beak-like nose and light blue eyes. A mariner, Athelstan concluded, a true son of the sea. Kyrie clasped Athelstan's hand then pulled him closer to exchange the kiss of peace. For a while there was a little confusion. Kyrie went searching for another chair. Mine Host hurried across to breathlessly announce that Culpeper could not be found. Cranston rapped the table.

'Never mind, never mind,' the coroner declared. 'We'll catch the little bastard sooner or later. In the meantime, bring me and my two companions a jug of ale and three clean blackjacks.'

'So Sir Edmund?'

Cranston and Kyrie exchanged pleasantries once the ale was served and the new arrival toasted.

'Sir John, Brother Athelstan, I have information.'

'Good man,' Cranston breathed. 'Little friar, I asked my comrade here if he had any information about the *Ludovico*, or indeed any cog bound out from London for a harbour in the Middle Sea, Italian ones especially. Edmund replied he did. So, when we berthed at Queenshithe, I sent Brother Moleskin to ask my friend to meet us here.' Cranston spread his hands and grinned. 'And so he has. Edmund, what can you tell us?'

'Some months ago, Master Thibault summoned me to a meeting in the Tower. Only he was present. He asked me to prepare sea charts for a small flotilla of war cogs, which would shadow the *Ludovico*, or any ship owned by the Bardi bankers. If necessary our cogs would follow such craft out of London port and down through the Gates of Hercules into the Middle Sea.' Kyrie's voice fell to a sharp whisper. 'Thibault insisted our ships fly no colours. Indeed the cogs must not carry anything to show that they were commissioned by him or indeed anyone associated with the English Crown.'

'This is not unusual?'

'No, Sir John, it is not. Thibault was in fact ordering us to be pirates, and the only colours we could display would be the red and black banner of anarchy.'

'So you would have had,' Athelstan retorted, 'English cogs,

warships of the Crown, closing to attack, pillage and sink some other vessel?'

'At the time,' Kyrie laughed sharply, 'I thought it was the usual mischief. Thibault and his coven enriching themselves at some poor bugger's expense. Then I heard about the great robbery at Westminster. I began to wonder if Thibault had been planning to hand the money over to the Bardi, then secretly seize it back.'

'It's not just possible,' Cranston murmured, 'but more than probable. Thibault was instrumental in repaying the heavy loan, and that's because he intended to seize it back. However, even our best-laid plans make God laugh, and someone pre-empted Master Thibault. Unless of course, Thibault decided to change his plan and steal the treasure another way. Athelstan, we have been down this path before We must not forget: Thibault's honesty is a faint, flickering light.'

'Our Master of Secrets could well have changed his mind,' Kyrie offered. 'After all, an attack by sea is highly dangerous. The *Ludovico* and its escort would be very well armed, their crews trained and skilled, resolute in resistance. Finally,' he sighed, 'there's Old Mother Sea. What if the *Ludovico* and its treasure sank to the bottom, never to be seen again. No, no, if I was advising Thibault, I would certainly warn him about the consequences of such rash action. Why steal a treasure at sea when an attack on land would be much simpler and indeed safer. But still the treasure's gone!' The admiral scratched his head. 'And I have heard rumours,' Kyrie continued, 'how the Lords and Commons are deeply suspicious, not to mention furious, at what has occurred. They have little love for Gaunt or Thibault, and they hold that precious pair solely responsible, be it on a charge of incompetence or, of course, theft and murder.'

'Thank you my friend,' Athelstan replied. 'So let us, for sake of argument, suggest that Thibault was responsible for the robbery. If so, he would need help both within and without. One of those clerks or, indeed, someone else, like Albinus or Wolfrich.'

'Oh I've heard of him,' Kyrie interjected. 'Albinus, strange-looking man. He mined many a wall in France.'

'Yes, that's our Albinus,' Cranston declared. 'He's Thibault's instrument of wickedness, and where the master goes the dog always follows. However, I also wonder about what you said, little friar. Was it one of those clerks? Could it be Whitby? Was that why he was killed here in The Hanging Tree?'

'Or did he discover something?'

'Again possible, little friar.'

Athelstan pressed a hand down on the table as he pushed back to make himself more comfortable. He exclaimed in annoyance as the table top, drenched by the ale from their blackjacks, had turned sticky to the touch. He rose, lost in thought, and crossed to the lavarium to wash his hands.

'Brother?'

'My friends.' Athelstan now rubbed his clean hands together. 'Let us put aside Thibault's possible involvement and concentrate on the stolen treasure. If I had such gold, I could not trade it in this kingdom. If I did, I could easily be caught and suffer the most cruel punishments.'

'Agreed, oh wise one.'

'So, my friends, I must somehow get the treasure out of this kingdom, even though its ports and harbours are being closely watched, ships searched from stern to prow.'

'True true,' Kyrie murmured. 'London's ports are rigorously guarded by bailiffs and beadles.' The admiral scratched his head. 'The same is true of the southern harbours, be it Southampton or any of the Cinque Ports.'

'Consequently,' Athelstan declared, 'if I am the thief, I am going to try and smuggle the treasure out by the safest means. Sir Edmund, help me. What would you suggest?'

'The south coast may be attractive but, as I've said, its harbours and ports make it as busy as a Cheapside thoroughfare. The south coast lies open to the eye of Master Thibault and that of the Crown. Of course, you could cross country, travel deep into Devon and Cornwall, but that is a long, arduous land journey. The treasure would be vulnerable, heavily guarded carts might eventually attract the attention of royal officials and manor lords, not to mention roaming bands of outlaws.'

'So, Sir Edmund, if you were a smuggler?'

'Oh I would transport anything I could in the dustiest, dirtiest cart. I would leave London, then strike northeast along the road to Mile End, Bow, then skirt the great Forest of Epping. Eventually I would reach the eastern coast, make camp in some inlet or cave deep in the darkness of Essex or Norfolk. The countryside there is wild and desolate and extremely lonely. Unlike the Narrow Seas, nothing more than a gulf between the shores of England and France. Moreover, the Northern Sea can render a cog almost invisible with its surging waves, deep mists, and an emptiness which strikes at the soul. The Northern Sea is highly dangerous, difficult to cross and so the best place to hide. Oh yes, I'd go east.' The admiral drained his blackjack and put the tankard down on the table. He made to rise, cursing at the stickiness on the table. The admiral rubbed his hands on the side of his jerkin and beamed at his companions. 'Sir John, Brother Athelstan, is there anything else?'

'Yes there is, Sir Edmund. Can you please maintain a sharp and wary watch on any ship or cog bound for the Middle Sea and some Italian port, be it Genoa or anywhere else?'

'Of course.'

'I also,' Athelstan rose to his feet 'want you to keep the sharpest eye on the *Ludovico*. If it prepares for sea we must be told.'

'I will, Brother Athelstan. You think the Bardi are responsible?'

'To be honest, Sir Edmund, I don't know, but I am certainly acting on what you have just told us. Someone stole that treasure, and that someone has to get it out of this kingdom.' Athelstan sketched a blessing in the air. 'It's as simple and as logical as that.'

The admiral nodded in agreement, made his farewells and left. Athelstan retook his seat and stared around. The tavern was filling up. Athelstan even glimpsed the group of the Italian mummers he had met earlier. They sat gathered around a table across the taproom. They'd pushed back their colourful masks, were laughing and shouting whilst downing tankards of ale.

'We all wear masks,' the friar murmured, 'even if it's just to face all the other masks.'

'Brother Athelstan, you are praying again; it's time we left.'

'Oh no, Sir John, let us cast about for a while. Let us see what we can learn from Master Culpeper.'

Cranston agreed, calling across Mine Host and demanding that he took them up to Culpeper's garret. The taverner seemed hesitant. However, after Cranston grabbed him by the shoulder and gave him a sharp squeeze, the taverner became more compliant. A short while later, huffing and puffing at the steep climb, Mine Host pushed open the door and ushered both his visitors into Culpeper's ill-lit, fetid garret. Cranston insisted that the taverner leave his lantern, which he did before hurrying off.

The coroner sat wearily down on the bed whilst Athelstan surveyed the room. He glimpsed the writing tray on the battered table. He pulled this across, peering down at the quill, inkpot and pumice stone, the type of shabby chancery to be hired in every tavern. Athelstan picked up a quill, turning it in his fingers.

'So Culpeper is literate, he can read and write?'

'Of course, little friar! Like so many of his tribe, Culpeper is a defrocked cleric, skilled enough to write as well as recite the "Hanging Verse" . . .'

'Have mercy on me, oh God, in your kindness . . .'

'Precisely, my friend, and Culpeper has used such skills on more than one occasion to claim benefit of clergy and so escape a hanging.'

'In which case, Sir John, like any clerk, he would marshal his thoughts and write them down, but where are they? Where would a rogue like Culpeper hide his scribblings?'

'He could have taken them with him.'

'I don't think so, Sir John. I suspect Culpeper only carries what he needs to.'

'Of course he could have destroyed them.'

'In which case, why write them down in the first place? No.'

'So up we get, little friar.'

Athelstan watched Cranston strip the bed. 'It's the only place,' the coroner declared, 'where you could hide anything in this miserable chamber.' Athelstan silently agreed. Everything else was open. Moreover, in a dirty little room such as this, anything left would soon be nibbled by the vermin. 'Ah got it.' Cranston had shaken the bolster from its stained cover and plucked out a small scroll tied with twine. Cranston handed this to Athelstan, who undid the knot and took the parchment over to the lantern for closer scrutiny. The vellum was old and creased but still useable. Athelstan studied the diagram freshly scrawled there and, with Cranston looking over his shoulder, declared that Culpeper had drawn a rough outline of the treasure chamber at Westminster.

'See, Sir John, this is the door leading into the stairwell. Here is the first fortified door and the steps winding up to the treasure chamber. Beneath it, scrawled in Latin "*porta prima, porta solo prima*" – the first door, only the first door.' Athelstan folded the scroll and slipped it into the wallet on his belt. 'Sir John, we are done here, and we should be gone.' He tapped the side of his head. 'However, my learned coroner, the mist, the murk is beginning to thin. The truth is emerging but,' Athelstan fastened on his cloak, 'tomorrow beckons.'

'Let us . . .' Cranston broke off at a sharp knock. The coroner hastily hid what they'd done, then strode to open the door, keeping Mine Host on the threshold.

'Brother Athelstan, Sir John, you have visitors.'

'Not my parishioners.' Athelstan groaned. 'Not here, not at this hour.'

'No Brother, Dominicans like yourself. They come from Blackfriars and wish . . .'

A brief while later, Cranston and Athelstan were ushered into a comfortable chamber on the first gallery, where two friars, hooded and cloaked, warmed their fingers over a fiery red brazier. They both rose as Cranston and Athelstan entered.

'Prior Anselm!' Athelstan exclaimed, and then peered through the dim light at his superior's white-haired, stooped companion. 'Brother Ignacio, in Heaven's name, so good to see you. But why are you here?'

'In a little while, we will say.' The stern-faced prior smiled and bowed at Cranston and Athelstan. 'My friends, we needed to see you, but first . . .'

All four clasped hands with each other and exchanged the kiss of peace. Cranston then went to the door shouting for Mine Host, demanding that he bring two more chairs as well as a tray of what the coroner called 'comfort at Compline's hour'. Once all this had been done, the four men sat warming their hands over the coals, their flickering light casting dancing shadows across the chamber.

'Well,' Athelstan began. 'Prior Anselm, Brother Ignacio, as I said, it is so good to see you.' He turned to the venerable ancient, who sat perched on his chair, his lean, bony face redeemed by eyes as bright as those of a spring sparrow. Ignacio was a friar whom Athelstan deeply respected as a teacher and as a mentor. Athelstan had first met Ignacio when, as a young friar, he studied at the schools of Padua and Florence, a firm bond of friendship had been formed. Ignacio had eventually returned to London, the city of his birth, his father being a wool merchant, his mother the daughter of a Lombard banker.

'Athelstan, you have not changed.' Ignacio chuckled, leaning forward to grasp Athelstan's hand. He gently pulled at his former student. 'You still stare at people as if you are drinking their very souls.'

'My apologies, Brother, but it is so good to see you. Father Prior?' Athelstan turned to his hawk-faced superior, who had taken personal responsibility for Athelstan. Anselm had been instrumental in Athelstan's appointment as parish priest of St Erconwald's. Anselm, as did Ignacio, knew all about Athelstan's journey through life. The devoted son of a yeoman farmer, Athelstan had run wild in his youth. He had served in the King's Array across the Narrow Seas. He had attended universities in Northern Italy before being drawn back again into the world of chivalry and war. He had volunteered for the great chevauchées in Normandy and taken his younger brother with him. The dream, and Athelstan's brother, had died in the filthy mud of Northern France. Athelstan's parents were heartbroken, the news had hastened their death. Athelstan had then taken another path, entering the Dominican Order to devote his life to others and so make reparation for his many sins.

'Oh yes,' Ignacio exclaimed, 'you haven't changed much, Athelstan. I remember drinking with you in the piazzas of Florence. You would suddenly pause, your goblet halfway to your lips, as you stared at someone who had caught your attention.'

'So Brother,' Athelstan spread his hands, 'I have not changed. But my question still stands. Why are you here and how did you know where to find us?'

'We appreciate how busy you are,' Friar Anselm retorted, 'so we thought we would come to you rather than summon you back to Blackfriars.'

'And I love London taverns,' Ignacio interjected. 'I always have. You can enjoy a good jug of ale and see life in all its colours. I can sit . . .' The old Friar lapsed into silence as Friar Anselm tapped him on the arm. 'Sorry, sorry,' Ignacio apologized, fingers going to his lips.

'We left Blackfriars for Queenshithe,' Friar Anselm explained. 'Now, as you know, finding a good barge master is difficult. Then

I remembered Moleskin, your parishioner. I captured two birds in the one net. I found Moleskin and his crew busy at their victuals. I asked the noble barge captain if he knew of your whereabouts, and he did, so here we are.'

'And why?' Athelstan persisted.

Anselm felt beneath his robe and brought out a scroll of expensive parchment with red and blue seals.

'This,' he explained, 'arrived at our mother house some months ago.' Anselm narrowed his eyes. 'Yes, just before the end of Advent. It's a letter from one of our brothers, Theodore, head of the Faculty of Law at the University of Bologna. The letter is in Italian; it is a request to me to allow you, Brother Athelstan, to lecture in the Faculty of Law at Bologna, specifically on criminal law and other aspects of English jurisprudence. Theodore claims he and his scholars are fascinated by your work and,' Anselm pointed at the coroner, 'your good self, Sir John. You were also included in the invitation.'

'I didn't know that our fame had spread,' the coroner mocked. 'Surely Italy has its own *periti* – skilled men – in our law as well as that of other kingdoms?'

'No Sir John, English law is quite unique. Its aspects most fascinating. The Commons, the Lords, the role of the Crown, the writings of jurists like Bracton, who espoused the principle that "what affects all must be agreed by all". Such teachings strike a chord in the heart of many Italian citizens.' The prior waved a hand. 'They are intrigued by the way the Commons propagates statutes of common interest. How they have the power to impeach and try royal officials, indeed all those who wield power in the name of the King. No, no, Sir John, what I have listed is enough to whet the appetite of any scholar in law, and there's more. They have also learnt about your role, and that of Athelstan, as maintainers and defenders of the King's peace.'

'But the invitation came in months ago?'

'Yes it did, Brother, I put it to one side. You and Sir John are busy enough. Since the collapse of the Great Revolt, you have moved from one murderous mystery to another. Isn't it only a few weeks ago that you were caught up in that business at Westminster Abbey over the Coronation Stone? You work for the Crown which, in practical terms, means my Lord of Gaunt and Thibault, his

Master of Secrets. I have no desire to alienate them by taking you away from what they want you to do.' Anselm smiled bleakly at Athelstan. 'You are a very busy priest, my Brother.'

'I accept what you say,' Cranston demanded, 'but what is the relevance of all this now? Why have you come to inform us about an out-of-date invitation?'

'It is not out of date, Sir John.' The prior sighed noisily. 'Though perhaps it is now.'

'For God's sake, Father Prior, tell us what you want.'

'Very well, my Lord Coroner.' Anselm turned to Ignacio. 'Now you must explain.'

'Prior Anselm,' the old prior replied, chomping on his gums, 'told me about the invitation. I would have supported you both going. However, you and Athelstan were very busy, then the great robbery at Westminster occurred. You became involved and I began to wonder.'

'What?'

'The original invitation to you may well have come from the Dominican House and Faculty of Law at Bologna. However, unknown to those scholars, the actual invitation could have been inspired by the Carbonari: powerful figures in the city and university who nourish a secret allegiance to this den of thieves.'

'Impossible!' Athelstan breathed.

'No, listen.' The old friar closed his eyes then opened them and smiled. 'No doubt, Brother,' he declared, pointing at Athelstan, 'you are famous but—'

'Not that famous,' Athelstan retorted.

'Precisely, my Brother. Now the Carbonari plundered the treasury at Westminster. They are proud of their achievements, you know that. Perhaps what you have not realized is how painstaking the Carbonari are at plotting such a crime. To be blunt, the Carbonari committed this crime in January, the year of our Lord 1382. However, I would go on oath that they must have been planning it for months. In doing so they listed the possible dangers, challenges and threats they might face . . .'

'And we are included in that?' Cranston countered.

'Yes, you are. The Carbonari took every precaution in plotting their crime and its possible aftermath.' Ignacio gestured around. 'And they were correct yes?' Cranston and Athelstan could only gape back in amazement. 'Do you think I romance? That I am some troubadour, a minstrel with a tale to tell? Listen, my friends,' the old friar continued. 'Many years ago, the jewel house of the dukes of Mantua was broken into and plundered. Now the jewel house was a squat, circular tower; its walls were at least a yard thick – great, heavy blocks cemented into each other. Anyway, the Duke decided to strengthen the jewel house, removing its sole window, as well as fortify the only entrance with an iron-plated door. No other aperture existed.'

'Yet the jewel house was pillaged?'

'It certainly was. The Duke of Mantua failed to realize that the Carbonari had suborned the master mason refurbishing his treasury. Whilst he was busy on the Duke's behalf, he was also secretly working away at dislodging one of the great stone blocks, hacking at the cement until the stone became so loosened it could be slid in and out. Once done, the gap, broad enough for a man to crawl through, was smoothed so the stone could slide in and out like a polished bolt. Any mess created was swiftly cleared or dismissed as part of the refurbishment. Early one morning, after the work was considered done, the jewel house was robbed. Caskets and pouches full of precious stones were taken, and a sack of mouldering charcoal ash left as a mocking farewell. No one could understand how such a robbery could have taken place. In fact, once it had, the stone block which had been used to allow the robbers in and out, was repositioned and made fast by a quick-drying cement that the master mason had carefully created. Moreover, the stone in question was on the base, in a darkened corner of the jewel house. No one would even suspect what had happened.'

'So how was the theft discovered, and by whom?'

'By myself.' Ignacio grinned. 'Brother Athelstan, as you may well know, I was once an inquisitor like yourself. I was commissioned to investigate. My real challenge was not who had broken in but how? I scrutinized every inch of that jewel house; floor, wall and ceiling. It was just a matter of time and logic that I eventually discovered lines of cement slightly different from the rest.' The old friar shrugged. 'And so it was. The master mason was questioned and confessed his guilt.'

'And what happened to him?' Athelstan asked.

'He was torn apart by horses in the piazza at Mantua.'

Athelstan swiftly crossed himself.

'I quote that,' Ignacio continued, 'to demonstrate my point. The Carbonari always plot well in advance and it is true here. To put it bluntly, they wanted you and Sir John out of the kingdom before they struck. They had correctly guessed that once the robbery occurred, the investigation would be entrusted to you.' Ignacio tapped the table. 'And so it was. The Carbonari, through their secret associates in Bologna, arranged for that invitation to be sent. When Prior Anselm first told me about it, I thought: what an honour! However, when the robbery occurred, I became highly suspicious. I mean why you? They also made a further mistake. Why now? It's winter. Sea passages are rough. Travel by roads is equally uncomfortable and dangerous. Why didn't they keep their invitation to the spring or full summer?'

'So the Carbonari wanted us out of the kingdom and, when that failed, they tried to murder us?'

'Now that I do find puzzling. So tell me,' Ignacio declared, 'what exactly happened?' Athelstan did so, describing the attack in the crypt, on his own house in Southwark, as well as the execution of Luke Whitby in the very tavern where they were now meeting. Once he had finished, Ignacio sat, eyes closed, hands clasped, lips slowly moving. He then opened his eyes and stared pityingly at Athelstan.

'I am so sorry, Brother.'

'For what?' Athelstan asked.

'For the enemy within. Listen, the Carbonari very rarely resort to murder. They are not assassins. They do not nourish deep, devious plots against Church and Crown. They are thieves, as simple as that. Great thieves, but nothing more.'

'Except in this situation.'

'No, Sir John, two things! Remember my story about the master mason of Mantua. Well, the Carbonari suborned him.'

'And they have done the same here?'

'Certainly, my Lord Coroner. Someone in the service of Richard, King of England, was their catspaw. In a sense, their key to the treasure chamber. This is the enemy within.'

'And who might that be?' Anselm demanded.

Athelstan just shook his head.

'Secondly,' Ignacio continued, 'the attack on you and the murder of Whitby? I suspect that – during the robbery – a potentially serious mistake was made.'

'Yes yes,' Athelstan replied. 'Whitby maintained something was wrong. He spoke in parables. How their plainchant that morning had been sorely disturbed.'

'And who would inform the Carbonari about what Whitby had said?'

'God knows, Sir John.' Ignacio shrugged. 'Whitby could have been overheard. What he said relayed from one mouth to another. After all, I do understand that details about the robbery spread like a mist over the city. More to the point, the Carbonari and their associates realized that a mistake, whatever that might be, had been made. Consequently, Whitby and, indeed, anyone else such as yourselves who might fasten on that mistake, had to be silenced.'

'They have not tried again.'

'No, no, they won't, Brother Athelstan, which means they have the treasure and are close to spiriting it away. They believe the danger you and others posed is receding. And that,' Ignacio sighed, 'is all I can say.'

The old friar gathered up his cloak. Both visitors got to their feet, as did Cranston and Athelstan, to clasp hands and exchange the kiss of peace.

'Prior Anselm, Brother Ignacio, we are most grateful for your help.'

'Sir John, it was our duty to inform you about what we suspect. We had to speak to you.' Anselm sighed. 'Let me know what happens.'

'One thing,' Athelstan declared. 'Brother Ignacio, how do you know so much about the Carbonari?'

The old friar grinned, a boyish smile which made him look much younger.

'Brother Athelstan, I know so much about the Carbonari because in my ill-spent youth, I was one of them.' He chuckled. 'Indeed, I know them better than they know themselves.' Ignacio patted Athelstan on the shoulder. 'Just be very careful. The Carbonari may have the treasure but they also know they are cornered. This is not their kingdom, their country. They must also be aware of you and Sir John closing fast. Swift and sure as hawks on the wing. If trapped, they will fight and it would be to the death.' Ignacio sketched a blessing. 'God be with you, Brother.'

PART SIX

'Much more often I am compelled by greed.'

Brother Ignacio was correct. The Carbonari believed they had eluded the trap and were preparing for the end of their journey. The chosen ones, those skilled in the English tongue, gathered in a derelict woodman's cottage deep in an ancient copse on the edge of Epping Forest. They had unhitched the two powerful dray horses which pulled their battered cart, which was carrying the treasure as well as a good store of weaponry and heavy sacks of hay. Indeed, they looked the part, garbed in soiled tattered jerkins, hose, cloaks and mud-splattered boots. Six of the Carbonari had been chosen for this perilous journey. Three rode on the cart, the rest trudged behind them. They had plotted well. It was a common enough sight to see peasants tramping from one holding to another, apparently bereft of anything of value except their horses and cart. However, these would be well protected by the swords, daggers and arbalests hidden away but easy to grab and wield. Outlaws, of course, would not dare to take on a party of six labourers. The wolfsheads who roam the lonely places hunted for more attractive quarry, some plump merchant or the occasional well-furnished pilgrim or tinker. The Carbonari had carefully mapped out their route, keeping to the lanes, farm tracks and coffin paths. At night, they would gather, as they did so now, in some derelict farmhouse or cottage. There were certainly enough of these since the Great Pestilence had swept the land some thirty years previously, wiping out entire communities in a matter of days. Ghostly, haunted places. The Carbonari were glad they had lit a fire, whilst the lanternhorns they carried on the cart also flared brightly. Light and fire kept the darkness at bay.

'I'll be glad to be out of here. We are going to the coast?' one of the Carbonari asked their leader. 'I just want to be away from the trees and empty fields.'

'Of course we head for the coast. Others will soon join us,' the leader replied. 'God willing, we will reach an inlet known only to me. Once we do, we must wait for the *Ludovico*. When that arrives, we will all be safe.' The leader stretched and pulled his cloak closer around him, staring into the leaping flames of the fire burning in the centre of the cottage floor.

'Master Thibault will be beside himself with fury.' Another of the group spoke up. 'I heard all the gossip along the quayside. They say he is riding for a fall, and what a fall it will be!'

'I've also heard,' the leader retorted, throwing more dry bracken onto the fire, 'that Thibault and his master face a veritable storm of problems, and it serves them right. As you know, he began this dance. The English Crown owes vast sums of money to the Bardi. We gave the English Crown generous loans in good faith. Since last autumn, we have been preparing to receive repayment in full. Indeed, we gave Gaunt more time due to the recent revolt, and what does he do? According to our spies, Thibault, like the snake he is, was preparing to lunge at the hand that fed him. We heard stories – received sound information –that when the gold was repaid and safely stowed on board the *Ludovico*, Thibault would strike. The *Ludovico* would have sailed out of London and, somewhere on the Northern Seas, be attacked by a small fleet of English cogs masquerading as pirates. They would attack, insist on the crew surrendering and so seize the gold.'

'But he could do the same now.'

'Could he?' The leader mocked. 'How does Thibault know we have the treasure? After all, it's been robbed.' He paused at the laughter of the others. 'Moreover, Thibault has, due to the robbery, lost both power and influence. I do wonder if he has the authority to unleash some murderous venture by sea, an attack, my friends, which would be resolutely beaten off.'

'How so?' one of his companions asked.

'When we reach the place we are journeying to,' the leader replied enigmatically, 'we have to wait for the *Ludovico*.' He paused, scratching at his beard. 'Listen now; it will not be coming alone. Our masters, who will join us soon, have hired Venetian carracks to escort the cog.'

Their leader's announcement provoked cheers and clapping from the group.

'Yet,' another called out when the laughter subsided, 'that great mountain of moving flesh Cranston, and his familiar Athelstan, could still check our plans. We should have killed them along with all those clerks when we had the chance. Remove anyone who could threaten us.'

'I agree,' the leader replied softly. 'It's now a race between us getting this treasure safely out of the kingdom and that little ferret of a friar, Brother Athelstan, closing with us fast and exploiting the mistakes which have been made . . .'

Cranston and Athelstan sat long after Prior Anselm and Ignacio had left.

'Interesting,' Cranston murmured. 'An invitation to the sun-drenched vineyards of Italy. At this moment in time, a most attractive prospect.'

'Come Jack,' Athelstan teased. 'Perhaps we will journey there and take Lady Maude and the poppets along with us. We could make such a journey when spring arrives and this business has finished.'

'True, true,' the coroner replied. 'Indeed, we may have no choice but to go. Well, I am speaking about myself. A short stay away from this kingdom, or even longer, might be necessary.'

'Sir John?'

'The theft of the treasure is a most grievous blow to both Gaunt and Thibault for many reasons. Little Friar, Gaunt and Thibault could fall, and what a fall it would be! If they do, the net will be cast far and wide. Fingers will be pointed at any who Thibault favoured, and that includes us. No, no,' Cranston held up a hand, 'let us be honest. I know, you know, we know what we really think of our Master of Secrets. Nevertheless, because of our work trapping this murderer or that; because, on more than one occasion, we have saved him from acute embarrassment, Master Thibault has rewarded and patronized us both. Now you, my friend, cannot be touched. You are a priest, a cleric and a much-loved one. Both Holy Mother Church and your Order would give you every protection. I cannot say the same about myself. Oh yes, I know the role I act. Honest Jack! Blunt Jack! Jack who likes his beer, sups his ale and feasts on the softest meat and the best Bordeaux. Nimble Jack! Good old Jack! Rest assured, Athelstan, all that could change at the drop of a coin. I have enemies both in the Guildhall and at court. You know how they act, like a wolf-pack beginning to stir. They'll scent the air for prey. Some will want to settle old scores; others just love the hunt and the prospect of blood.' Cranston's face became harsher, leaner, even younger, his light blue eyes were not so merry. 'I'll have to protect Lady Maude and the poppets. Some of those lords at the Guildhall have about as much compassion as a fox on the hunt. In short, Brother, matters could turn very nasty.'

'Perhaps not. Remember, Jack, you have friends, very powerful friends.'

'Such as?'

'First myself, and secondly the young King, who has, on more than one occasion, solemnly vowed his patronage and protection.' Athelstan leaned over and squeezed Cranston's hand. 'This is Sir John Cranston, Lord High Coroner of London, who stood by his young King and single-handedly confronted Wat Tyler and his horde of rebels at Smithfield not so long ago. Young Richard may have many faults. He sees himself as God's vicar on earth, and God help Gaunt when Richard comes of age. But you, Jack, he will never forget. You are his sworn man, and I believe one of Richard's greatest virtues is that he has, he does, and he will, stand by his friends. Merry Jack, rest assured, if your enemies move, so will I.'

Cranston gazed at Athelstan in amazement then burst out laughing.

'Sir John?'

'I'd forgotten, little friar, how highly young Richard regards you. So,' the coroner breathed out, 'on the day of the great slaughter, when the strongholds fall, I will put all my trust in you, little friar. Very well, back to the business in hand!'

'Jack.' Athelstan peered at the coroner. 'I believe Thibault intended to steal the treasure, but . . . wouldn't that be obvious, if the English Exchequer suddenly received, as it were, a gift from God?'

'Oh, believe me little friar, Master Thibault is master of the coin. Oh, he'd probably use the money to secretly pay off Crown debts; or in refurbishing this property or that. Can you imagine the power and resources it would also give him? The bribes, the rewards, the creation of a secret exchequer, a treasure house controlled only by him and his master. But he didn't steal it, so who did?'

'I believe the Carbonari are involved,' Athelstan replied. 'I listened carefully to what Ignacio said. This is a deviously plotted robbery. I keep thinking of that stonemason in Mantua. He was the key to that mystery. All we have to find, Jack, is the key to ours. Now we should . . .' Athelstan broke off at the sound of running feet down the gallery, followed by a pounding on the door. Cranston rose as it opened, and a highly distraught Mine Host almost fell into the room.

'Sir John, Brother Athelstan, you must come. One of the clerks, Philip Crossley, has been murdered. I found his corpse in the cellar.'

Cranston and Athelstan followed the taverner down to the taproom. The hour was late and the tavern had begun to empty. Athelstan, curious about how quiet it was despite the murder, whispered a question to Mine Host, who put a finger to his lips.

'Sir John, Brother Athelstan, I have told no one else but you. I have just discovered the corpse. My wife too . . .' He pointed across at the buttery table where Isabella stood rigid, head down, staring at the empty platters. Mine Host called her across and told her to go and wait in their chamber. The woman, all pale-faced and agitated, simply nodded and fled. The taverner watched her go, then led Cranston and Athelstan along a side passage to a door which opened up onto the steep steps down into the cellar. Both Cranston and Athelstan gingerly followed the taverner. The inky darkness seemed to embrace them, though the strong smell of ale and wine was comforting enough. At the bottom of the steps, more lanterns blazed. Athelstan straightened up and stared down the narrow tunnel, which was cut by casks, tuns, barrels and locked storerooms. The Friar held a hand up as a sign for silence. He then closed his eyes as he repressed a shiver. He opened his eyes and murmured a prayer.

'Athelstan?'

'Nothing, Sir John, just a feeling.'

He and Cranston then followed the taverner a little further along the tunnel, where Crossley's corpse lay sprawled, face down on the wet, sticky floor. The blood from the wound in the back of his head had gushed out to colour the small puddles either side. Athelstan asked Cranston and the taverner to stand back whilst he scrutinized the corpse.

'He is fully dressed to go out,' Athelstan declared. 'Notice how he is cloaked, cowled and booted.' Athelstan crouched down. 'He has a belt on with wallet and dagger. The latter is sheathed, so his assailant struck suddenly with little, if any, sign of defence or resistance. One small, sudden bolt through the back of his skull.'

Athelstan turned the corpse over and grimaced at how the shock of death had contorted Crossley's pale, narrow face, his mouth gaping and blood-laced. Crossley lay, eyes rolled back, as if straining to see the cause of his death. Athelstan felt the man's clothing and searched both purse and wallet. But, apart from some small chancery items, such as sealing wax, a pumice stone and a small sheath of quill pens, there was really nothing of note. Athelstan got to his feet, fighting off a surge of weary tiredness. He stared down the tunnel, which cut past the barrels to disappear into a stygian darkness.

'Where does this lead?' Athelstan asked over his shoulder.

'Some distance,' the taverner replied. 'An ancient tunnel with narrow entrances sealed by heavy slats, barred from the inside.'

'And why should Crossley come down here?'

'God knows, Sir John.'

'He was definitely leaving,' Athelstan remarked.

'Escaping?' the coroner suggested.

'But where to, Sir John? Where could Crossley flee and why? He would become a fugitive, a felon, put to the horn as an outlaw. Remember Crossley has done no harm. He has broken no law. He was simply unfortunate enough to be caught up in all the tumult at Westminster. Do you know, Sir John, I just wonder if Crossley wanted to speak to someone in authority. Had he learned something, recalled some vital piece of information. I suspect Crossley came down here intending to leave, and he had good reason for that. Anyway,' Athelstan pointed at the taverner, 'did Crossley speak to you?'

'No.'

'Did he ever ask about the cellar and its blocked entrances?'

'Not that I know.'

'But he must have done,' Athelstan insisted. 'The only reason

Crossley would come down here, surely, would be to find a way out. What else is there? He didn't come searching for a jug of ale. Somebody in this tavern must know something. Crossley didn't just stumble along here by chance.'

'I agree,' Cranston broke in. 'Master Taverner, summon your entire household. Quick now, because the candle burns.'

The taverner hurried off with Cranston's insistence that all be summoned ringing in his ears. Cranston and Athelstan eventually returned to the taproom. The coroner stood imposingly before the buttery table, cloak thrown back so his warbelt, sword and dagger could be clearly seen. The coroner clapped his hands and gestured for the household to gather closer. He then told them in short, pithy sentences, what had happened to Crossley, whose corpse now sprawled, stiffening in the cellar below.

'So,' Cranston declared, his voice echoing around the taproom. 'Do any of you know anything about this horrid murder? You must tell us on your allegiance to the Crown. Did any of you here have words with Crossley before he died?' Cranston's question drew muttered denials and much shaking of heads. The scullions, maids and servants shuffled their feet and glanced nervously at each other. Cranston was about to repeat his question when a young boy, a scullion of the spit, edged forward, hand raised. Athelstan beckoned him closer.

'Don't be frightened,' the friar urged. 'We mean you no harm. Indeed, we intend you all good. So what is your name?'

'Shutup.'

'I beg your pardon.'

'Shutup. That's what people here tell me to do. So often, it's become my name.'

'And what name were you given over the font?'

'Simon, I think, but I am not too sure. I am a foundling of the parish, hired here as a spit boy. I like Shutup, I've got used to it.'

'Very well, Master Spit Boy.' Athelstan paused and glanced at Sir John. 'My Lord Coroner, this young man might be of assistance. Let's talk to him in a more comfortable place.'

A more comfortable place was soon found. Cranston and Athelstan took the boy up to the same chamber where they had met Prior Anselm. All three waited until a slightly agitated taverner had made them comfortable with warming pots, a jug of light ale and a platter of crispy pork strips. Once they were settled, and Cranston ensured that the gallery outside was deserted, Athelstan took the two pennies the coroner had given him and placed them on the table before the boy.

'Well, Master Spit Boy. Did the clerk Philip Crossley speak to you? Why and when?'

'He constantly moaned about the cold so he would come down and sit on a stool close to the hearth. I would be in the inglenook, turning the spit, basting the meat with different juices and keeping the flames strong. I mean,' Shutup wiped his dripping nose on the back of his hand, 'it's an important task.'

'I am sure it is,' Athelstan declared. 'But Master Crossley?'

'He would come down to warm himself by the fire and then,' Shutup screwed his face in concentration, 'he asked how, if he wished, he could steal away from this tavern without being seen.'

'And why did he ask that? And when did he ask it?'

'Oh recently, a few days ago. He said he had to get out. He needed to cross to Southwark.'

'Southwark?'

'Yes Southwark. But he didn't say why. He simply said he had to get there. He said he needed to speak to someone about keys. Good masters, that's all he said.'

'Did he mention my name, Brother Athelstan?'

'No, but he did mention yours.' Shutup pointed at Cranston. 'He said he would like to speak to the Lord High Coroner, but he claimed it was too dangerous to walk the city, whilst Southwark was only a short journey across London Bridge. He would talk to me like that, chatter as if to himself. He seemed frightened, cowed.'

'And?'

'He offered me coins so I told him about the cellar. The long tunnel and the narrow blocked posterns.' Shutup paused. 'I think he stole down there once or twice.'

'And tonight?'

'Brother Athelstan, I don't know anything about that. I am sorry he died. He seemed pleasant enough. I'm frightened now.'

'Don't be,' Athelstan soothed. 'You have no more to tell us?'

'Nothing, Brother.'

'Very well, then go down and tell Mine Host I want to see those clerks in this chamber and here.' Athelstan scooped up the coins and pressed them into the boy's hand. 'Go now, you've earned your reward.'

The three clerks looked frightened and beaten as they sat on the wall bench Cranston had pulled forward. Mailed clerks yet, Athelstan ruefully conceded to himself, they were men who had been threatened time and again, be it by Thibault's anger or that hideous assault in the taproom below.

'Why are we here?' Beaumont demanded. 'Why can't we be released from this benighted place?'

'True,' Athelstan replied. This is a house of murder. Whitby died here and now Crossley. Do any of you, Beaumont, Calpurne and Bloxham, three of Crossley's closest colleagues, know anything about why such a killing should take place here and now?'

'No,' all three chorused.

'In which case, do you know of any reason why Crossley should have gone down into that cellar? Look,' Athelstan asserted himself against a wave of tiredness, 'you are being kept in honourable house arrest because of the robbery at Westminster. No one has accused you of anything. All sorts of theories thrive about how the robbery was perpetrated but there is no reason to accuse you or this tavern of any involvement. Yet Crossley was murdered here. I cannot see any tie between his death in The Hanging Tree and the plundering of the royal treasure chamber. So why was Crossley down in that cellar?'

'We don't know.' Bloxhall almost screamed, froth bubbling at the corner of his mouth.

'Adrian, Adrian,' Calpurne grasped him by the shoulder and shook him gently, 'peace now. Brother Athelstan must question us.' Calpurne turned back to the friar. 'Nevertheless, I wager that none of us can tell you much about Crossley's final hours. He was with us until late in the day, then he disappeared.'

'Talking of disappearances,' Athelstan interjected, 'you may recall an individual known as Culpeper who was lodged here at our expense?'

'A snooper, a spy and an eavesdropper,' Beaumont retorted. 'Always trying to draw us into conversation or listen in on ours. He was an annoying little man, yes my friends?' The other two clerks muttered their agreement.

'Do you know his whereabouts?'

'Of course not, Brother Athelstan, he was here then he was gone. True, he was interested in us, but I got the impression he was more intrigued by this tavern.'

'So, to return to Crossley. Did he make any mention of trying to escape from The Hanging Tree?'

'No.'

'Then let me inform you of what we've learnt. Crossley was determined to leave this tavern without being seen. He intended to cross London Bridge and, I suspect, meet with me in my parish church. Now why should he plot that? Did Crossley learn something fresh about the robbery?'

'Not that we know, Brother.' Beaumont scratched his brow. 'Why should he go to Southwark? Why not meet you here?'

'That, Master Beaumont, is part of the mystery. Only Crossley could explain why and what he did. Now apparently this tavern is built over ancient tunnels, sewers or ditches, with narrow posterns all boarded up. Crossley apparently learnt of these; I suspect he intended to use the tunnel to escape. He went down into that cellar and was murdered. Oh, by the way,' Athelstan raised a hand, 'I am sure that Sir John, on his return to the Guildhall, will arrange for Crossley's corpse to be removed to Westminster. The cadaver will be dressed properly for burial and handed over to his family.'

'He has family,' Bloxhall declared. The clerk now seemed more composed.

'He will be given every dignity,' Cranston affirmed. 'So, back to Crossley before his death. Did he say or do anything which might explain why he so desperately wanted to speak to Brother Athelstan?'

'He did,' Calpurne declared, 'make reference to Whitby's declaration that "our plainchant had been sorely disturbed on the morning of the robbery". I still believe that was a superficial comment on Despencer not ringing the bell in answer to ours. I cannot understand why Crossley became so fascinated with that declaration.'

'He also mourned young Whitby,' Bloxhall interjected. 'We all did, but Crossley and Whitby were firm friends. Crossley began to wonder if Whitby's death was simple, fickle, cruel chance. Or did our visitors from Hell come here to murder Whitby from the start. Yet why? What had Whitby done or said different from us?'

The clerk sighed noisily. 'Except for that remark about plainchant.' Bloxhall pointed to the door. 'One thing I did see, and I wondered if it was connected to the robbery. On at least two occasions, I found Crossley standing by the door to his chamber, doing nothing more than pushing the key in and out of the lock. God knows what was going through his mind.'

'Yes, God knows.' Athelstan stared at the clerks and abruptly wondered if one of these men had loosed that deadly bolt at Crossley. The thought startled him so much he had to hurriedly compose himself. He glanced at Cranston. 'My Lord Coroner, we are finished here yes?'

'We certainly are, except for one question,' Cranston added. '"Our plainchant was sorely disturbed." Did Whitby say that when you entered the treasure chamber?'

'No, no,' Bloxhall replied. 'He said it whilst we were going up the steps.'

'In which case, gentlemen,' Athelstan pointed to the door, 'you may go. But be careful, prudent.'

The three clerks left. Cranston and Athelstan sat in silence until their footsteps faded. The coroner rose and opened the door to ensure the gallery was empty. He then returned to his seat next to Athelstan.

'The hour is very late. The candle ring burns away, it's time we slept. Athelstan, what did we learn here?' He glimpsed the friar's half smile. 'Little friar, you have found something, haven't you?'

'Oh yes, Sir John, I can hardly believe my luck. My good friend, please go down to the taproom and bring young Shutup here. I want to question him again. But first, Sir John, you ask what we've learnt? Crossley definitely had discovered something, or at least entertained suspicions. He was hurrying away from here to talk to me. But why Southwark? Is there something or someone, which frightens him, a situation he does not trust? Secondly, Crossley was following the same path as I am. He was deeply interested in Whitby's remark about plainchant but he was also entertaining a suspicion that Whitby's death was not cruel fortune but deliberate. Those Carbonari came to this tavern to kill him. To silence him.'

'Then there's the business of the key.'

'Yes, Sir John, there's the business of the key. What was Crossley doing playing with the key to his chamber? Pushing it in and out of the lock?' Athelstan smiled. 'I think I know Sir John. Anyway, fetch young Shutup.'

Cranston left, and returned clutching the heavy-eyed spit boy.

'I was going to sleep,' he mumbled. 'Sirs, I am tired.'

'Just one question, boy, and I want you to tell me the truth. You must think and think hard.' Athelstan produced a penny from his purse. 'And this will be yours. Tell me, boy, does this tavern have an armoury? A cupboard where weapons are stored in case of attack?'

'Oh yes, Brother.'

'And where is it?'

'Close to the pantry at the rear of the tavern.'

'Take us there.' The boy looked as if he was going to refuse, but Athelstan picked up the coin and pressed it into his hand. Shutup seemed to come to life. He grasped Athelstan by the hand, tugging gently for him to follow. The friar glanced at Cranston and winked. 'I think we have our guide, Sir John.'

They went down to the deserted taproom where shuttered lanterns glowed. The boy went into the inglenook, took a key from a hook, and handed it wordlessly to the friar. He then grasped Athelstan's sleeve again and pulled him down the passage leading to the cellar, but then turned into an enclave and pointed to a narrow door. Athelstan took the key and unlocked it. Cranston followed, carrying a lantern. The armoury was no different from that found in many a tavern. A crossbow hung from the wall but it was a powerful, Genoese type with thick barbed quarrels, which could shatter a man's head. Athelstan scrutinized this carefully before handing it to Cranston, who agreed with Athelstan's whisper that the arbalest had not been used in Crossley's murder. The friar glanced around at the rusting daggers, battered shield and a number of war bows with quivers of arrows.

'Nothing here.' He murmured. 'Nothing at all. Master spit boy, we thank you.' Athelstan ushered Shutup to the door and told him to go back to his bed under one of the tables in the taproom. He and Cranston then went down to the cellar. Crossley's corpse still sprawled on the floor, the horrible crossbow bolt still lodged deep in the back of his head. Athelstan and Cranston inspected the corpse, kneeling either side.

'We found nothing,' Cranston murmured. 'No weapon which was used in this killing.'

'Sir John, I'll wait here and pray for poor Crossley's soul. I want you to go to our three clerks, they are probably drinking in one of the chambers, drowning their sorrows or easing their pain. Ask them, on their allegiance to the Crown, what weapons do they carry and insist that they show you, be it a dagger or a club, it doesn't matter. Once you've done that, Sir John, I think we've finished.'

Cranston hurried away, breathing heavily as he climbed the steep steps. Athelstan heard him go and knelt back down again beside the corpse. He could not anoint Crossley; after all, his soul had long gone.

'Or has it?' Athelstan murmured to the darkness. 'Is it still here, desperate for justice?' Athelstan closed his eyes and recited the '*De Profundis*'. Once he had finished, the friar got to his feet and pointed to the steps at least nine yards from where Crossley lay. 'You came down here,' he whispered to himself, 'booted and cloaked, ready to go, but your killer crept up behind you, softly, like the Angel of Death he was. He carried a weapon, a small crossbow. Now he would find it very difficult to conceal this as he came through the tavern. So . . .' Athelstan walked slowly back. To his left and right were shelves, roughly hewn planks fastened to the wall. All sorts of items lay there. Athelstan returned to the corpse and stared down at it. 'Was your killer waiting for you here or did he follow you down? He certainly let you walk on and then he released that bolt. But,' Athelstan rubbed his face as he murmured a swift prayer for divine help, 'your killer must have reassured you, so much so you turned your back on him, and that's when he struck. The bolt is embedded deep so he must have drawn close.' Athelstan continued to reflect, trying to keep his eyes from closing as he pondered the possibilities. He shook himself awake as Cranston made his noisy descent down into the cellar.

'Well, my Lord Coroner?'

'Nothing, my friend. The clerks were not allowed to carry weapons, except for the dagger in their belt. Nothing more. So why, Brother, why this interest?'

'Why this interest, Sir John? Well, I believe I have solved one mystery and I am on the verge of resolving a second. So, let us be gone. We need to sleep, to reflect and then return to the hunt.'

Athelstan sat in the luxurious, exquisitely furnished chantry chapel in St Erconwald's. This was his pride and joy, hidden behind its beautifully carved trellis screen and carpeted with dark blue turkey rugs. The very air sweetened by the fragrance from the pure beeswax candles specially supplied by the best chandler in Cheapside. The chapel was dedicated to the patron saint of the parish. Athelstan had used generous donations from the young King, Gaunt, Thibault and Cranston to buy the very best, be it the polished oaken furniture, the gold tasselled cushions, the snow-white altar cloths, or the gold and silver sacred vessels. The chapel was warmed by three capped braziers. Athelstan had pulled these close because the nave of the church was truly freezing, with wisps of mist moving like clouds through the air. Athelstan strained his ears but the church lay eerily silent. The friar had locked himself in as he was always wary. Athelstan fully accepted that being the secretarius of the Lord High Coroner was an extremely dangerous task. It was a matter of logic. If Athelstan drew up an indictment against any felon, any secret murderer, then it usually held fast. Consequently, the only way to prevent that indictment from being laid was to kill its creator. Time and again Athelstan had encountered assassins determined to kill him, and the present troubles proved this. The Carbonari, who held sway with those powerful Italian bankers, had made the ruthless decision to remove him from Southwark under the pretence of friendship. When they failed, they turned to murder.

Athelstan sat back in his chair and reviewed the last two days. He had returned across London Bridge following the lantern men, Cosmas and Damien, whom Cranston had insisted on hiring. Both dwarfs, chattering like squirrels on a branch, had seen him safely home. The friar had hastily checked both his house and the stable but all was well. Bonaventure was toasting himself before the banked fire, whilst Philomel lounged in his stable. Athelstan had come across to the church to pray as well as to marshal his flitting thoughts. He was certain he now had keys to unlock the mysteries confronting him, but how was he to do it? The friar crossed himself and quietly intoned the '*Veni Creator Spiritus*', his favourite hymn to the Holy Spirit. He reached the enchanting verse 'if you take your grace away, nothing good in me will stay'. Athelstan glanced up. 'True, true,' he whispered. 'On our darkness,' he continued, 'pour thy dew . . .' Athelstan put his face in his hands and fervently prayed for guidance. In the end, Athelstan did not sleep well that night. In the morning, after he'd celebrated a sparsely attended dawn Mass, he returned to his studies. He immersed himself in all the information he had garnered, well into the next day when Cranston abruptly appeared, sweeping like a storm into the parish. Athelstan met him in the chantry chapel; sitting on the wall bench with Cranston slouched behind him.

'I came,' the coroner declared, 'because I have heard from Kyrie. The *Ludovico* is preparing for sea. My spies report there is little haste but gradual preparations. Moreover,' Cranston nudged Athelstan, 'your questioning of Kyrie was most useful. The admiral's spies have repeated quite sound rumours that the *Ludovico* might not simply leave the Thames and turn south for south-west but veer sharply north by north-east.'

'In other words,' Athelstan observed, 'the *Ludovico* is not going to slip through the Narrow Seas but sail up the east coast of England. It's time, Jack, time we moved! That ship is the key to one of the mysteries we face!'

'True true, my little mariner. So what is to be done?'

'Sir John, here is my indictment.' Athelstan began to talk. He informed the coroner slowly and measuredly about the conclusions he had reached and the evidence he had collected and studied. He made close reference to what Ignacio had told him and all he had learned at The Hanging Tree. Cranston heard him out, whistling under his breath or whispering some startled question. The hour candle burned, its flame moving from one red ring to another, but Athelstan pressed on. Once he had finished, taking a generous sip from the coroner's miraculous wineskin, Athelstan sat in silence. He stared fixedly at the chantry chapel's trellis screen. He then crossed himself and turned to the coroner.

'So, my friend,' he murmured, pulling himself up on the wall bench, 'I have told you what I have discovered. I have also described how we can trap and punish all the perpetrators. The murder of the hangmen must wait a while. Time passes, those responsible for the robbery at Westminster must be dealt with first.'

'And you want Thibault brought in?'

'Of course, Sir John, we need him for so many things. True, Thibault is treacherous, he may have had his own plans for the treasure, but that is in the past. Sir John, we must act and do so quickly. You must inform Thibault. Search him out and tell him to get the people we need and the arrangements to be made. As I have told you, you can free the clerks. Inform them that they are innocent, though we need one last meeting with Master Beaumont.' Athelstan rose to his feet. 'Come, Sir John, we have work to do. Tomorrow morning I shall celebrate my dawn Mass and join you in the Tower.

PART SEVEN

'My own sin is greed.'

'Master Henry Beaumont, I do impeach thee of high treason against our Sovereign Lord. Master Henry Beaumont, I do impeach thee of murder. Master Henry Beaumont, I do impeach thee of robbery . . .' Cranston's powerful voice, the sombre words he uttered, echoed like a death knell around the cavernous questioning chamber deep beneath the great White Tower. Cranston's words rolled out like the ominous beat of a tambour. The coroner stood behind a table, reading from the script Athelstan had prepared. The friar now sat on Cranston's right, staring at Beaumont, whilst on Cranston's left, Master Thibault just glared hatefully at his treacherous clerk.

Beaumont himself sat on the other side of the broad, bench-like table, gaping open mouthed, eyes all fearful, his face an ashen grey. Athelstan, however, was not convinced. Beaumont was a killer, an assassin, a ruthless soul who hid behind a number of masks, be it the loyal official or, as now, the timid chancery servant. Athelstan had to remind himself that Beaumont was a mailed clerk who had fought in the King's Array and had seen his fair share of bloodshed. Athelstan always felt a twinge of compassion for those he indicted. Sometimes they deserved mercy, Beaumont certainly did not. This man was responsible for a whole host of murders. He truly was an Angel of Death, dealing out destruction on every side. He deserved to die. Whitby and the other souls demanded that. God needed to have words with Beaumont. Cranston finished what he had to say and sat down.

'You sir,' Athelstan began, pointing at Beaumont, 'are on trial for your life.' Athelstan fell silent at a hideous yell, which pierced the dark dank gallery outside, only to be echoed by further blood-chilling cries and agonized shrieks. Beaumont went to speak but Thibault slammed the top of the table time and time again.

'That,' Athelstan declared when the shrieks faded, 'is the sound of two of Conteza's men. They will not be missed – well, not until it's too late. They are petty officials who, Conteza might suspect, have deserted his retinue to stay and revel in this great city. The truth is we have kidnapped them because they are dagger men. They took part in the assault on us at the treasure chamber. They attacked me again in my own parish and, of course, they were members of that murderous pack who stormed into The Hanging Tree and executed poor Whitby. He was chosen specially, wasn't he? Because he witnessed the one great mistake you made. You rang that bell three times at the foot of the tower steps. However, you never paused or questioned why Despencer failed to reply. A dire mistake. After all, that's why the bell system was implemented, wasn't it? But, of course, Despencer could not respond: you had murdered him. In those first hours after the robbery, you were free enough to despatch a message to Conteza and your fellow conspirators, warning them about your mistake and Whitby's comment. Those two gentlemen, now screaming their hearts out in that torture chamber, have confessed as much.'

'I don't know what you mean,' Beaumont yelled.

'Oh you will.' Athelstan beat his breast in mock contrition. '*Mea culpa*, *mea culpa*, my fault my fault. At first, I approached what happened on that stairwell from the wrong perspective. A silly mistake, let me explain. You rang the bell, Despencer failed to reply. Whitby remarked how their plainchant, a reference to the usual horarium or daily routine, had been sorely disrupted that morning. At first, I thought he was referring to Despencer's failure to reply. However, as I said earlier, that was not the truth. Whitby, Crossley, and eventually myself, realized Whitby was actually referring to the way you, Master Beaumont, ignored what had happened. You rang the bell, there was no reply. There was no comment from you, no response. You simply pressed on, acting as if you knew full well that Despencer would never, could never reply. Whitby made that comment before he entered the treasure chamber, before he saw the hideous carnage. He was sharp-witted with a keen mind. Whitby was the first to pick up on your dreadful mistake.' Athelstan pointed at the accused. 'Of course, you might ask why Whitby did not confront you?'

'Obvious thing to do?'

'No, no, Master Beaumont. You were the trusted Magister, a

royal chancery clerk. Whitby would be surprised, deeply so; he needed time to reflect before asking very disturbing questions – which explains your haste, as well as that of your fellow conspirators, to silence him for good.'

'This is ridiculous.' Beaumont stammered. 'How could I?' He fell silent as fresh screams echoed through the room. 'I thought I was to be freed, summoned here to be informed of that.'

'Oh no,' Athelstan retorted. 'Master Thibault, if we could visit that chamber?'

Gaunt's henchman sprang to his feet. He would have lunged at Beaumont but Cranston swiftly intervened, so Thibault just flailed a hand in the air. The Master of Secrets swept around the table, throwing open the iron-studded door leading into a dimly lit gallery, where the walls and floor glistened with grease and dirt. Puddles of filth and blood reflected the flickering flames from the sconce torches. The air reeked rancid, whilst the horrid sounds from the torture chamber rang out like some hellish music. They all followed Thibault down to an enclave at the far end of the gallery. Thibault pushed open the door and led them in. The room was a square box with an earth-beaten floor, its rough-hewn walls covered in filth. Against one of these, at the far end, hung two prisoners by their wrists from manacles driven into the stones above their heads. Both prisoners were naked except for a loincloth, though that provided little dignity as both men's hair and beard were drenched in blood, with rivulets running down their chest and legs. Albinus and Wolfrich supervised the torture, issuing orders to three executioners, garbed in thick leather aprons with grotesque masks over their faces: these prowled like wolves before their two hapless victims. Albinus turned and lifted his slender, white willow-wand; the end of the rod was cruelly splintered and stained with globules of blood.

'We have learnt more,' Albinus shouted, 'about the *Ludovico*.'

'Good good,' Thibault retorted. 'We simply came to view what was happening. So let us return.' Thibault shoved Beaumont in the chest. Again, Cranston intervened, and all four returned to the chamber guarded by Flaxwith and his bailiffs. Once they had retaken their seats, Athelstan just sat staring at the prisoner. He was totally convinced of Beaumont's guilt. Cold logic alone dictated this royal clerk had been responsible for the murders and the theft. Athelstan felt he could demonstrate this before any justice of Oyer et Terminer, or before the royal judges on King's Bench at Westminster. Indeed, the sheer simplicity of the crime had at first confused both him and Cranston. Now this simplicity was analysed, it would be easy to convict but that was not all. Beaumont had been caught, accused, and would be convicted but problems remained. The treasure was still missing and, just as importantly, Beaumont's fellow conspirators were scrambling around scot-free, ready to flee the trap. He needed to break Beaumont yet, at the same time, win him over, and that might prove most difficult. Beaumont, like all Cain's offspring, was arrogant. He truly believed he would walk unharmed and wealthy from this kingdom. He still might, because Athelstan was prepared to use him as a lure. The silence in the chamber was abruptly shattered by more pitiful cries and groans.

'Listen and listen well, Master Beaumont,' Athelstan remarked. 'That is your fate. You can avoid it. No!' Athelstan held a hand up at Beaumont. 'For the moment, remain silent. You must hear the indictment and then you can respond. But I advise you, do so carefully, prudently, for not only does your life depend upon it, but also the manner in which you might leave this life. You stand accused of dreadful crimes so you deserve a dreadful death. Now listen.' Athelstan tapped the sheets of vellum before him. 'You were Magister of the Clerks of the Light. On that fateful evening, before the murders, you finished your last honest day's work. You left the treasure chamber in good order. Despencer and his clerks were safely ensconced. Your companions heard the door at the top of the steps be locked. You and they went down the staircase. Of course, you went last, refitting the trip cords along every eighth step. You reached the stairwell; your companions were tired, cold and weary, eager for good food and warmth. What happened next is what happens every night after they have finished their work at the treasury, and why should that night be any different? But it was.' Athelstan abruptly rose and walked to the door. He opened it, called in Flaxwith and closed the door behind him, rattling the key in the lock. Athelstan had practised this before the meeting began and he was certain that the stratagem would work. 'Master Flaxwith.' The bemused bailiff clerk turned.

Brother Athelstan?'

'Master Flaxwith, what have I just done?'

'Why, Brother, you just called me in here.'

'And so I did. What then?'

'You closed the door and locked it.'

'You are sure?'

'Yes.'

'It is not locked!' Athelstan pulled hard on the door and it opened, Athelstan snatching the piece of thickened parchment he had secretly used to wedge the door closed. 'That,' Athelstan held up the wedge, 'made it seem like the door was locked.'

'But you turned the key.'

'No Master Flaxwith, I fiddled with the key. I rattled it in the lock but I didn't fully turn it. I pushed the door to and, as I did, inserted the wedge. I then rattled the keys as if I was locking it. Doors are closed and locked throughout the day, we rarely give it a second thought or glance. This is what happened on that fateful evening in the shadowy, cold stairwell of Flambard's Tower. The Clerks of the Light, your comrades, Beaumont, were eager for home. They saw and heard the door being closed, the key being inserted in the locks, then they were gone in a matter of heartbeats.' Athelstan paused. 'Master Beaumont, do you remember Culpeper, the little snooper? And indeed he was! Culpeper was a *peritus*, an expert, in getting into places supposedly locked. Amongst other business assigned to him, Culpeper was asked to study the robbery, or rather the place where it occurred. He visited the treasure chamber at Westminster and came to a similar conclusion,' Athelstan shrugged, 'to the one I eventually reached. Culpeper wrote down his conclusion "*porta prima, porta solo prima*" which, as you know, translates "the first door, it can only be the first door". Culpeper's conclusion was that someone somehow managed to get through that first locked door. He was correct. So, to return to my indictment. Flambard's Tower settles down, Despencer and his clerks are busy within, whilst you, Master Beaumont, are equally busy without. Your comrades have left. You have surrendered the keys, then you returned to Flambard's Tower garbed in black from head to toe. You slink through the night. Albinus and Wolfrich do not pose any real challenge. They come regularly every three hours. Like everyone else, they are tired, cold, and believe everything is secure enough. They perform their guard in a perfunctory manner. You know when they will come and when they will leave so you continue with your plot. After all, you have so many things to do. You slip into the crypt or cellar of Flambard's Tower. You'd probably laid out there what you needed, especially a large strong hempen sack, sturdy enough to hold the deluge of gold coins you are about to cascade from the treasury.'

'I am sorry I don't . . .'

'Don't be sorry, Master Beaumont, don't stutter, don't act the innocent. So let me continue, then you will understand. You slip like a shadow into the crypt of Flambard's Tower. You have, as I said, made preparations, a wheelbarrow, a large sack and a hooded lantern. You fire the lantern and prepare to attach the hempen sack to the end of the jakes chute which falls vertically down from the treasure chamber, to hang just above the cess barrel. You first put the lid back over the barrel and fasten the sack to the end of the chute. Oh I concede,' Athelstan smiled, 'it was messy, odiferous and cold. But what is that compared to seizing a king's ransom in treasure?'

'You have proof of this?' Beaumont stammered, eyes blinking.

'You are the proof, the evidence, Magister, as I will continue to demonstrate. So let me press on. You had prepared the crypt, the sack, the barrow. You faced no real danger: Albinus and Wolfrich are not due for some time. You collect something else from the crypt, something you've left there.'

'What?'

'Oh you know what it was. It was your birthday, wasn't it? Or is that also a lie, a pretence? Anyway, it gives you a reason for carrying that jug of the best Bordeaux, laced with a most powerful sleeping powder. You opened the door to the stairwell, pulling out the wedge of parchment. You then ring the bell three times and Despencer replies.'

'No, no, wouldn't he be suspicious? Wouldn't he refuse?'

'Of course not. Why should Despencer and his clerks be alarmed? The first door has been opened, the bell rung. Who has the keys to that door? Who knows how many peals the bell must make? Either you or Master Thibault. Why should that alarm Despencer?' Athelstan paused as another chilling cry pierced the air. Cranston stirred, tapping the table.

'They must have decided to rack them,' Cranston murmured. As if in answer, more strident screams rang out. Athelstan glanced swiftly at Beaumont. The clerk was now ashen-faced, lower lip quivering.

'You'll be next,' Thibault snarled. 'If you do not cooperate.'

'I am sure he will,' Athelstan soothed. 'Now back to Flambard's Tower. Carrying the wine jug, you carefully climb the steps, avoiding the trip cords you yourself prepared. Despencer awaits you. The door is open, and in you sweep like Herod dancing amongst the innocents, smiling all sweet, when you meant all murder and so you did.' Athelstan caught his breath at fresh screaming followed by Albinus and Wolfrich yelling at their victims. 'Behind the Judas smile you meant all ill. That is what you inflicted; all ill on those innocent men: fathers, brothers lovers and cousins. You slaughtered royal officials who had taken an oath to the Crown and kept faith with it. You didn't give a whit. You didn't care. You poured the tainted wine, goblets all brimming. You would chatter about your birthday, about the wine being the best Bordeaux and the finest way to celebrate. You toast yourself to a long and comfortable life of leisure whilst you sent those souls, before their time, to judgement. They drink that wine, gulp it down, savour its full richness. You did not. They fell into a deep slumber but you did not. Once all lay quiet, you acted. You're a mailed clerk who has seen service in France. You have probably used the twine of a war bow to strangle or garrotte enemy sentries. In that murder room you met with no opposition, no threat, just five men deeply asleep, whom you callously and cruelly choked to death. You arranged it so the corpses sat in their chancery enclaves. Perhaps the wine and the potion made itself felt. They would go to the only place they could really rest, namely their chancery chairs. In the end, you have your way. The clerks were an obstacle quickly removed.

You then turned to what lies at the heart of your wickedness – the theft of the gold and silver coins. You first get rid of what is left of the tainted wine in the jug, pouring it down the jakes hole. You do the same with what's left in each goblet, replacing it with dregs of untainted wine. Just to make sure, you'd use water from the common butt to cleanse away completely all the drops of tainted wine in jug, cup, as well as the chute itself. To all intents and purposes, the chamber now only contains goblets holding good wine. The jakes hole, in fact, is now your real concern. It is a sheer vertical drop to hang above the cess barrel.'

Athelstan paused again as more pitiful wails rose and fell. He glanced at Beaumont. Athelstan was surprised how cold and reserved the clerk now appeared. True, Beaumont showed apprehension and fear, yet he seemed to control them well enough. Athelstan narrowed his eyes. He had met such mailed clerks before, more ruthless and violent than any city riffler. The garb of a clerk only disguising their true violent nature. Athelstan smiled to himself. Of course this confrontation was totally different from any other Athelstan had faced. Beaumont still held the dice for one crucial throw which would account for his abrupt shift of mood. He knew where the stolen treasure now lay, as well as when and where Conteza intended to move it. If he had to, Beaumont would trade such information for his life. Athelstan was determined to make his opponent do exactly that.

'Brother Athelstan?'

'Yes, Master Thibault, I am just thinking about Beaumont being all satisfied in that chamber. How everything was now in order for the last part of his villainy. The removal of the gold and silver. Of course that was simple enough, wasn't it Beaumont? The long jakes plunger pole ensured the drop was clear. You then used that same pole as you emptied the sacks one by one into the chute and down to the waiting net.' Athelstan shook his head. 'Easy and swift enough. The chute is totally vertical, a sheer drop, its smoothed stone made even more so by any liquids freshly poured down it. Of course,' Athelstan added, 'you had this plunger rod to ensure nothing was missed. The small sacks you gather up to be burned in some God-forsaken spot by your allies.

'Once the treasure was gone, you stared around that chamber. You had woven a true mystery. Five clerks garrotted, with no sign of violence or any resistance on their part. Fortified doors opened and locked again by some invisible hand. The tainted wine thrown away and replaced with the dregs of good Bordeaux. You had the jug you brought your potion in safely with you. You then made the final touches to your hideous slaughter. You took some of the empty bags, filled them with charcoal and left them in one of the chests. A clear declaration that the Carbonari, the charcoal burners, were responsible for the robbery. Of course, to a certain extent that is true, for such a gesture removes any suspicion from you. You also seal the mystery in the most cunning way . . .'

'The keys.' Beaumont now asserted himself. 'The keys,' he repeated. 'How did I lock those doors, eh Brother Athelstan. Thibault held my set.' Beaumont looked contemptuously at the Master of Secrets. 'And Despencer had the other.'

'Oh, that was subtle enough,' Athelstan replied. 'You got into the chamber by jamming the first door with that stiffened parchment. Despencer innocently allowed you in through the second so that you could celebrate your birthday with them. Finally, strangely enough, it was the dead Despencer who allowed you to mysteriously disappear. You took his keys and replaced them with a ring of keys taken from elsewhere, not a difficult task in a place like Westminster. You then left, locking the door, going carefully down those steps, clutching both the keys and that wine jug. You reach the bottom, lock that door and quietly leave. Albinus and Wolfrich are not due. You make sure that is so, then you enter the cellar or crypt.' Athelstan picked up a piece of parchment and studied what he had written there.

'And so we come to the actual theft. I concede this may be pure speculation, but you must have been helped. I am sure Conteza's ruffians would find it easy enough to hide at night in the dark, dank vegetation and shrubbery to the north of Westminster. They could have easily stolen in and, when you entered the crypt, assisted you with securing that heavy bag, loading it and the empty sacks onto some wheelbarrow. You and your accomplices then wheeled that into the night, hurrying through the dark to the waiting cart. You and Conteza had formed an unholy alliance, both dependent on each other. You certainly fulfilled your part. You then retreated to your lodgings, to return all innocent the next morning to resume your usual horarium.'

'He certainly did,' Thibault rasped. 'Came all clear and collected to receive the keys. I handed them over.'

'Of course you did,' Athelstan soothed. 'And you, Master Beaumont, began your usual routine. You unlocked the first door, rang the bell three times in honour of the Trinity and began to climb those steps. You then made that dreadful mistake. So intent on reaching that treasure chamber, to ensure all was how it should be, you failed to be aware, let alone acknowledge, that Despencer had not replied. Of course, we now know the reason. And what a mistake, wasn't it?' Athelstan paused. 'The bell had been rung.

Despencer was supposed to reply. Whitby brought that to your attention. A mistake on your part which became the direct cause of Whitby's murder. Now of course *I* made a dreadful mistake. I dismissed Whitby's words as a passing remark about Despencer not replying. I don't think so. Whitby was more concerned that you had failed to acknowledge Despencer's silence, which leads to a further question. Why did you? The reasons for a lack of any reply became more than apparent when you reflect on what happened in Flambard's Tower that morning. No no.' Athelstan shook his head, pointing at Beaumont. 'You rang the bell, there was no reply, and you continued on. It was Whitby who first fastened on your mistake. Anyway, you entered the treasure chamber. Of course your comrades are shocked, frightened at what they see. You hastily use that time to ensure all was how you wanted it to be. Above, all you replace the keys on Despencer's corpse and removed the false ones.' Athelstan leaned back in his chair. 'And so all is done.'

'Listen.' Cranston, who had sat silent through most of the proceedings, abruptly lifted a hand. 'You, Beaumont, are a traitor, and if you'd had your way, you would have killed both myself and brother Athelstan.'

'I am also certain,' Thibault spoke up, 'that if Albinus and Wolfrich had posed any danger to you, Conteza's rifflers would have swiftly intervened. You are a killer, a creature of the night.'

'I am not . . .'

'Oh yes you are,' Cranston retorted. 'You informed your hellish allies that Brother Athelstan and I were skilled in the hunt for any assassin. The Bardi tried to remove us from England, well away from London, when they were plotting their crime. You know what I am talking about. They failed. You made your mistake in Flambard's Tower and you advised more drastic steps. Conteza took your message seriously. Brother Athelstan and I were nearly burnt alive in the crypt of Flambard's Tower. You failed there, but your allies crossed to Southwark to try again.' Cranston wiped the spittle from his lip. 'Whitby was another of your victims. He noticed your mistake on the staircase. He was keen-witted with a sharp curiosity. He began to probe what happened and, actually, the more he did, the deeper he would reflect. After all, Whitby was a high ranking clerk . . .'

'Sharp as a knife,' Thibault intervened. 'He died for that. Your allies silenced him.'

'Yes, your allies,' Athelstan declared. 'The Bardi, the Carbonari, or whatever name they want to take. How did it start, Beaumont? Are you Italian?'

'No, my grandmother was.'

'And she taught you the tongue?'

'Yes.'

'And Conteza made a mistake over that. Petty but telling.'

'What do you mean?'

'When we met at Westminster, we all gathered in that council chamber. You were acting the cowed clerk. Conteza shouted at you in Italian. Something like "courage, my friend". Harmless enough, after all you did business with the Bardi and with Conteza in particular, yet it also showed some form of friendship between you.'

'Do you speak Italian?' Beaumont demanded.

'Enough to understand Conteza's remark. A slip wasn't it? Ah well.' Athelstan lapsed into silence. Secretly he was surprised at Beaumont's diffident attitude. Was it time to test the reason for it?

'When?' Athelstan asked abruptly.

'When what?'

'When will Conteza move the treasure? How and where?'

Beaumont forced an icy smile.

'You find it amusing?'

'Yes, Brother Athelstan, I do. Here am I being questioned about a robbery, yet there are others in this godforsaken place who are guilty of the same.' Beaumont shrugged. 'At least in thought. Didn't you, Master Thibault . . .' Beaumont flicked his fingers at the Master of Secrets. 'Weren't you zealous in trying to discover how, where and when the Bardi would store their treasure before safely despatching it out of the kingdom? We would meet with the Bardi occasionally and, at your behest, Master Thibault, we were all under instruction to discover the answer to those questions. I suspected you were preparing to play the pirate. I told the same to Conteza. We would meet at this tavern or that alehouse around Lombard Street. We'd exchange chatter. I believed you were going to rob the treasure, Conteza agreed, and so the dance began.'

'Never mind that,' Athelstan snapped. 'My questions, where, when, how?'

'Tell us.' Thibault banged the table. 'Beaumont, you have seen men executed for treason. You will suffer the same punishment, but only after my henchmen, Albinus and Wolfrich, take out on you what they are inflicting on those two miscreants only a walk away. Once they have finished you'll be dragged on a hurdle to Tyburn,' Thibault snarled, banging the table with the flat of his hands.

'Oh the drums will beat and the pipes will play,' Beaumont retorted, 'and the Friars of the Sack will sing songs of sadness and hymns of mourning. The crowds will gather. The hot-pot girls and the pudding-pie boys will be busy. A great day for the city! I'll be half hanged, my innards torn out, my head severed, my limbs quartered. My body will become a tangle of flesh and bone. Oh yes, I will be dead,' he taunted, 'but you won't have the treasure. You have lost that and have to pay again. Or perhaps,' Beaumont laughed behind his fingers, 'maybe you won't! Maybe the Commons might impeach you, eh? Gaunt will forsake you and, if I am dragged on a hurdle to Tyburn or Smithfield, it won't be long before you follow the same path in a similar fashion. So listen well, Thibault.' Beaumont fell silent, eyes closed, lips murmuring as if he was reciting a prayer. He then opened his eyes and pointed at all three of his accusers. 'I want a letter of full pardon for any and all crimes committed, as well as licence to leave this kingdom. No hurt or injury to me and mine either here, now or in the future. I also want two hundred pounds in good sterling, a warbelt and weapons. Oh yes, I will be gone, unscathed. I want the letter drafted under your seal, Master Thibault, witnessed and guaranteed,' Beaumont languidly waved a hand at Cranston and Athelstan, 'by these two worthies. You are a liar, Thibault. You are a criminal and a felon. I wouldn't trust you as far as I could spit and that's not far.' Thibault lunged forward, his face quivering with anger. Cranston, however, swiftly intervened, and the Master of Secrets drew back.

'Enough of your insults,' Thibault grated, 'or I'll stab you here and now.'

'But then what will happen to the treasure? So stop interrupting me, Master Thibault. I want the letter, sealed and signed by you and witnessed by two men I do trust in this vale of tears, Fat Jack and his friar.'

'Come, come!' Athelstan murmured. 'Provide the information we need.'

'Did you get anything from those two unfortunates now being tortured?'

'Minions, nothing but minions,' Cranston countered. 'They know nothing, you know everything, Beaumont. Tell us now, or what befell them will certainly befall you. Come.'

Athelstan peered at the prisoner and decided to gamble on what he'd learnt from Sir Edmund Kyrie.

'This is what we've discovered so far. The treasure is being moved, probably to the east coast, where it will be picked up by the *Ludovico* at the appointed time and in the appointed place. Yes?' Athelstan watched the shift in Beaumont's eyes and realized this criminous clerk agreed with what he'd said. 'Come come,' Athelstan pressed on. 'Let us bring this nonsense to an end.'

They summoned Flaxwith and two of his bailiffs to guard the prisoner whilst Thibault led them up some steps into a small chancery chamber. The Master of Secrets dismissed the clerk working there and, assisted by Cranston, hastily cut and prepared a cream-coloured sheet of the best parchment. Thibault, a trained clerk, wrote out the letter of pardon in an elegant black, cursive script. He inscribed the letter 'to all bailiffs, beadles, etc.', asking them 'to provide assistance, without any trouble whatsoever, to Master Henry Beaumont of Colchester, who must enjoy safe journey throughout the kingdom'. Thibault wrote swiftly. He then read out the full terms of the licence, which Cranston and Athelstan witnessed under the coroner's seal, Thibault placing his next to it. They returned to the chamber. Thibault thrust the document at Beaumont, who took it over to the light to read carefully. Athelstan glanced quickly at Thibault and repressed a shiver. The Master of Secrets had that half-formed, sneering smile he assumed when plotting destruction. Athelstan truly wondered if Beaumont would ever use the licence he was studying. Once he'd finished, Beaumont glanced up. 'I want the two hundred pounds in good sterling immediately, a warbelt and weapons. Oh, and by the way, I want to clear my chamber in Aldersgate.'

'Agreed,' Thibault replied, 'except for your chamber. Sir John will arrange that. You must stay in the Tower. You will now write a letter to Conteza, informing him that you are busy, having been appointed to the Royal Mint. You are now a member of a cohort of specially chosen clerks preparing to mint fresh coins to replace those lost. You must play the part. You will be given comfortable lodgings, good food and drink and all the necessities of life. Conteza, cunning as he is, will need evidence. He'll undoubtedly have spies in the Tower, so you must play the role of the noble clerk and, more especially, be seen lounging and walking about as if you haven't a care in the world.'

'And then will you break your word? Once I have revealed all, a swift knife thrust, my corpse tossed into the river?'

'No no, Master Beaumont, we need you alive,' Athelstan declared. 'If you disappeared, Conteza would become deeply alarmed and highly suspicious. But enough of that. The treasure – where, when and how?'

'The treasure is already on its way. A woodcutter's cart, lumbering across the Essex countryside towards the coast.'

'Where?'

'Orwell, a desolate coastline—'

'I know it well,' Athelstan interrupted. 'Whereabouts?'

'The deserted priory of St Osyth, on a headland overlooking a narrow cove. The treasure has to be there by the Feast of the Chair of St Peter in five days' time. On that day at midnight, if Conteza is ready, he will light a beacon fire. From that day onwards the beacon will be lit every day at midnight until the *Ludovico* replies with its own light. Once the cog and its escort are in position, boats will be lowered.'

'And Conteza, you, your escort and the treasure will disappear into the dark. Is that what's planned?' Athelstan demanded. 'Is that what you want, Master Beaumont? Is this what they promised you? Some small farm or villa in the beautiful countryside outside Florence? A new life, comfortable and luxurious. A far cry from the freezing mists and the ice-cold winds of London. Did Conteza buy your soul piece by piece? Did he weave a tapestry of what your life would be?' Beaumont just gazed coolly back. Athelstan joined his hands as if in prayer.

'Master Beaumont, I have one question for you, a small favour. All I want is the truth.'

'What is it?' Beaumont demanded.

'Your comrade Crossley. Are you responsible in any way for his death? Were you involved in his murder?'

'No, I was not, and I can speak for the others. For God's sake, Athelstan, use your logic. We had no crossbow, and why should we kill Crossley?' Beaumont smiled slightly as if savouring a joke. 'Haven't you heard, Brother?'

'Haven't I heard what?'

'Well, as you know, I and the others have been locked in The Hanging Tree. We grew sick of it. We had to listen to the chatter, the futile gossip of greasy scullions and dirty slatterns.'

'And?' Athelstan demanded.

'You may recall, Master Thibault, that you were going to ask me and Despencer to investigate the murder of London's hangmen? Of course, that's all in the past now. Are you aware, Athelstan, how people who frequent that tavern entertain deep suspicions about who is really responsible?'

'And?' Athelstan declared. 'Forget the mummery, Beaumont. Say what you have to!'

'Well, some people allege that your parishioner, the Hangman of Rochester, that eerie grotesque, is responsible.'

Athelstan fought to keep his face and voice passive.

'And why should he be accused?'

'Think, Brother Athelstan. He is a skilled hangman, yet the Guild regard him as a newcomer. He's not really one of them. He has no claim on their treasure or on what they have lodged with Galliard the City Goldsmith. Moreover, the more hangmen who die, the more business is created for those who survive and, my dear friar, we have all got to earn a crust one way or another. The Hangman of Rochester could well be settling scores as well as culling the herd so he can be more fully admitted.'

Athelstan just shook his head in disbelief and turned away.

'You have your orders,' Thibault intervened. 'I want to be gone from here. You, Beaumont, will draft that letter to Conteza. You will add a postscript how, when the time is right, you will slip from the Tower and join them. You will assure Conteza that all is well and going to plan. Yes yes.' Thibault tapped a booted foot against the floor. 'You will write your letter, a royal courier will deliver it. You must pretend all is well then, sometime over the next few days, disappear from view.'

'Where to?'

'Why, my traitorous friend, you will accompany us to St Osyth.' Thibault beckoned at Cranston and Athelstan, who followed him out of the room, now closely guarded by Flaxwith and his bailiffs. Thibault led them into the torture chamber, where the two prisoners now sat with their backs to the wall, grinning from ear to ear as they supped from tankards of ale. Albinus and Wolfrich slouched on a bench nearby, sharing a jug. All four scrambled to their feet. Cranston stood before the prisoners, bowed mockingly, then clapped his hands.

'All hail,' he proclaimed, 'to those master masquers and mummers, the "Uffizi Brothers". You performed well.' Cranston pinched his nostrils and waved a hand in front of his face. 'Devils tits, what a smell! Master Thibault, I want these two men washed clean of the pig's blood. They are to be scrubbed, scoured, shaved and shorn so even their mothers will not recognize them. They are to be properly dressed in good costume with sound leather boots and belt. Then they can leave. My friends,' Cranston opened his purse and brought out three silver coins, 'for your troubles.' The coroner dropped the coins into their outstretched hands. 'You're getting what we agreed,' Cranston declared, 'and a little more.'

'Gentlemen.' Athelstan stepped forward. 'I give you my blessing.' He sketched a cross in the air. 'Not a word to anyone yes?'

The Uffizi nodded in unison. 'What was all that about?' one of them declared. Athelstan stepped closer and stared into the man's laughing eyes.

'You love life, don't you?' the friar demanded.

'Brother, life, good red wine and a soft plump lady.'

'Of course,' Athelstan breathed. 'So not a word to anyone, or the Lord High Coroner here will swoop like the hawk he is and hold you fast in his talons.'

'Is this about the robbery at Westminster?' one of the Uffizi asked, wiping the blood from his face on the back of his hands.

'Yes it is,' Cranston declared. 'And what do you know about that?'

'We don't know anything, Sir John, though we've heard the Carbonari are active and have played a part in that mischief.' The man shrugged and made a face. 'Just chatter, my Lord High Coroner. Gossip amongst the Italian community – to be honest, they are laughing behind their hands.'

'I am sure they are,' Cranston retorted. 'However, we have a phrase in England "whoever laughs last, laughs loudest". Now, my friends, silence and all will be well.'

Cranston and Athelstan followed Master Thibault out of the torture chamber. As they left the White Tower, the freezing daylight was beginning to fade. The people of the garrison were now busy preparing for nightfall. Somewhere a drum beat, trumpets shrilled and horses neighed. The air was thick with all kinds of odours, some sweet, some sour. A gibbet, black and stark against the icy blue sky, was being relieved of its gruesome burdens. The corpses of malefactors were being cut down and tossed into the waiting cart to be taken to some city burial pit. The gruesome sight provoked memories of The Hanging Tree. Athelstan was tempted to go there but realized he had to complete the business in hand.

Thibault did not dally, but took them across into the cold darkness of St Peter ad Vincula, the Tower chapel, a barn-like building with its raftered roof and crude wooden furniture. They gathered around a blazing brazier, hands spread out towards the glowing heat.

'We are here in the sight God and Man,' Thibault began sardonically. 'To plot and prepare. We now know that Conteza, God damn him, holds the treasure . . .'

'Which is rightfully his!' Athelstan broke in.

'Yes, but wrongfully taken, Brother.'

'True,' Athelstan conceded.

'So what do we have?' Cranston demanded. 'The Uffizi Brothers have played their part and will be gone soon enough. Beaumont now understands the threats facing him; he will write his letter then be detained here. Conteza's henchman Genaro is undoubtedly moving the treasure towards Orwell. He will do so in some battered cart, he and his confederates disguised as poor woodmen. I strongly suspect Conteza will join them for the last few miles before Orwell. The *Ludovico* and its escort must be preparing to leave Queenhithe. They will slip from the Thames then turn north, hugging the Essex coast. More than that I cannot say.'

'So what do you intend?' Athelstan turned to Thibault.

'What do I intend? Why, Brother, that we work to settle matters with Signor Conteza.'

'Which means?'

Thibault grinned. 'Wait and see.'

'Are we needed for this?'

'Yes, my Lord Coroner, we certainly are.' Athelstan answered tersely. 'I think Beaumont would demand that. He will insist that we, his guarantors, are present.'

'I agree,' Thibault snapped. 'And it's time we moved. We shall leave the Tower at first light the day after tomorrow. In the meantime, I will immediately despatch Albinus, Wolfrich and a comitatus of mounted Tower archers to seize Osyth Priory, fortify it, then wait and watch. We shall join them there.' Thibault drew a deep breath. 'Sir John, Brother Athelstan, I am grateful, very grateful, for what you have done, but it is not yet finished. We have thrown the dice; let us find out how they lie. Prepare yourself for a swift, hard ride.'

Thibault's words proved prophetic. They left the Tower just after dawn on the planned day. Six Tower archers accompanied Athelstan, Cranston, Thibault and Beaumont. The Master of Secrets had insisted that their mounts be the best, sturdy garrons, well harnessed and properly shoed. Athelstan had returned swiftly to Southwark, left instructions with Benedicta over the house, church and God's Acre. The parish appeared surprisingly quiet, and Athelstan fervently prayed that it would remain so. He was determined to be present at the impending confrontation with Conteza, and resigned himself to a hard, long ride. Cranston teased him about this but the coroner soon apologized when Athelstan demonstrated that his own season of campaigning in France had improved his riding skills. Athelstan ruefully conceded he needed these.

Thibault proved to be a hard taskmaster. They left the Tower, moving along to Mile End, past Bow Church before turning east, following the roads which skirted the great Forest of Epping. Thibault loudly wondered if they might encounter Conteza's band also moving east. Cranston, however, put him right. The coroner explained how there was a wide choice of trackways as there were carts and labourers moving between the different hamlets. They paused to rest at a lonely tavern in Woodeforde, The Traveller's Friend, then continued on, deep into the Essex countryside.

The weather was ideal for their journey; harsh and cold but no biting wind, whilst the trackway remained hard and solid. Athelstan tried to pray as the horsemen thundered around him, but gave up except for the occasional, whispered invocation. He became aware of the change in the countryside, bleak and foreboding, a land of black-garbed copses, clumps of trees and wild gorse. They pounded through the occasional hamlet or village, lonely places, and eventually caught the salty tang of the sea creeping like a shadow over the heathland. The countryside grew even more desolate. Open fields, ancient twisted trees, strange stone plinths, the crumbling relics of some long-lost cult. They galloped on; conversation was fragmentary. Cranston and Athelstan grew tired, wary of Thibault and even more so of Beaumont, whose life now depended on what would happen when they reached the coast.

Early on the morning of the third day after leaving the Tower, they breasted a hill, the land falling away beneath them, before sweeping up to a promontory and the brooding ancient building of St Osyth's Priory. Beyond this, the sea glinted in the early morning light, surging strongly towards the land as a tide swept in. A truly lonely place. The home of sea birds wheeling noisily above them. They gathered the reins of the horses and made their way carefully down, then up to the main gate of the Priory. This swung open after one of their archers gave a noisy blast on his hunting horn, promptly answered from the priory. Athelstan sighed with relief as he glimpsed figures moving along the parapet of the priory's crenellated wall.

Thibault led them in to be greeted noisily by Albinus, Wolfrich and their comitatus. The riders quickly dismounted, moaning about the pain in their back and legs, Cranston loudly declaring he needed a hot meal, some strong wine and a good night's sleep. Athelstan echoed such comments. Thankfully Albinus and his comitatus had established themselves. They had fired ovens, braziers, as well as the well-stocked fire hearth in the refectory. At least two of the comitatus were skilled cooks. Athelstan immediately noticed the supply carts crammed to the brim, half pushed into an outhouse, and he wondered why Thibault needed so much provender.

Whilst the food was being prepared, Cranston and Athelstan walked around the priory, but not before Cranston had whispered to Thibault to keep Beaumont under close and constant guard. The Master of Secrets promised this would certainly be done, the criminous clerk being closely confined in the sacristy of the bleak priory chapel. As he walked, Athelstan quietly prayed that the business plotted here would soon be done and they could return to London.

St Osyth was an eerie, even sinister, dwelling, despite it being a former house of prayer. The priory building still stood intact; very little of its stone or woodwork had been removed. Athelstan had found the same elsewhere in the kingdom. The Great Plague or Pestilence had swept in some thirty years earlier and harvested a host of souls. Buildings such as St Osyth were abandoned and left forsaken. Local peasants feared going anywhere near such sacred yet ghostly places. They became shells of their former life, shadows of what had been. St Osyth was certainly one of these, especially on a bleak January afternoon, with a sea mist curling in to break into wisps, as if a multitude of disembodied spirits gathered for conclave. Thibault only deepened Athelstan's unease; he said as much to Cranston who fully agreed. The Master of Secrets truly deserved his title here at St Osyth. Gaunt's henchman became strangely silent and watchful: a sinister presence locked in his own dark thoughts. Thibault held whispered conversations with his two retainers, placing a close guard around the church where Beaumont was being kept. It also seemed as if the church was being used to house many of the supplies brought in by the carts. In the end, Athelstan and Cranston had no choice but to watch and wait.

At last, on the afternoon of the day following their arrival at St Osyth, an excited, keen-eyed archer, who had been placed on watch, breathlessly hurried down from the top of the church tower. Wiping the sweat from his face, the young archer reported he was certain he had glimpsed a massive war cog far out at sea.

'I am sure,' he said in a singsong voice, 'I glimpsed its lights high on the stern and prow. I believe it has escorts though I couldn't see much of them.'

'It must be the *Ludovico*,' Thibault declared. 'I wonder where Conteza is, eh?' He smiled wolfishly at Cranston and Athelstan. 'So now we must wait for our false friend to join this deadly banquet, yes?'

Thibault's question was answered the following day. Just as dusk deepened around the priory, an archer, sent back along the trackway to watch, hurried in to report there was a heavy supply cart, pulled by powerful dray horses, approaching St Osyth's.

'Three men on the cart,' he declared. 'With a mounted escort. Master Thibault, it must be coming here.'

The Master of Secrets agreed. He ordered all lights to be

immediately doused, the gate left half open. Thibault and his comitatus hid in the shadows overlooking the stable yard. Cranston and Athelstan took up position in an outhouse where, once inside, they stood by a window which had clear sight of the darkening yard.

'Where is Beaumont?' Athelstan whispered. 'He was locked in the sacristy. Does Thibault intend to produce him? Sir John, I have a premonition something terrible is going to happen. This is no longer a house of God, it's more like a gate to Hell.'

'I agree, Brother, but we are committed. There is nothing we can do but bend before the coming storm. I believe,' the coroner continued, 'this truly is a struggle to the death. I suspect what Thibault is planning. Don't forget our Master of Secrets is fighting for his very life. If he returns to London unsuccessful, he will be arrested by a writ from the Commons within the week. He intends confrontation,' the coroner squeezed Athelstan by the wrist, 'but enough said, here they are.'

They fell silent as the main gate to the priory was flung open. A man entered, carrying a torch, followed by a heavy, high-sided cart. Two men were on its seat, with another standing in the cart, whilst a fourth guided the powerful dray horses. Outriders followed. One of these dismounted, pulling back his hood as he shouted orders in Italian. He then moved into the pool of light thrown by the torchbearer.

'Conteza!' Athelstan whispered.

'Now!' Thibault's shout echoed across the yard. Immediately Tower archers emerged from the shadows, bows strung, arrows notched. Conteza and his retinue could only turn and stare. Albinus and Wolfrich lit cressets and tossed them onto the cobbled yard so the cart and its escort became clearer against the dark. Thibault emerged into the light, flanked either side by bowmen.

'Signor Conteza. So good to see you, and I am sure,' Thibault pointed to the cart, 'you have the plunder stolen from the King's own treasure chamber.'

'Master Thibault, we have simply regained what is rightfully ours. This treasure is now our treasure, lawful repayment by your King of the loans granted by my masters.' Conteza paused and spread his hands. 'We found the treasure,' he mocked. 'It's wonderful what you can achieve, Master Thibault, if you have the energy and commitment. Bearing in mind what has happened, I decided not to inform anyone of how we resolved this matter or, indeed, that we had. After all, the treasure was stolen once, why can't it happen again? I believe it is crucially important to get this treasure on board the *Ludovico* for its journey back to its rightful owners.'

'Why didn't you inform us?'

'Sir John, as I have already said, it is our gold. The English Crown lost it and we have found it!' Conteza drew off his gauntlets, throwing his cloak over his shoulder so Thibault could see the warbelt and sheathed blades. 'Master Thibault, you have questions for us? I certainly have for you. How did you discover all this? Master Beaumont, I presume?' Conteza grinned. 'Such is life. Where is our clerk?'

'Oh, he's resting and you shall be with him shortly.' Despite Thibault's soft tone, Athelstan repressed a shiver. 'Signor Conteza,' the Master of Secrets continued, 'you must have ridden hard and far, you want refreshments? Some wine, a platter of hot food?'

'Master Thibault, No.' The *Ludovico* is undoubtedly closing fast and we wish to be gone. Your countryside,' Conteza declared, 'even at the best of times, is hardly congenial. In the depths of winter, it is truly ghastly. So, I must prepare the beacon light and be gone.'

'Not yet, signor.' Thibault's words hung like a noose in the air. Conteza immediately stepped back, hand going for his sword, as his retinue gathered closer.

'Not yet, Master Thibault, not yet? What does that mean?'

'It means nothing, signor. You have your treasure, yes? The English Crown's repayment of certain loans?'

'Long overdue,' Conteza interjected.

'Never mind that, signor. All I want from you is a receipt. You have your gold; the English Crown has repaid its debts. It has been handed over. A receipt is demanded.'

Conteza laughed and the tension visibly eased.

'Signor,' Thibault pressed on. 'Remember I have to answer to my master, not to mention the Lords and Commons. You must have heard the rumours rife in London?'

'Yes, I certainly have,' Conteza conceded. 'Chatter, gossip about an indictment, the possible impeachment of your good self.'

'Precisely, my friend. I need to go back to London with proof. Now,' Thibault waved towards the church, 'leave two of your men here then follow me. I have set up a small chancery in the sacristy. We really should hurry. I suspect you are right, signor; the *Ludovico* could well be lowering its boats within the hour.'

'You've certainly been well informed,' Conteza retorted.

'Master Beaumont was most knowledgeable, signor, but come, sign that you have the treasure, then we can all be gone.'

The Lombard agreed. He left two of his retinue guarding the cart and, accompanied by the rest of his cohort, followed Thibault across the yard, through a side door into the dank, dark nave of the priory church. A few cressets flared against the freezing, inky darkness. Athelstan tried to remain calm. Cranston had fallen strangely silent. Athelstan wondered what was to happen. He truly believed they were now spectators to a confrontation, which, despite all the diplomatic niceties, would end in blood.

Athelstan glanced quickly at the grim-faced coroner and realized that Cranston probably felt the same, yet there was little either of them could do to escape the gathering storm. They climbed the sanctuary steps, turning left into the sacristy, a large square-like room with a long trestle table running down the centre. This had been cleared and transformed into a chancery desk. Candles flamed in their spigots to illuminate the large rectangle of parchment held down by small weights at each corner. Next to this were inkpots, a tray of quill pens, pumice stones, sealing wax and a sander. Thibault immediately stretched across the table and pulled the manuscript closer, giving Athelstan a good view of it.

The document was an Indenture, drawn up in the Exchequer at Westminster. It listed the monies handed over in full quitclaim of the debts the English Crown owed to the Bardi. Conteza, with his minions milling around him, scrutinized both the top part of the Indenture then the bottom half, which accurately copied what was written above. Conteza, stubby fingers tracing the words, read the remittance aloud, as did his henchman Genaro. Athelstan stared quickly around. He wondered where Beaumont was. He sensed Thibault's wariness.

Albinus abruptly left the sacristy, leaving Wolfrich sitting on a long chest at the far end beneath the window. Archers clustered near the doorway. Cranston made to leave, saying he needed fresh air, but Thibault asked both him and Athelstan to remain and sign the Indenture as the Crown's witnesses. Cranston shrugged and sat down on a chair at the end of the table, Athelstan beside him.

'The storm is brewing fast,' Athelstan whispered. 'But God knows, Sir John, how and when it will break.'

Conteza, however, seemed happy enough. He finished his scrutiny then signed and sealed both copies of the Indenture. Thibault did the same, Athelstan and Genaro signing as witnesses. Athelstan noticed that the document was dated two days earlier and proclaimed that it had been drawn up at Westminster, an obvious lie, but Conteza did not seem to care. He had the treasure, whilst the *Ludovico* was closing fast.

'We are done here.' Thibault gestured towards the door. 'My Lord Coroner, Brother Athelstan, if you could help Albinus and the archers build a pyre for our guest. Signor Conteza, if you could please wait here with your retainers and I shall bring Beaumont to you. Brother Athelstan,' Thibault gestured at the expensive cloth he had laid out over the makeshift chancery table, 'if you could fold that cloth and put it back in the chest.' He pointed to the one Wolfrich had been sitting on before he hurried out searching for Albinus. Athelstan hid his surprise at being asked so bluntly. He picked up the cloth, walked to the chest, opened it, and then stared down in horror at the dead, contorted face of Magister Henry Beaumont of Colchester. The clerk had been cruelly garrotted, the cord biting deep into the soft flesh of his throat, eyes popping out at the shock of death, mouth open, the swollen tongue thrust out.

Athelstan glanced over his shoulder. Thibault and Conteza were now cutting the Indenture in two with a chancery knife. Athelstan threw the cloth in and closed the lid. He walked back to Thibault, who was now rolling up his copy of the Indenture as he thanked Conteza for the banker's cooperation. The Master of Secrets then repeated his request that Conteza wait in the sacristy until he brought Beaumont, before ushering Athelstan out of the room. Once outside, Thibault silently pulled the door closed, gently turned the key and, holding a finger to his lips as a sign for silence, lowered the bar into the iron clasps.

'What are you . . .?'

'Never mind, Brother, come come.' Tugging Athelstan by the sleeve, Thibault hurried across the sanctuary, down the steps and out of the church. The cart and horses were being moved through the main gate of the priory. Cranston was having words with Wolfrich, pointing down at the two corpses of the men Conteza had left on guard.

'What is happening, Thibault?' Cranston rasped.

'Hush, my Lord Coroner, in a while, in a while! In the meantime, Wolfrich take these corpses back into the church, lay them down close to the sacristy door. Hurry now, and I mean hurry!'

Wolfrich, snapping his fingers at the Tower archers, had the corpses lifted and carried into the church.

'Come, come. Sir John, Brother Athelstan,' Thibault urged. 'Come, it might not be safe to linger.' He hurried them through the priory gate. Wolfrich and his archers returned. Athelstan glanced at Sir John standing next to him.

'I think,' the coroner whispered hoarsely, 'I know how the tempest is going to break. Ah and here he is; our storm-bringer.'

Albinus, a dark, darting shadow, except for his snow-white hair floating around him, came hurrying through the gate.

'Master Thibault,' he gasped, 'all is done. The fuse is lit.'

Athelstan glanced back at the church, holding a hand up to still Sir John's questions. The archers milled around them. They too now realized what was intended. A night bird shrieked piercingly. Athelstan startled, then froze. A sheet of flame abruptly surged up, illuminating the narrow windows in the church tower. This was followed by a deep rolling thunder and a bursting second sheet of fire, which seemed to lift the church slightly off the ground before it fell back in a torrent of crackling wood and tumbling masonry. Another explosion, like the blast of a trumpet, shook the ground, and the priory church just disappeared with a hideous crack and a surging pall of the deepest grey smoke, which rolled towards the priory gate. Coughing and spitting, Thibault and his cohort fell back; only Athelstan stayed, head down, eyes closed. He stood murmuring the verses of the death psalm until Cranston grasped him firmly by the arm and led him back to where Thibault sheltered behind the treasure cart.

'You are shocked, Brother Athelstan?' the Master of Secrets mocked.

'Of course, that was callous murder.'

'No it wasn't.' Thibault stepped closer. 'No it wasn't, was it, Sir John? I too carry a commission of Oyer et Terminer. I am a royal justiciar. Conteza was our enemy. He is not a subject of our King. He has no loyalty to the Crown. He is an alien, a foreigner. He in fact conspired against the Crown. He violated the royal and sacred precincts of Westminster. He robbed the King's treasure and was responsible for the slaughter of five innocent royal clerks. He arranged the murder of another at The Hanging Tree. He attacked and tried to do the same to Sir John, a royal official, not to mention yourself both at Westminster and in Southwark. My indictment could go on.' Thibault paused as another part of the priory church collapsed in a roar of falling masonry and ancient timbers. 'Finally,' Thibault turned, 'remember Brother Athelstan: the lost treasure could have led to me being impeached as a traitor with a Bill of Attainder being passed against me. Now I am hero of the hour.'

'What about the *Ludovico*?' Athelstan asked. 'Does it pose a threat?'

'I doubt it,' Cranston retorted. 'Its master may think these flames, this smoke, is a beacon light and land some of his crew to investigate. But what's the use? All they will find is total destruction. Moreover, they have no right to be here. They have no horses, and whatever supplies they need they'll have to buy. It wouldn't take long, desolate though this place may be, for the sheriff to be summoned. I doubt very much if the Bardi want that.'

'There's little they can do,' Thibault agreed. 'Oh, I am sure the Bardi will complain and protest. Nevertheless, I have the treasure and, above all, I have that Indenture which proclaims for the world to see that the English Crown repaid its debts and the Bardi have acknowledged that.' Thibault gestured back at the priory church where the flames still raged. 'Oh I agree, I am responsible. Albinus prepared that, my judgement on the Bardi! Of course they'll question, they may even point the finger,' Thibault grinned, 'but I have an answer. I'll tell them to hunt the Carbonari. Now you and I know that the Carbonari were led by Conteza, but they loosed that threat at us and we have sent it hurtling back.' He shook his head, that beatific smile on his face as he tapped Athelstan on the chest. 'So Brother,' the Master of Secrets whispered, 'the devil does look after his own.'

'So it would seem, Master Thibault, so it would seem.'

PART EIGHT

'Flee avance, flee!'

Deep in the taproom of the ancient Mitre tavern, which stood under the shadow of the great Abbey and Palace of Westminster, the two royal clerks, Bloxhall and Calpurne, sat hunched over a bowl of roasted pike, sliced and mixed with spiced vegetables. They had pocketed the dice they had rolled, both clerks revelling in their new-found freedom. As they kept reminding themselves, it was only about ten days ago that a royal serjeant had arrived at The Hanging Tree with writs signed and sealed by Master Thibault. These letters declared that the three royal clerks, Beaumont, Bloxhall and Calpurne were now free to leave, though Master Henry Beaumont of Colchester, was to hasten to the Tower where urgent business required his attention.

'Do you think Beaumont will return?' Bloxhall popped a piece of fish into his mouth. 'Do you think he will? He always seemed distant from us, didn't he? Quiet, as if he was watching something we couldn't see. Well, Beaumont went off to the Tower. He seemed startled about that and wondered if all was well. Anyway,' Bloxhall mumbled, his mouth full, 'he was glimpsed strutting like a peacock around the fortress. So, my friend,' Bloxhall stretched over and patted Calpurne on the shoulder, 'what shall we do? Here we are in The Mitre where we have our chambers. We've rested and eaten well. So far we have not been summoned back to the chancery, though I am sure we will be.'

'I'm tired of taverns,' Calpurne retorted. 'I truly am. I don't think I'll ever forget poor Whitby's death, so swift, so callous, so cruel. Oh yes, I am tired of all this. I think we have every right to request leave of absence from our duties. Perhaps we should take the Pilgrim Road to Canterbury? Or, when the weather breaks, we could go south to Glastonbury? I would love to visit the Holy Thorn and see where Arthur and Guinevere lie buried.'

'Strange, isn't it?' Bloxhall mused, lost in his own thoughts. 'We were lodged, or at least put under house arrest, and made to stay at The Hanging Tree; now that's the Guildhall for the Hangmen of London, members of which have been murdered. Apparently Beaumont was going to investigate those killings. And you've heard the rumours?'

'What?' Calpurne demanded testily.

'About who the killer could be. On a number of occasions I listened to tavern chatter, just gossip, slipping from prattling mouths: how that macabre character, the Hangman of Rochester, might be the perpetrator.'

'That's possible,' Calpurne agreed. 'And wasn't it strange that he was in the taproom when Whitby was executed? And, do you know something, Adrian, I wonder if he was responsible for Crossley's death. Rumour has it that Crossley was trying to escape from The Hanging Tree. Nevertheless, I still can't understand why someone such as the Hangman should murder him for that.'

'Neither can I,' Bloxhall retorted. 'But that's what the gossips say.'

'Oh by the way, what were you doing sitting at the chancery desk in our chamber?'

'I am trying to earn the good graces of Brother Athelstan and Sir John,' Bloxhall replied. 'I've done what any good and loyal subject of the Crown should. Look we were prisoners in that tavern but perhaps it wasn't a complete waste of our hours. To cut to the quick. I have informed Brother Athelstan about the rumours regarding his parishioner the Hangman of Rochester.'

'Was that wise?'

'Yes Ralph, we may well go on pilgrimage either here or across the Narrow Seas but, at the moment, I feel tainted. Ralph, no less than seven of our comrades have been slaughtered. Despencer and his cohort, Whitby and Crossley. Master Beaumont doesn't seem to give a fig about anyone but himself. As I said, I am trying to earn the good favour of our masters, but,' he clambered to his feet, 'in the meantime I need the jakes.'

Bloxhall, who had drunk deep on strong tavern ale, lurched across the taproom and out into the yard. For a while Calpurne just played with the dice, casting them on the table time and again.

He glanced at the hour candle. 'Where are you, Bloxhall?' he murmured. 'Oh don't say you've fallen asleep on the jakes.'

Calpurne got to his feet, throwing his cloak about him. He crossed the taproom, nodding at the buttery maid, and went out into the yard. It was so cold, a hoar frost was already forming. Calpurne took a torch from its sconce and walked across the yard to the line of narrow jakes closets. Most of the doors hung open except for the one in the centre. 'Bloxhall,' he whispered, 'I'd wager you are there.' He went across, lifted the latch and pulled the door back. He stared in horror. Bloxhall was on the jakes seat, his head thrown back, the garrotte cord around his throat so tight and fast, his eyes were popping, swollen tongue poking out between blood-chapped lips.

Calpurne dropped the torch and backed out of the jakes closet. He meant to turn but the garrotte cord slipped easily over his head and around his throat, his assailant pulling fast. Calpurne didn't even have time to murmur a prayer. He flailed his hands, fought for breath and died choking on his own spittle. The two assassins who had waited for the clerks simply dragged the corpses out through a narrow gate to a cart standing in the alley beyond. They were lifted up and tossed in as if they were sacks of rubbish. A canvas sheet was pulled across and both assassins climbed onto the cart, one of them grabbing the reins and gently urging the dray horses forward.

Cranston and Athelstan, standing either side of the broad mortuary table, stared down at the two corpses sprawled there, soaked in blood and river water.

'I thought I should summon you,' the Fisher of Men declared, 'as soon as the corpses were brought here to the Chapel of the Drowned Men.'

'You did well, you did well,' Cranston reassured him. 'In God's name what happened? Two corpses, each with their head severed. Any sign of either.'

The Fisher shook his head.

'So you dragged both cadavers from the river last night: their clothes are filthy and stained, what made you think we would be interested?'

'Because of this,' the Fisher of Men replied. He went across and picked up a tray from the nearby table. 'I found these in the wallets which kept them fairly dry, bills from The Mitre tavern in Westminster. One was issued under the name Adrian Bloxhall, the other to Master Henry Beaumont.'

'Impossible,' Cranston declared.

'Sir John, what do you mean?'

'Let me assure you, my friend,' the coroner patted the Fisher on the shoulder, 'Master Beaumont does not lie in a watery grave but in a more sombre one out in the wilds of Essex.' The coroner gestured at Athelstan. 'True Brother?'

The friar nodded and blessed both corpses. He inspected the bills and once again murmured a prayer against the hideous evil responsible for these savage murders. Athelstan pulled up his cowl and walked to stand before the stark crucifix nailed to the end wall of the Chapel of the Drowned Man. Cranston let him go. He recognized the signs; his little friar friend was about to become absorbed in his own meditations. Instead, the coroner beckoned the Fisher of Men across to learn more about his gruesome discovery.

Athelstan, fingering his ave beads, reflected on what had happened since they had left St Osyth four days ago. Time was turbulent. Events rushing into each other. He and Cranston had returned as swiftly as possible from Orwell. They left Thibault, as Sir John declared, 'immersed in his malicious machinations'. The Master of Secrets moved just as swiftly. He entered the city and summoned up, as a huntsman would his dogs, the riffler chiefs, the gang leaders and those who control the street heralds; the sower of the seeds of gossip and chatter. Master Thibault's minions were given one juicy morsel to play with. They were to proclaim from one end of the City to the next how Master Thibault had found the treasure. How he had handed it over to the Bardi and how Master Thibault had documentation proving this.

More good news followed. Master Thibault now controlled the Exchequer, promising that all the Crown's debts would be paid, that they would disappear like smoke in the wind or wax before the fire. On his return to the Guildhall, Sir John had discovered the same. All the great and good of London were now a choir singing of the Master of Secret's prowess; the Commons had openly declared themselves delighted, all chatter about impeachment faded. Indeed, there were rumours that Master Thibault might be given one honour after another. Festivities and banquets were being arranged at both Westminster and the Guildhall and, of course, the guest of honour would be Master Thibault, henchman of my Lord of Gaunt. Even in Athelstan's own parish where everything else was peaceful, the likes of Watkins and Pike had seized on the good news, as indeed they would do anything to celebrate and rejoice in The Piebald. At the same time, however, Thibault was also busy exerting his authority, summoning people to task and enforcing decisions. Both Cranston and Athelstan had received curt messages demanding that the mystery surrounding the murder of London's hangmen be resolved.

'Well it's going to be . . .' Athelstan whispered to himself. He walked back to scrutinize the corpses, almost oblivious to Cranston and the Fisher of Men talking in hushed tones. The friar leaned down and studied the bruised, bloody, jagged necks. He tried to impose order, a logical sequence of events and, as he did so, talked quickly to himself.

'Brother Athelstan, Brother Athelstan.' The friar peered up at Sir John, who was gently shaking him by the shoulder. 'Brother Athelstan, the hangman has arrived.'

'Oh yes, yes of course. Please ask him to join us, Sir John.'

The coroner did so and the hangman strode in; he immediately knelt before Athelstan.

'Father,' he murmured, 'your blessing.'

'Gladly my friend.' Athelstan blessed the hangman who then got up, his light blue eyes watchful.

'I have been away, Father. I was visiting the grave of my wife and children in that little churchyard outside Rochester on the Canterbury Road.'

'Of course.'

'Father, I came back this morning, just after you'd left to join Sir John. Benedicta said you wanted to see me, that it was urgent?'

Athelstan opened his wallet and handed over the letter Bloxhall had sent him, Benedicta had held this until Athelstan's return to St Erconwald's. The hangman opened it and read the message, lips soundlessly moving as he spelled out the words. The hangman then thrust it back into the friar's hands.

'Lies,' he declared. 'Lies, all lies and, by the way, I have heard the same. I have just visited my wife's grave, wept tears over her and my children, that's my true home. I know who I am, Father, I am a stranger here.'

'Not to me.'

'Thank you, Father, I just wish others would share your charity. I look eerie, I act strangely. I once heard you give a homily, Father, on the scapegoat, and I thought of myself. Well of course, I do understand it. I was in the taproom of The Hanging Tree when Bloxham's comrade Whitby was slain. People asked if that was a coincidence? Such gossip is only fanned by jealously from the Guild. Sir John, you know how the sheriffs wish to hire me as opposed to others.' The Hangman smiled. 'People might even say how it is strange that I have never been attacked.'

'They could say the same of others.'

'True, Brother Athelstan, I would also add that I very rarely visit The Hanging Tree. I have little, if anything, to do with the other hangmen.'

'So why do you think Bloxhall wrote that?' Cranston asked.

'Sir John, there's gossip in the taproom of The Hanging Tree as there is in every tavern and alehouse across London. Gossip, gossip, gossip! It thrives like weeds in a field. I am a hangman, a most skilled one. What Bloxhall says simply reflects some people's nasty tongues. Look at Bloxhall, trying to mitigate the disgrace he and his comrades suffered after the great robbery.' The hangman cleared his throat. 'But above all, they do not understand, they do not realize . . .'

'What?'

'Brother Athelstan, I am a hangman. I execute felons mercilessly and swiftly.'

'I would certainly agree with that.'

'Thank you, my Lord Coroner. What you do not know is I cannot stab another human being.' He shook his head. 'Hanging is simple. You thrust the hood on, you push the condemned up the ladder, down I come. I twist the ladder and the condemned man or woman falls like a stone and their neck is snapped as easily as you would a twig. However, that is very different from using the knife. To hold someone close, as you would a lover, only to cut the very life breath out of them. No, no,' the hangman waved a gauntleted hand, 'Brother Athelstan, Sir John, for many reasons, you must believe my innocence in those murders. I have simply informed you of one more.'

'Oh we do, we do.' Athelstan leaned over and squeezed the hangman's wrist. '*Pax et bonum*, my friend. I know your soul. I just wanted to hear your response. No, that's not the full truth. We are also going to need your services. Now my friends,' Athelstan pointed to the Hangman and Fisher of Men, 'what I am going to say is part of a story, a deadly tale. I am talking *sub rosa*, so what I say is highly confidential.' Athelstan cleared his throat and pointed at the corpses. 'One is Adrian Bloxhall, the other is Ralph Calpurne, both royal clerks, both caught up in the dire events following the great robbery at Westminster. They were released along with Beaumont, the real sinner. Beaumont was invited to the Tower where he was trapped into compliance with us. Now I call Beaumont a real sinner and he was. A killer to his very marrow. He was determined, absolutely determined, to flee this kingdom and create a new life in the sun-drenched valleys of Northern Italy. God knows when this rottenness appeared, what truly motivated him. However, let me make it very clear: Beaumont's involvement was crucial to Conteza's plot. If Beaumont had not cooperated, I doubt very much that the robbery would have even been planned. Now Beaumont demanded a high price.'

Athelstan paused to sip from the beaker of water that the Fisher of Men thrust into his hand. 'I'm sure some of the treasure would have been given to him in order for him to resurrect a new life hundreds of miles away from here. Beaumont used the Carbonari to deal with any threat, either to himself or the robbery. However, he demanded more. He wanted people to think that he had died. So, part of his cooperation with Conteza was that when he and the others were released, they should make it look as if Beaumont had been murdered, along with Bloxhall and Calpurne: seized, beheaded, their remains flung into the Thames.' Athelstan leaned down and touched one of the corpses. 'Master Thibault released three men, Beaumont was seized as soon as he entered the Tower, Calpurne and Bloxhall were allowed back to their lodgings and their old way of life. Now remember, Conteza did not realize Beaumont had been seized until he reached St Osyth. Of course, by then it was too late to change arrangements. Indeed, it was too late for anything. Conteza had promised Beaumont that the two remaining clerks, Calpurne and Bloxham, would be murdered, but evidence would be left on one of the corpses to suggest that it was the cadaver of Master Henry Beaumont.'

'Which explains, does it not,' Cranston intervened, 'why their heads were removed. I am sure they were tossed into a weighted sack and now lie rotting at the bottom of the Thames.'

'I agree,' the Fisher intervened. 'Because the heads were removed, we would label each cadaver according to the information found on them.'

'And what about Calpurne?' the hangman demanded.

'Oh, I am sure people would think he had been murdered as well. After all, some corpses are never found. To all intents and purposes,' Athelstan continued, 'Henry Beaumont of Colchester simply ceased to exist. Unbeknown to anyone, he would board the *Ludovico* and sail south to his new life of wealth and ease.' Athelstan smiled thinly. 'On one matter, my good teacher Brother Ignacio was wrong – perhaps matters have changed over the years. The Carbonari will kill and kill again to protect their interests and further their plans. They sent two of their men to Galliard with those coins proclaiming that the treasure must be somewhere in London. They whetted the appetite of the riffler captains and gave false information about Genova and his cog the *Serafino*, who paid a most terrible price. The Carbonari didn't care; the chaos and confusion only deepened. Oh yes, they are Murder's own sons.'

'Do you think,' Cranston asked, 'that Conteza will let Beaumont live?'

'Oh Sir John, I agree thieves turn on each other, but there's every possibility that Beaumont would be allowed to profit from his wickedness. Bloxhall and Calpurne are dead. Beaumont would also want that for another reason. You see, Whitby, and I am sure Crossley, began to think, to reflect and to remember. Sir John and I reached certain conclusions – maybe those remaining clerks might, in the months – even years – ahead, reflect and recall things. They might emerge as a real threat to Beaumont and Conteza, so their murder was a logical conclusion to the benefit of men who would kill for their own profit.' Athelstan fell silent. He was tired, weary.

Cranston opened his wallet and shook two coins out onto the table.

'My friend,' he pointed to the Fisher of Men, 'give these two unfortunates honourable burial. Arrange for some priest to sing the requiem. Brother Athelstan, are we finished here?'

'I think we are, Sir John, and I will pray for all the dead, nine clerks; nine royal clerks, slaughtered. I am sure in the months ahead, Master Thibault will make his displeasure known to the Bardi. However, we have more pressing business. My friend,' Athelstan plucked at the hangman's jerkin, 'we need your presence, perhaps your skill.'

'Brother for where, for what?'

'The Hanging Tree. It's time other demons were brought to judgement.'

Athelstan reflected on these words hours later as, sitting beside Cranston, he stared at the two individuals the coroner had summoned to this summary Court of Oyer et Terminer in the taproom of The Hanging Tree. Both Mine Host and his wife Isabella looked highly nervous. The tavern had been closed, the taproom emptied except for Cranston, Athelstan, the accused and Master Flaxwith with three of his bailiffs.

'This is a lawful inquisition into an unlawful killing,' Cranston began. 'In your case,' the coroner thundered, 'more than one such killing.'

'Sir John, Brother Athelstan, we have just been summoned. Tiptoft served the writ immediately after the Angelus. We have had no time to prepare our defence.'

'Do you need a defence?' Athelstan countered. 'This is only an inquisition. If you are innocent you could be back to serving ale by Vespers.'

'And who brings the indictment?'

'I do,' Athelstan retorted. 'And I admit this indictment has not yet been proved but if it is, you must know that you are subject to summary judgement. So.' Athelstan picked up a sheet of parchment. 'You, Isabella Penon, were the sole and only child of your parents, who owned The Hanging Tree tavern. Yes?'

'Yes.'

'You married Columba, son of Clement the Key-Master?'

'Yes I did.'

'Now Clement the Key-Master fell from grace in a most spectacular manner. He had fashioned four unique locks with special keys for the royal treasury at Westminster. Clement, a royal appointment, had promised, even sworn, that all documentation and anything else used in the fashioning of those keys and locks would be destroyed. Clement, for God knows what reason, did not do this. I suspect he simply forgot. He was careless. Other people were not, and somebody informed Master Thibault and the Exchequer about this serious lapse. Clement's house and workshop were raided and the evidence found. Clement was disgraced in the eyes of everyone: the court, the city and the Guild.'

'We know this,' Isabella stammered.

'Of course you do. I suspect you, mistress, informed the authorities about Clement. No, no,' Athelstan raised a hand, 'don't object.'

'I do object. Why should I do that? Why?' Her voice rose. 'I was Clement's daughter-in-law, I had married his son, my beloved Columba. I was part of the family. I had no reason to do that.'

'That's what protected you.' Athelstan retorted. 'People would say you had no motive for such a betrayal, a few may even describe what you did as part of your civic duty. It must have been you, mistress. A Key-Master's workshop is carefully guarded, but you knew exactly what Clement had done and where the evidence could be found. Who knows, you may have learnt something, though unwittingly, from Clement or Columba. Anyway, the real reason for your betrayal was a hidden secret. At the time, you just hoped both father and son would be caught and punished vigorously. I understand Clement and Columba were mentioned in the information given. However, in the end the family's only punishment, because of their former good service, was nothing more than disgrace and destitution. You must have been surprised at such leniency?'

'I loved Columba.'

'Perhaps you once did, until you met the strapping Robert here and both of you were swept up in illicit lust.'

'Nonsense,' Mine Host shouted, making to rise then changing his mind as Flaxwith stepped forward and his mastiff Samson growled threateningly.

'It's the truth, mistress,' Athelstan continued. 'You were tired of Clement, tired of Columba and, after their fall, matters only grew worse. Both men were broken. Clement was publicly disgraced and Columba tarred with the same brush. For all I know he may have even mistakenly blamed himself for his father's disgrace. I doubt whether either man would think of blaming you.' Athelstan drew a deep breath. 'You became impatient, desperate to see the back of your husband and his moody ways, his absorption with the past and his father's failures. You, Isabella, were gravely smitten with Mine Host here. Perhaps even before Columba's disappearance, you were playing the two-backed beast with your lover.'

'Never, we did no wrong.'

'Aye, but you certainly did no right.' Athelstan tried to maintain his temper. 'You decided enough was enough. Clement and Columba were disgraced. You, mistress, regarded them as a millstone around your neck, so you both plotted murder. You eventually carried it out where, I believe, you perpetrated other abominations.'

'This is—'

'The truth, Master Taverner. God's own truth. Oh, by the way, you may soon hear sounds from your large cavernous cellar.'

'Oh my God no!' Isabella moaned.

'Oh my God yes,' Athelstan retorted. 'Some of Master Flaxwith's bailiffs are supervising a group of men who have their orders—'

'My orders,' Cranston interrupted, quietly marvelling at the sheer speed of Athelstan's attack.

They had arrived at the tavern around the time of the Angelus bell. Cranston, at Athelstan's behest, had confined Mine Host, his wife and household whilst he ordered a thorough scrutiny of the place. Secretly Athelstan must have also given orders to the leader of the labourers to dig as well as to search. Cranston turned in his chair to stare at the little friar, now fully absorbed as he pored over his sheets of parchment. Athelstan had outlined his indictment earlier. Cranston had asked about evidence but Athelstan had countered with the enigmatic reply, 'The dead would rise to indict the living.' Cranston now understood what the friar meant; this precious pair sitting opposite him would be condemned by their own house.

'Oh yes, my Lord Coroner's orders. To continue the indictment.' Athelstan raised his head and pointed at the accused. 'You lured Columba down to the cellars beneath this tavern. You murdered him, then buried his corpse somewhere in that unholy crypt. You then cleared away all his personal items so it would appear that Columba had finally broken and fled. Time passed. No one could prove otherwise so you were left to revel in your sins.' Athelstan paused to collect his thoughts. 'The years roll by. Columba has disappeared completely from hearts and minds, except for that of his poor father. Now Clement of course drifted back to this tavern and you made a most dreadful mistake, or eventually you did. The Hanging Tree is an ancient hostelry. I've been down to its cellar; it's sprawling, with a path leading down into the darkness. You probably hired Clement as a temporary cellar man. Perhaps you gave him some menial tasks to do but, of course, that cellar is a death pit, isn't it? It houses so many mysteries and murders.'

'What do you mean? If I had anything to hide in that cellar, why would I let anyone go down there?'

'Because if you didn't, that would raise suspicion, alert people to the possibility that something was wrong. Oh no,' Athelstan shook his head, 'at the time you were not frightened of any gruesome or grisly discovery. Anyway, you were wrong, because Clement took to wandering the cellar and discovered something deeply disturbing.'

'What?' the taverner shouted. 'What did he find?'

'This.' Athelstan bent down, opened his chancery satchel and held up the Walsingham, turning it to catch the light. The taverner just gaped whilst his wife put her face in her hands. 'Clement found this,' Athelstan declared softly. 'We discovered it on him whilst we were preparing his corpse for burial.'

'A statuette, a pilgrim's gift,' Mine Host yelled.

'Ah yes, but a special one. Eh Isabella? Columba took this everywhere, didn't he? He had a deep devotion to the Shrine of Walsingham. Didn't he?' Athelstan insisted harshly. 'Didn't he?' He shouted so his voice echoed around the taproom. Isabella reluctantly murmured her agreement.

'Finding this,' Athelstan declared, 'transformed Clement. He knew Columba would never have gone anywhere without this statuette, what he called "the Walsingham". Clement began to talk about his son's disappearance. Only the good Lord knows what he reflected on.'

'I don't give a horse's turd,' Mine Host retorted. 'My Lord Coroner, this is not evidence. This is not proof.'

'Isn't it? The Walsingham made Clement ponder on the past. Why? Because if you feel the base of this statuette, you'll find a thick stickiness, as if it's been standing in something like ale or wine for a long time, possibly years.'

'I don't understand,' Isabella stuttered.

'Don't you? Mistress, look around this taproom; the goblets, tankards and blackjacks spill their contents, which dry into a glue-like substance. Now, they are not experts, but the washerwomen in the Tower say this substance, spillage of ale or wine, is very difficult to clean. I shall return to these ladies and the secrets of their laundry tubs. However, in the meantime let me press on.' Athelstan picked up his beaker of water and sipped at it carefully, watching the two prisoners. Mine Host looked truculent, seething with rage, but one glance at Isabella reassured the friar. She was a murderess, a killer, who knew she was being brought to judgement. It would not take much to break her completely. 'As I have declared,' Athelstan continued, 'Columba was never parted from that relic, so why had it been left lying in some dark recess of the cellar? I am certain that is where Clement found it. There is no other explanation. I understand that when Columba disappeared they made good search. They found little. So I ask you, Isabella, why should it be found down there, a place only you and your paramour controlled?'

'I don't know,' she mumbled.

'I think you do. Columba was carrying it at the very moment you and your husband murdered him in that haunted place. A blow to the back of the head yes? The garrotte or a knife slid between the ribs. Columba falls and, in the chaos, the Walsingham slips away to lie in its puddle until Clement, and God works in wondrous ways, stumbled on it by accident. Clement must have begun to reflect, to view both of you in a different light. He might have even wondered about The Hanging Tree and the murder of the hangmen who regard this tavern as their Guild house. After all, it's not a great leap of logic. If you have killed once, why not kill again, and again, and again? Clement was intelligent, a master craftsman. He would meditate on all that had happened to him and his son. He would wonder who really provided the information to the authorities? What had Columba been doing down in that cellar when he and the Walsingham parted company? What had truly happened to him? Clement must have asked you questions as well. But he could only go so far. Clement, deeply troubled, turned to his distant kinsman and friend Crispin the Carpenter, a parishioner in St Erconwald's, who advised Clement to speak to me. God knows what Clement would have told me. Perhaps he hoped that Sir John and I would investigate, even carry out a thorough search of the cellars beneath, which is certainly happening now.' Athelstan paused, straining his ears, until he heard the satisfying sound of mattock and spade against stone. 'In a while,' he breathed, 'however, to return to my indictment. The more I have reflected, the more I realize that for you, Mine Host, murder is the way you solve most of the problems you encounter. Now Clement was emerging as a real danger, a threat to the dark secrets of this place.'

'No no,' Isabella wailed.

'Oh yes,' Athelstan declared. 'Clement had to be silenced.' Athelstan pointed at the taverner. 'You learned about his meeting with me so you followed him across to St Erconwald's. You waited for the right moment and seized it, or thought you did. Imagine Clement standing alone in that bleak, dark nave. Clement was sickening, an old man who had his own death gnawing at him. He was weak prey. You strangled him easily. Then, to deepen the mystery, you hurried to the sacristy to collect a candle to place by the corpse. Whoever came in, and by chance it was Benedicta, would see a light burning where it shouldn't and hurry across. You would then slip from the church and disappear.'

'And how would I know which door they would come through?'

'What did it really matter? You would hear them approach, the insertion of a key, the door creaking open and the visitor hurrying across. St Erconwald's certainly is a hall of shadows. Whatever, you proved it could be done, though you made one mistake, a terrible oversight. Blodwyn the Blessed, our sanctuary man, was cowering in the enclave behind the high altar. He had been asleep, the after-effects of being pursued and drinking strong wine, but then he awoke. He had become curious and crawled forward . . .' Athelstan paused as the foreman of the labourers burst into the taproom and hurried across to kneel by Sir John, gabbling so quickly Cranston had to tell him to speak more slowly.

'Enough!' the coroner rasped, clapping the man on the shoulder.

'Well done, my friend, but continue with the search.' Cranston waited until the labourer left then rapped the table. 'Three corpses,' he declared, 'and, God save him, I believe one is Culpeper.'

'He probably suffered the same fate as Blodwyn.' Athelstan continued. 'You see, our sanctuary man was one of those little people who live in the twilight, a true dusk-dweller. Sometimes a felon, at other times a creature who assisted the hangmen of London, you in particular. In the dancing light of my church, Blodwyn recognized you.' Athelstan pointed at the taverner. 'You truly are a killer to the deep, dark marrow of your sinful soul. Blodwyn recognized you and he fled for shelter with Thomas the Toad. He told Thomas that he was to make some money and that Thomas could share in his good fortune.'

'You did know Blodwyn?' Cranston broke in.

'Oh shut up.' The taverner's face had turned truly ugly, as if the demon he housed now showed itself. 'Let your little ferret,' the taverner gestured at Athelstan, 'let him babble on.'

'And so I shall,' Athelstan replied. 'Blodwyn crept in here; he told you what he'd seen. He demanded money for his silence. You arranged to meet him at Dowgate; you once mentioned that you went there to purchase wines. You met Blodwyn, strangled him and threw his corpse into the Thames.'

'And Culpeper?' Cranston barked. 'A snooper, a crawler through the dark with more than an eye for mischief.'

'We'll view his corpse soon enough,' Athelstan declared, 'and the circumstances of his death, but now we come to an even more deadly indictment. The gruesome murder of at least six of London's hangmen.' Athelstan sifted amongst the manuscripts before him. 'Recently we met Galliard the Goldsmith. As you know, the Guild of Hangmen lodge money with that goldsmith, in particular monies from the plunder seized in France, which of course is diminishing. There's less to share out, isn't there? Made worse by a further problem.'

'Which is?' the taverner asked, glancing hatefully at his spouse, keening as she rocked herself backwards and forwards on her chair.

'The number of hangmen,' Athelstan declared, 'members of your Guild, have increased quite significantly at a time when your revenue has shrunk. I mean there are no more wars across the

Narrow Seas; the Great Revolt has been crushed, and the imposition of the King's peace in London and the surrounding shires has led to a fall in the number of executions. So,' Athelstan held his hands up as if weighing something, 'so on the one hand you've got a shrinking revenue, and on the other an increased number of hangmen in your Guild. There is also the popularity of the Hangman of Rochester, an executioner much preferred by the Guildhall and the sheriffs for execution days at Tyburn and Smithfield. Fees which should have gone to the Guild now go to him, a matter I shall return to shortly. However, to revert to my main indictment: too little silver, too many hands outstretched so, like the devil's huntsmen you are, you and your paramour decided to cull the herd. Oh yes you did.' Athelstan raised his voice to carry over Isabella's wailing and her husband's foul-mouthed curses. 'You selected your victims, God knows how and why, and you lured them down to that hellish cellar, a true slaughter yard. Perhaps they were sodden with ale. You stabbed them to the heart and then you stripped them. Why? Ah well.' Athelstan fidgeted with the parchment sheets on the table before him. 'As I have already mentioned, when I was in the Tower, I encountered the washerwomen busy at their tubs. These lovely ladies proved to be a truly valuable source of wisdom for an ignorant little friar. They informed me that the stink and stains of ale, wine and beer are the hardest to get rid of.' Athelstan nodded towards Isabella. 'You would know that. The bodies of those poor hangmen would be hidden away for a while. Once ready, you would strip the corpses. After all, if these cadavers were found and all their clothes stank of the same smell, people would soon suspect that all these hangmen were murdered in some tavern or alehouse where the floors slopped with ale or wine. Places like The Hanging Tree would soon come under close scrutiny. That is why you removed and probably burned the clothing of your victims. You then pinned that scrawled message about vengeance as if former rebels were settling scores. Of course, that was a total nonsense. Now, the cellars beneath this tavern consist of ancient, winding tunnels. You would take the corpses of your victims along to one of those narrow posterns, barred from the inside, which lead out to some lonely, desolate yard with a bier or barrow hidden in the shadows. You would load your victim onto this and, under the cover of night, hooded and visored, push the barrow to some midden heap. Before you did, you probably placed the usual stark wooden cross on top of the cloth covering the corpse to signify that it contained a cadaver for burial. I've noticed,' Athelstan pulled a face, 'indeed it is well-known, that the carriers of the dead are very rarely challenged; indeed they are given a wide berth. So, you would toss the corpse onto some lay stall or midden heap, then hurry back the same way to this den of iniquity.'

Athelstan gave a noisy sigh as he shuffled the sheets of vellum before him. 'Do you know, Sir John, when I was a boy, visitors from here and there would sometimes call in. A good number were tellers of tales. My mother would give them a sumptuous meal in exchange for news of what was happening over the hill, or down the lane or even sometimes from across the sea. I remember one visitor, a huntsman; he had journeyed to France, hired as a verderer in the province of Alsace. He told us a terrifying tale, I can still recall it. Across this ancient province of France stretches a deep, ancient forest. Wolves prowl there. Sometimes they are a danger, sometimes not. As you may know, wolves very rarely attack a healthy armed adult. However, this changed with the emergence of two wolves, male and female, as leaders of the pack. They would attack anyone anywhere; they seemed to have no fear. More frightening was that wolves kill for food but this pair from hell seemed to thrive on killing, be it man or beast. I thought I'd never meet such creatures,' Athelstan shook his head, 'until I encountered Mine Host and his wife here.' Athelstan pointed at the accused. 'You enjoy murder and all its aftermath. You threw the corpses of your victims onto lay stalls or midden heaps well away from this tavern. You acted the same over poor Clement. You followed him out across the river and murdered him in God's own house. Now the arrival of the clerks here must have disturbed you. Like the wild creatures you are, you are sensitive to any change. Oh, you must have heard about the great robbery at Westminster. You may have even suspected for a while that the clerks' presence here was somehow connected with your litany of sins. However, the murder of Whitby would have reassured you that the clerks' enforced lodging in your tavern was closely connected to the robbery at Westminster rather than anything else. Nevertheless, you remained vigilant. Culpeper the snooper arrived in The

Hanging Tree, a possible threat. After all, Culpeper had the sharpest appetite for information. You would certainly notice him darting around the tavern, poking his nose where he shouldn't. Now Culpeper was one of those little people like Blodwyn. No one would really miss him because no one really cared. So you invited Culpeper down to the cellars and cruelly despatched him. If anyone came searching for him, you could shrug it off. Culpeper, in your eyes, was a nobody. Crossley was different.'

'What do you mean?' Mine Host was now not so angry but more fearful as Athelstan dug away, pulling down the façade this precious pair had built up over the years.

'Oh yes Crossley. You must have learned about his conversations with Shutup the spit boy. You would have certainly noticed Crossley slipping down to the cellars. You perceived this as a possible threat. What you didn't know was that Crossley couldn't give a fig about you or your tavern. All he wanted was to escape so he could meet with me. Only God knows what he would have said but, as God knows, you took care of him. You followed him down into the cellar; you reassured him that he was most welcome to go where he wished. You then took an arbalest, hidden away close to the steps. Crossley walks on; you come swiftly up behind him and loose the bolt into the back of his head. You hide the crossbow away and return to the taproom. No one would suspect you. What motive would you have? People would gossip. They'd probably reach the conclusion that the assassins who murdered Whitby had returned to take care of Crossley.' Athelstan crossed himself. 'I do that for protection, Master Taverner, because I realize that I am in a place of great evil, facing a soul deeply malevolent. I do wonder just how many people you have murdered. How many corpses lie under this tavern or elsewhere? You were a soldier in France? One of those killers who just roam the face of the earth, hacking and cutting to your heart's content? I suspect you had your eye on another victim.'

'What do you mean?'

'The Hangman of Rochester. I noticed when he came here he was ill at ease. You hate him, don't you, because of his skill? I mentioned this earlier. Were you torn between killing the Hangman of Rochester and using him to distract attention from yourself? Rumour and gossip are fires easy to fan, their flames soon take hold. People began to wonder if the person murdering the Hangmen of London was my good friend and parishioner. I am sure the gossip originated in this tavern and I am certain its true source was you. Rest assured,' Athelstan smiled bleakly, 'you'll be given time to face the truth, not to mention the Hangman of Rochester. You and I are done for the moment. Sir John,' Athelstan turned to the coroner, 'we should view the corpses.'

Cranston and Athelstan left the prisoners under strict guard and followed Flaxwith out of the taproom to the steep steps leading down into the cellar where the labourers waited. Athelstan, remembering his previous visit, cautioned Sir John to be careful as they both went gingerly down, taking each step carefully, until they reached the pool of light thrown by the lanterns placed there. These also provided clear view of the three corpses, stretched out side by side on the floor. A truly gruesome sight, whilst the foul smell of corruption poisoned the air. Athelstan and Cranston took out their pomanders. Athelstan knelt by the bodies. He murmured a prayer and blessed the corpses though their souls had long gone to judgement. Each cadaver was wrapped in a canvas sheet which reeked of pinewood juice as well as the strong tang of stale ale and beer. One corpse had virtually rotted away. Athelstan suspected this was Columba; the second was also much decayed, with little indication of who he was or how he'd died. Athelstan immediately recognized the third corpse. Poor Culpeper! A truly grisly sight, his throat clasped tight with twine. The agony of a cruel death had contorted Culpeper's face, a sight made more gruesome by the onset of decay.

'Where were they found?'

'Deep down in the cellars, Brother.' The leader of the labourers shuffled mud-caked boots. 'Sir,' he pleaded, 'can you give us a special blessing? We believe this truly is hell's pit where demons swarm.' He pointed to the three corpses. 'God save us but there may be more.'

'I am sure there are,' Athelstan responded. 'But first my blessing. "May the power of the Trinity . . ."' Once he'd finished the benediction, Athelstan walked around the corpses, following the soaked runnel which ran by barrels, tuns and hogsheads. A deep, dark, dank tunnel which seemed to stretch for ever. The occasional glint or glow of a lantern spluttering against the ever-encroaching shadows was the only light. He heard footsteps behind him and turned to smile at Cranston and the leader of the labourers.

'I am well protected.' He smiled.

'Thank you for your blessing, Brother; this truly is a grim place.'

'Where were the corpses? How did you find them?'

The labourer tapped his boot against the paving stones, which formed the floor.

'These slabs, Brother, are of high quality and undoubtedly laid by a master mason. They lie even and square. Very precise, skilled work.' He hurried on. 'I noticed certain slabs were not quite square, slightly twisted or raised. I thought that strange. I mean, this is a lonely place, not a constantly used highway, so why should slabs, carefully cut and precisely laid, be out of line? Anyway, I started on one and found a corpse. After that,' he shrugged, 'it was just a matter of following a trail. Brother Athelstan, Sir John, there are certainly more. This passage snakes a great distance. There are gaps and ancient outlets served by crumbling steps leading out to God knows where. I'll show you.'

'No, no. Thank you,' Athelstan replied. The friar took a deep breath, he felt slightly sick. He believed he was in a place reeking of evil. He murmured a prayer of thanks because he now had the truth and it was time to move to judgement. He and Cranston thanked the labourer and returned to the taproom. Before they went in, Cranston told Athelstan exactly what he intended. Athelstan made to object. However, the coroner explained that the process he was about to follow was legal, appropriate and just: it was in full accord with the ancient usage of Infangentheof, whereby malefactors caught red-handed could be immediately dealt with.

'It's very similar,' Cranston whispered hoarsely, 'to when the King unfurls his banner and rides against a rebel. Once that banner is unfurled, anyone caught in arms against the King is guilty of high treason. These are killers Brother, caught red-handed in the very place of murder. Heaven knows what horrors this hostelry houses. Moreover,' Cranston added, 'I have no pity for this precious pair. Think of the dead! All those innocent souls brutally murdered! So come, their souls, as well as the angels, gather to witness judgement.' They entered the taproom where the taverner and his wife sat bound in their chairs. Cranston and Athelstan took their seats. Flaxwith crossed to the coroner and whispered how the

Hangman of Rochester was waiting outside. 'We summoned him,' Cranston murmured. 'And now we certainly need him. So let us move to judgement.' The coroner rapped the table. 'Henry Penon and his not so good wife Isabella. How do you plead to the indictment laid against you by Brother Athelstan? I ask you. Guilty or Not Guilty? Let me hasten to add that if you plead the latter, you will be committed for trial before King's Bench at Westminster. Once there, if the indictment is upheld as good and true, you will both be sentenced to a traitor's death, being hung, drawn and quartered above Tyburn Stream. However, if you plead guilty now, on the ancient legal principle of Infangentheof, that you were caught red-handed, the victims of your wickedness lying below this tavern, then judgement will be swift. You will be sentenced to hang immediately, here on the very ground where you committed your crimes.' Cranston paused. 'So how do you plead, guilty or not guilty?'

Both taverner and wife murmured 'Guilty', slouching further down the chairs, not bothering to strain against the ropes which held them fast.

'I ask you again,' Cranston bellowed. 'So, in a clear voice, guilty or not guilty?'

'Guilty,' they both chorused together.

'Then judgement must be carried out.'

The prisoners' bonds were released and, under the close guard of the bailiffs, escorted to another chamber. Athelstan asked Flaxwith to go out into the street and find a Friar of the Sack to hear, if they agreed, the last confession of the condemned, to shrive them and pray for God's absolution.

'Satan's tits, Brother, they are being shown more mercy than they did their victims.'

'Oh Sir John, I don't think this precious pair will find the journey to God an easy one, but they must be given the chance . . .' He broke off as the Hangman of Rochester came into the taproom. He had a hushed conversation with Cranston, then asked both Coroner and Friar to join him outside, where the Hangman soon came into his own. Garbed completely in black, he had ladders brought from the stable, carefully placed so he could fashion two nooses from the stone arch above the main gate. Cranston and Athelstan crossed the thronged courtyard and sat on the chairs

Flaxwith had organized. The bailiffs pushed the curious back from the main gateway, now a macabre sight with two nooses hanging down next to the long siege ladders. The prisoners were brought out, hands bound. The Hangman moved swiftly. He pulled hoods over each of their faces and then pushed Isabella to the foot of a ladder before forcing her up the rungs almost to the top. Once there, using the second ladder, he slipped the noose over her head, tightened it carefully then slid down nimble as a squirrel. He glanced at Cranston who raised his hand then dropped it. The Hangman twisted the ladder and the condemned plunged as fast as a falling stone to break her neck. The Hangman next grabbed the now moaning taverner and pushed him up the ladder. The condemned man tried to resist but the executioner punched and pushed him up to suffer the same fate as his wife. In a matter of a few heartbeats, both corpses were swaying on the end of the ropes, their macabre creaking the only sound to break that baleful silence which always follows an execution. A silence which deepened even further as Cranston rose to his feet.

'Justice has been done,' he declared. 'Judgement has been passed. Let both corpses hang for a day and a night.' The coroner paused to take a deep breath before he loudly proclaimed that The Hanging Tree tavern and all it contained was now forfeit to the Crown. 'Master Flaxwith,' Cranston summoned his bailiff closer, 'you will, once the corpses have been moved to the death house at St Mary-le-Bow, ransack this tavern from cellar to garret. All valuables are to be impounded. The cellar is to be ruthlessly searched. I want every paving stone raised to discover if any more corpses rest in such unhallowed grounds. These proceedings are now at an end.'

Cranston crossed the yard to have words with the Hangman. Athelstan continued to stare at the still swaying corpses, lost in a reverie, until the coroner returned to shake him by the shoulder. 'What are you thinking, Brother?

'Oh Sir John, I recall the words of Master Thibault. What he said in St Osyth's Priory. How the devil always looks after his own.'

'And?'

'I think he does. But he always comes back with the bill.'

AUTHOR'S NOTE

The Hanging Tree, of course, is a work of fiction set in medieval London. I believe my novel captures the very essence of the city and the people who lived, worked, prayed and died there. London was a busy, bustling place. Trade was vigorous and closely intertwined with the murky, bloody politics of both the city and the court.

Certain strands of this novel are historically accurate. The summary executions carried out under the legal principle of 'Infangentheof' (the word has many spellings) were commonplace. Justice and judgement were as simple and as stark as that. Caught at seven in the morning, convicted at eight, hanged at nine. Only those who pleaded benefit of clergy could escape the inevitable.

The Lombard bankers were powerful merchants during the medieval era even though families such as the Frescobaldi and the Bardi were eventually bankrupted by the English Crown. The Carbonari did exist and, by the nineteenth century, had emerged as a powerful political force, playing a key role in the process of Italian unification. Of course the Carbonari in this novel simply reflect their activities elsewhere in Europe and these were certainly not fictional.